# DEUCE'S WILD

## ABOUT THE AUTHOR

Noted mythologist, trained psychologist, and sought-after public speaker Clyde Ford is a native New Yorker who now lives north of Seattle. He is the author of both nonfiction and fiction, including *Hero with an African Face*, *Red Herring*, and *The Long Mile*. Clyde has been a featured guest on *The Oprah Winfrey Show*, NPR, and many other television and radio programs nationwide.

THE SHANGO MYSTERIES

# DEUCE'S WILD

## CLYDE W. FORD

MIDNIGHT INK
WOODBURY, MINNESOTA

First Edition
First Printing, 2006

Book layout by Steffani Chambers
Cover design by Gavin Dayton Duffy
Cover image © 2005 by Rubberball, Digital Vision, Artville, PhotoDisc

Midnight Ink, an imprint of Llewellyn Publications

**Library of Congress Cataloging-in-Publication Data**
Ford, Clyde W.
  Deuce's wild / by Clyde W. Ford.
    p. cm.—(The Shango mysteries)
  ISBN-13: 978-0-7387-0809-6
  ISBN-10: 0-7387-0809-7
    1. Rap musicians—Crimes against—Fiction. 2. Police—New York (State)—
  New York—Fiction. 3. African American police—Fiction.
    4. New York (N.Y.)—Fiction. 5. Psychological fiction. I. Title.

PS3606.0724D48 2006
813'.6—dc22                                        2006042021

Midnight Ink
Llewellyn Publications
2143 Wooddale Drive, Dept. 0-7387-0809-7
Woodbury, MN 55125-2989, U.S.A.
www.midnightinkbooks.com

Printed in the United States of America

*To Chelsea,*
*With much love.*

# ONE

Nothing says "starting over" like sitting alone in an empty apartment. But here I sat on a borrowed couch in the middle of bare wood floors and naked white walls. The one-bedroom apartment, in a newly renovated brownstone, had a view out the living room window to other newly renovated brownstones across the street. And, if I craned my neck and strained hard, I could see a sliver of northern Central Park just a few blocks down from my building. Light green coated the trees. Spring had already arrived in the city.

Nora Daniels helped me land this apartment, which had a long waiting list. But she had a client, who had a friend, who knew someone, who worked for a man, whose son did this remodel as well as others in Harlem. So, after slipping an associate of the man two hundred fifty dollars for the man to give to his son, I found myself promoted to the head of the list. I craned my neck a little more to see how much of the park I could take in.

Suddenly, the downstairs doorbell went off. I flinched. The ring tone on the high-tech system played a computerized version of "Stars and Stripes Forever," and I fully expected a band of tiny toy soldiers to emerge from underneath the couch and march across the living room floor. I went over to the small monitor sitting next to the front door and fumbled with a few buttons until the screen flashed on.

"Meow. Meow."

A cat's face stared at me from the screen. Then a high-pitched, contrived voice came on behind it. "We just stopped by to say hello."

Finally, Nora poked her head from behind the ball of white fur and waved. I found the right button to push. "Stars and Stripes" played again. I cringed.

I opened the door before Nora got there so John Philip wouldn't get going once more. She turned the corner from the staircase with a wrapped package in one hand and Madame Meow at the end of a leash in the other. Nora had on jeans and a fitted sweater the same white as Madame Meow's fur.

"Hi," she said. She strolled in. "A house warming gift for you." She handed me the package.

I closed the door behind her, and she let Madame Meow off the leash. The cat took one look at me, sniffed the air, then, claws skidding over wood, raced around the living room and disappeared down the hall.

"Apparently she's not waiting for the cook's tour," I said.

"Well, I am," Nora said. She slowly turned her head around the living room. "Not bad. It's got potential. Do you need help with decorating?"

"If I do, I know where to call . . . your office. And I'll tell Brendan that I have a 9-1-1 interior decorating emergency."

Nora laughed easily. "Queer Eye for the Straight Guy—Home Makeover Edition . . . He'd love it."

"First I need enough money to afford what Brendan would want me to buy."

"His tastes are good . . . and expensive. Tucker paid you for that airport assignment, right?"

"You mean the TSA guard who stole luggage then resold its contents?"

"Uh-huh. And we paid you for both investigations?"

"Uh-huh."

"So you oughta have something left over to decorate with."

"After a month's rent, a month's security deposit, an agency fee, a key fee, a utility deposit, a cable TV installation fee, and a telephone deposit, I had barely enough to buy a few pieces of furniture, and a television."

"Sorry," Nora said. "I forgot all about those minor details of starting over."

"The furniture won't be delivered for a week." I pointed to the television. "The television will have to sit on top of its box until I get a stand. It's kind of like camping out in the wilderness of my living room."

"You could have stayed at my place longer."

"I needed to be on my own. I needed a place for JJ and I to spend time together."

"Has he seen your new digs yet?"

"He should be here soon. Liz's dropping him off for two weeks while she goes to a workshop somewhere upstate."

"He'll love it. His dad's own place. It won't matter to him if it's furnished."

Nora reached out with her arms, giving me a big hug and a little kiss, setting off a tiny spasm of longing. She walked over to the couch and sat down.

"Truth is, it's only been one day and already I miss coming home to an apartment where someone else lives," I said.

Nora looked around. "Welcome to sex . . . I mean, being single . . . in the city." She smiled. "Where, unlike on television, you spend a lot of time alone." She sat on the couch and pointed to the package. "Open it."

I peeled off the wrapping paper to reveal a boxed bottle of California merlot—expensive, but one Nora and I both liked.

"Would you like a glass now?" I asked.

She waved me off. "No, I've got to go. I need to pack. Tomorrow I leave for a week-long conference of public defenders in Phoenix. Let's celebrate when I return."

"That's good," I said. "Because I only have paper cups. What do public defenders confer about for a whole week anyway?"

"You know the joke about lawyers going away to a conference?"

I winced and shook my head. "No."

"All bar exams take place during happy hour. Cross-examinations are done behind closed doors. Habeas corpus has a new meaning. And married or single, whatever lawyer you end up with will still bill you for their time at three hundred dollars an hour."

"Habeas corpus?" I asked.

She smiled. "Show me the body," Nora said. "In Latin."

"I see . . . Drinking and sex," I said.

"For some," she said. "For most of us it's a time to commiserate about the sorry state of affairs for the protection of civil liberties in the 'land of liberty.'"

The doorbell rang. Nora grimaced. "Stars and Stripes?" she said. "Oh, that's precious."

From somewhere down the hall, Madame Meow meowed as though the sound caused her great pain. I shrugged and pointed to the wall. "New high-tech security system."

"Yuck. Change the ring tone," Nora said. "Or the Madame will never come back."

I walked over to the security system panel.

"Hey, Dad." JJ's voice came over the speaker. He waved into the monitor. Elizabeth, my soon-to-be ex-wife, stood somberly behind him. I buzzed them in, then I turned to Nora.

"JJ'll have his laptop with him. The instruction manual for the security system said that you could use a home computer to download other ringtones from the Internet. John Philip Sousa's days are numbered."

Nora sucked in a breath. "Maybe I should go."

"Hell, Liz wanted to go through with the separation and divorce. If she can't handle seeing me with a friend, what will she do when I'm with a lover?"

John Philip beat me to the front door, and Madame Meow let me know of her displeasure. JJ "hi-fived" me as he sauntered in, dropping his bags on the floor. He glanced around the living room. "Cool," he said.

When Madame Meow came bounding down the hall, JJ went after her, then stooped down to pick her up. She jumped up into his arms. Liz stood outside the door, as though afraid to cross the threshold.

"Please, come in," I said to her.

"Thanks," she said. Her smile seemed tortured. She handed me a wrapped package about the same size as Nora's. "A housewarming gift."

Liz had on a pair of jeans, too, though she wore a thin leather jacket over a vibrant yellow blouse. Apparently, she didn't register Nora's presence.

"Hello Elizabeth," Nora said.

Liz did a double take. "Sorry, John. I didn't mean to disturb anything," she said.

The two eyed at each other. JJ looked up from Madame Meow and stared back and forth warily between his mother and Nora. Nora stood up and gathered Madame Meow from JJ's arms.

"Nothing to disturb," Nora said. "I was just leaving."

I opened the door and Nora slid sideways past Liz. She waved to me as she walked down the hall, raising one of Madame Meow's paws to wave as well. I closed the door and stepped back inside my apartment. Liz stood near the couch staring out the window. I stood with my back against the front door. I searched for words amidst my anger and sadness. Liz turned toward me and spoke.

"I'm sorry. I should have called first. It won't happen again."

I reached out toward her. Her body stiffened, so I pulled back.

"You don't need to apologize," I said. "Nora just stopped by to bring me a bottle of wine."

"Oh." Liz wrinkled her face. "So did I." She pointed to the package in my arms.

I motioned to the couch. "Have a seat," I said.

"No. It's JJ's time with you." She turned to leave, then stopped. "Here," she said. Liz handed me a multipage brochure. "It's the catalog for the Sigma Center."

"The Sigma Center?"

"It's in upstate New York. I'm going there—"

"Ah, yes. To find yourself."

"For a two week yoga and meditation retreat."

"To find yourself?"

Liz huffed. "There's an emergency number in the brochure in case you need to call." She turned to JJ and held her arms out. "Aren't you going to say goodbye to your mother?"

JJ sauntered over to Liz, then gave her a peck on the cheek. He closed the door behind her as she walked out. JJ leaned back against the door.

"Got any food?"

"Lemme see."

JJ's cell phone let out a funky, hip-hop ring tone. He raced for his backpack, which rested near the window. I walked into the kitchen and swung open the refrigerator door.

"Yeah, man, my dad's place is cool. You know when we got here, his 'ho was here too. At least I think she's his 'ho."

My body stiffened. I let the refrigerator door close but held on to the door handle.

"Yeah, my mom was cool. She dealt with it." He tapped on the windowpane while he listened. Then he said, "Nah . . . Nah . . . uh-huh, that's cool. Yeah, I'll see you tomorrow."

JJ snapped his cell phone closed. I let go of the refrigerator door handle and walked into the living room. I reminded myself to take deep breaths.

JJ pivoted around and took a few steps toward me. "What's to eat?" JJ asked.

I pointed to his cell phone. "Who was that?"

"Eddie."

"I heard you use the word 'ho in reference to Nora."

JJ shrugged his shoulders, and raised his palms. "'Ho. Bitch. It's just the way we talk."

I sat down on the couch and patted the cushion beside me. "Sit down, son," I said. "We need to have a talk about women."

JJ grimaced. "Is this the big 'sex talk?' I mean 'cause if it is, I can save you some time. I already got it in Health Ed."

I patted the couch again. "No. This isn't a talk about sex, as much as it's about your attitude toward women."

He threw his hands into the air. "What's the difference?"

I raised my voice and pointed to the couch. "Sit. And please don't make me ask you again."

JJ strode over to the couch, a cocky hop in his step, his arms swinging at his sides. When he sat, his gangly legs stuck out before him. I turned to face him, but he glanced off to one side.

"Nora's a friend," I said. "A good friend. And our relationship doesn't go beyond that. I lived in her apartment for six months. Are we attracted to each other? Yes. But we decided we'd be better off as friends. I like her and I respect her. But beyond that, even if we were romantically involved, I would never stand for anyone to call her 'my 'ho' or 'my bitch.' A bitch is a female dog. And a 'ho is slang for a whore. I know it's street talk, but you need to stop using those words to refer to women."

JJ shrugged his shoulders in protest, talking out the window, not to me. "It's not just street talk," he said. "It's hip-hop. It's rap. It's our music. Our poetry."

"Look at me, son," I said.

He sighed.

"Look at me," I said again.

Finally, he turned toward me, head over to one shoulder, a defiant gaze in his eyes.

"There's nothing poetic about calling a woman a whore," I said.

He waved me off. "What do you know about my generation, my music?" He patted his chest. "'Ho. Bitch. Those are the words we use. We know that parents don't like them, but they're our words to our music. Just like I'm sure your parents didn't like the words to the music you listened to."

I took another long, deep breath. "My parents would have smacked me for using those words," I said. "And while I'm glad you feel you can stand up for your beliefs, you need to think about what calling a woman a 'ho or a bitch does to the way she sees herself. If you had a little girl, would you want her growing up always being referred to as a whore?"

JJ sighed. "That's the problem," he said. "That's why you don't understand my generation. The words are part of songs. They don't stand on their own. There's a rhythm, a beat that goes with them."

I raised my eyebrows. "I just heard you refer to Nora as a 'ho and a bitch, and I didn't hear you singing a song or tapping your feet."

He huffed. "You don't get it. You just don't get it. The words come out of the music I listen to, and when I use the words I'm thinking about that music, not what the words mean in a dictionary like you are."

"Let's leave it at this," I said. "I would prefer that you never used those words to speak about women. And I insist that in my house, or in my presence, you don't refer to a woman as a 'ho or a bitch. I need your agreement on that, okay?"

He sucked in a breath, but said nothing. And I let him stew in his agitation for a few minutes. When I put my hand on his shoulder, he pulled away.

"I need your agreement," I said.

JJ huffed again, looked away, and then muttered under his breath, "Okay."

I shook my head. "No," I said. "Not okay. Look me in the eyes, even if you're angry, and then speak to me."

He gazed out the window instead. Then he finally turned toward me. With tight lips, he said, "Okay." His jaw muscles flexed.

"Thank you," I said.

JJ scooped up the remote control from the floor, pointed it at the television, and jammed buttons with his thumb as if firing a high-tech weapon. I got up to make us some lunch. By the time I reached the kitchen, a halting, staccato burst of words set atop a driving bass beat spewed from the television speakers. JJ had settled on a music video station, and I'm sure on a few choice words for me in his mind.

I walked back to the refrigerator and hung onto the door while I stared at the empty metal shelves. I listened to JJ's music in the background. I have to admit that if I tuned out the words, the intonation and rhythm of the male singer reminded me of Charlie Parker or John Coltrane soaring high in a wild flight of lyrical imagination. But the words always came crashing through, bringing me down with them.

*You my 'ho . . . don't you know . . . want some mo'; Need my fill . . . of your thrill . . . want it now, want it later . . . from behind's even better . . . You my 'ho . . .*

In the background, a young woman moaned with pleasure. I slammed the refrigerator door closed.

"JJ," I said.

With his eyes fixed on the television, I waited a while before he looked over to me.

"Yeah?" he said.

"There's nothing in the fridge. You want me to call out for pizza?"

"That's cool," he said, turning back to the television.

I called for pizza, but I hesitated to leave the kitchen, as though by crossing the threshold from linoleum to carpet would cause me to step into an unfamiliar world. Somewhere I read it's better to watch offensive television shows with your children and have discussions afterward than to forbid them from tuning in at all. So I took one more of what seemed like a thousand deep breaths, and went to sit down next to JJ.

A thin, striking young man sang and strutted on the music video. His dark skin stood in sharp contrast to his all-white robe and white skullcap. When he danced, he twirled and his robe fluttered up and out like a bird spreading its wings. Apparently, I'd caught the tail end of the video.

"Salaam Alaikum . . . Salaam Alaikum . . . Salaam Alaikum . . .," the singer whispered, twirling round and round while images of soldiers fighting in the Middle East faded in and out of other

11

images showing children with blown-off limbs, and police pushing young men up against cars in front of decimated buildings in America and abroad. "Salaam Alaikum," he whispered. Then a drumbeat crashed. The singer twirled once more before the camera focused on the tears in his eyes. "Peace be with you," he said.

The screen cut to black.

JJ sat, riveted, staring at the blank screen. When a tennis shoes commercial came on, he turned to me. "You'd probably like the new Deuce F," he said.

"Deuce F? Is that who that was?" I asked, pointing to the screen.

"Uh huh. Kinda New Style hip-hop," JJ said. "He used to be a gangsta rapper, then he changed. He wears all that white because he's now a Muslim." JJ made the peace sign with his fingers. "Peace. Love. No violence. Doesn't use 'ho or bitch."

"Do you like him?" I asked.

JJ shrugged. "I really liked the old Deuce F. His new stuff is kinda okay. Everyone thinks his beat's cool. But the way he dances. All that spinning. A lotta people think he's bogus. You know, he became a Muslim because it's controversial, and that's good for album sales. He changed his name too. Yousef something-or-other. I can't remember, but at least it rhymes." He looked at me, cocked his head, and gestured with his hand. "You know, Yousef and Deuce F. Get it?"

"Got it," I said.

JJ shook his head back and forth. "Yeah, I guess I do like Yousef, the new Deuce F." He smiled. "Hey, that rhymes too."

"Stars and Stripes Forever" chimed over the security system's speaker.

"Must be the pizza," I said.

JJ shook his head. "Now that music I hate," he said, pointing to the door.

I slapped him playfully on the knee. "At least that's one time our tastes in music agree. Did you bring your laptop computer?"

"Uh-huh."

"Stars and Stripes" came on again when the pizza delivery person got to the door. I shook my head, pointed at the door, then at JJ. "Then you get to figure out how to change the ringtone."

He finally smiled.

* * *

The following morning, I walked with JJ to the Dubois School, then I caught a subway downtown to City Hall. When I pushed through the doors of the Office of Municipal Security, I heard a familiar, deep, female voice sing out, "Good morning, John." And I turned to see Charlene Jordan, Ken Tucker's secretary, smiling. Today, she wore a fuzzy charcoal sweater with a string of pearls gleaming from around her neck, and one pearl hanging from each earlobe.

"Congratulations. I heard you just moved into your new place," she said. Then she reached under her desk, emerging with a long, wrapped box. She handed to me, and winked. "I hope you don't drink it alone."

"Thanks," I said. I took the wine from her. "It's a pleasure to walk into the office and to see you at your desk."

She smiled and fixed her gaze softly on me. I knew the look, which always seemed to telegraph that it would be all right if I asked for more when I walked through the office door. And I would have asked if she didn't work for Ken Tucker. Business and that kind of pleasure made for a combustible mix in my book.

"You can go right in," Charlene said. "He's expecting you."

I set the wrapped present on her desk. "Thanks again," I said. "I'll take this when I leave."

I knocked on Tucker's door and waited . . . and waited. Finally, I turned back to Charlene, who waved me in with a few quick backside flips of her hand.

Tucker held a telephone to his face with one hand, and with the other pointed to one of two empty leather chairs in front of his desk. Behind him, out his wide picture window, a blue sky reigned, sunlight glinted from the windows of Wall Street skyscrapers, and, in the distance, the Verrazano Bridge snaked its way across the narrows from Brooklyn to Staten Island. A package wrapped in silver foil stood like a miniature skyscraper in the middle of Tucker's desk.

Tucker hung up, then sighed. "Washington," he said. "Glad I'm out of the agency, working here and not there."

I imagined Ken Tucker's closet organized in rows of blue, gray, and black suits. Some with pinstripes, some without. He wore a dark gray suit and maroon tie today. He pushed the wrapped silver package toward me.

"Before I forget," he said. "It's a housewarming gift for you."

"Thanks," I said. I set the package in my lap and laughed to myself. Forget a bed and bureau. At this rate, I needed a wine rack more than any other piece of furniture.

Tucker's expression turned serious, and the already deep lines cutting across his forehead deepened more. "I just got off the phone with Homeland Security," he said. "We got tagged with a terrorist investigation. Seems some rap artist who lives here in the city decided to embark on his own diplomatic mission. Visited a number of Arab countries. Maybe even met with some terrorist groups. The State Department's furious because he asked them for permission, and when they denied it, he went anyway. The Justice Department has him on a terrorist watch list. We need to do a threat assessment on him."

"A threat assessment." I chuckled. "That include his music and lyrics, as well?"

Tucker failed to laugh. He picked up a sheet of paper from his desk. "Guy's name is Edgar Koontz, makes his home on the Upper Westside."

"Edgar Koontz? And you say he's a rap artist?" I shook my head. "Not with a name like that."

The lines crossing Tucker's forehead deepened even further. "Edgar Koontz," he said, as though barking an order. "a.k.a. Deuce F, who just changed his name to Yousef al-Salaam. And guess what, Shannon . . . ?" A sly smile swept over his face. He pointed. "Deuce's wild . . . he's your case."

# TWO

EARLY AFTERNOON SUNLIGHT SLICED down 94th Street, illuminating a group of whitewashed brownstones, which reminded me of the gleaming white Casbahs of North Africa. I counted house numbers as I walked. Edgar Koontz, a.k.a. Deuce F, a.k.a. Yousef al-Salaam lived in a brownstone in the middle of the group.

I bounded up the stairs of the rap star's building expecting to find his name beside a button. Instead, I found the building roster covered over with a single silver plaque embossed with the name "Deuce F." A lone button below the plaque pretty much confirmed that the he occupied the entire building. I mashed the button with my thumb and waited.

Finally, the hand-carved wooden front door swung open. I looked up into the flat, round face of a man several inches taller than me, and many inches wider. Standing in the doorway of a hip-hop artist, I assumed people called him Biggy. He wore a dark suit and a thin, closely shaven goatee almost lost amidst the folds of fat under his chin. I couldn't see his eyes behind his sunglasses, but I could see the bulge near his left armpit, which most likely meant that Biggy carried a piece.

"Yo." Biggy's deep, bass baritone voice resonated. He folded his arms across his massive chest, stoically waiting for me to reply.

I pulled out my wallet and flashed my badge.

"John Shannon, Office of Municipal Security," I said. "I'd like to speak to Mr. Koontz."

Biggy sneered. "Mr. al-Salaam does not wish to be disturbed."

He swung the door toward me, but I jammed my foot into it before it closed. Biggy's nostrils flared. He stripped off his sunglasses. His eyes widened. He made a move with his hand toward his weapon. I threw my jacket open, exposing the 9 mm in my shoulder holster. He stopped and eyed me. I stared at him and let my gaze soften, using a trick that Charles Promise had taught me in prison about projecting quiet strength through my eyes.

The front door swung open.

"I'll see if Mr. al-Salaam is available," Biggy said.

"And I'll wait here for him," I said.

Biggy glared at me before turning and disappearing down the hallway. The parqueted wooden floor groaned under his footsteps. No platinum and silver records lined the stark white walls. A shaft of sunlight stabbed through a skylight at the top of the staircase three floors above me, and the thick, cloying smell of incense hung in the air.

Suddenly, the floor-to-ceiling sliding doors next to me rumbled apart. Biggy stood on the other side, dwarfed by the height of the parlor ceiling. Sunlight streaming in through the front window dazzled off the plush white parlor carpet. In one corner of the room, a seated figure wrapped in white faced away from me, toward the street. I started across the threshold, when Biggy pushed me back.

"Shoes," he said, pointing down.

I looked down at Biggy's feet and stifled a laugh at the contrast of a big man in a suit and tie without shoes. I reached down and slipped off my shoes. Biggy slid the doors closed behind me, then walked through another door at the far end of the parlor.

Murmurs rising from the figure in the corner of the room, reminded me of the whispers at the end of the music video I'd seen with JJ. Suddenly, Yousef al-Salaam prostrated deeply toward Central Park, then spinning around to me.

A black butterfly in a white cocoon. That's what al-Salaam looked like wrapped in white silk from head to toe with only his piercing eyes and wide nose visible. He sat cross-legged and slowly unwrapped the fabric from his head, revealing the smooth dark skin of his face.

"Al-Salaam Alaikum." He bowed, then motioned to the floor. "Sit, please."

I folded my legs underneath me and sat across from him, watching a subtle smile work its way across his lips as he gazed at me. He ran his hand over his bald head, then pointed to mine.

"My sheikh said that baldness opens the mind to the exaltation of God and one's inner spiritual life."

"Means shaving more often," I said.

He extended his hand toward me. "Yousef al-Salaam," he said. Al-Salaam possessed a soft voice, but clear and resonant.

I shook his hand. "John Shannon," I said.

His delicate handshake reminded me of grasping a feather. Gangsta rapper? So far, I didn't see it.

"Willis said that you worked for some municipal agency, and you wanted to question me."

"That's right. The Department of Homeland Security asked the Office of Municipal Security, which I work for, to gather information about your recent travels in the Middle East."

Al-Salaam shook his head. "Travels? What travels?" He spread his hands wide. "I'm a musician, an artist. I just returned from a spiritual pilgrimage and a goodwill tour."

"Algeria. Senegal. Sudan. Egypt. Turkey. Iran. All Arab countries where you met with local groups opposed to the United States invasion and occupation of Iraq. Can you see how some in the government might not see your trip as a goodwill tour?"

"I don't care what 'some' in the government think," al-Salaam said. He clasped his hands together and pressed his fingers against his lips. He sighed, then let his hands drop. "Do you know what *tariqah* is?"

"I don't," I said.

"It's a journey toward God. A journey of enlightenment, self-discovery, and self-realization. A journey I embarked on when I converted to Islam."

"Sometimes people on journeys trying to find themselves do strange things. Suicide bombers talk about the rewards awaiting them after they've blown themselves up and taken others with them," I said. "I think Homeland Security's worried that your journey toward enlightenment may have dire consequences for others who do not choose to be enlightened at the wrong end of a bomb."

Al-Salaam sighed and shook his head. "Do you know what my name means?" he asked.

"No."

"Yousef is the Islamic form of Joseph, son of Jacob, despised by his brothers and sold into slavery in Egypt. Al-Salaam means 'the peaceful one,' 'he who brings peace.' My spiritual teacher, Sheikh Tariq Bashir, gave me this name because he said it was my duty on my journey to use music and words to bring about peace."

"Yet in each of the countries you visited you met with organizations on the State Department's terrorist watch list."

"If by that you mean groups that oppose the United States invasion of Iraq, yes, I met with such organizations. But, please, Mr. Shannon, tell me, since when is one a terrorist because one desires peace? Sufis desires peace, and the groups I met with were Sufi Islamic groups in the countries I visited. Groups that follow the teachings of Sheikh Muhammad Bashir."

"And this Sheikh . . . Muhammad . . . Bashir." I stumbled over the name. "He lives in what country?"

Al-Salaam shook his head and smiled gently. "Sheikh Muhammad Bashir died in thirteenth-century Persia. Modern-day Iran."

"So you were approached by followers of the Sheikh to join this group?"

Al-Salaam's frown reminded me of JJ's last night when he told me that I just "didn't get it."

"I converted to Islam because I had an *al-hal*, a revelation, an insight. I had just finished performing onstage. Rapping about shooting cops, screwing 'ho's, slapping bitches, doing drugs, and killing anyone who stood in my way. Gangsta rap, you know? And the crowd loved it. I got back to my dressing room drenched in sweat, completely exhausted. I couldn't even make it to a chair. I fell onto the floor on my back. And . . . I don't know . . . something happened. The room and lights, everything around me, grew distant and far away, like I was looking at the world through the wrong end of a telescope, floating above it all. I saw myself back onstage, and I heard the thunderous applause of the audience again. But their clapping grew fainter and fainter while another voice grew louder. And that voice said, 'Come to me. This is not you. Come to me.'

"I got up and I started to dance. More like spinning around and around. I didn't get dizzy. I felt exalted, as through some type of grace or energy had poured into my body. A seamstress who works with my wardrobe crew, an older woman, entered my dressing room looking for some fabric she'd used on my costume that night. When she saw me spinning, she sat. And when I finished I sat across from her. She told me about Sufism, about the whirling of the dervishes, about tariqah. And I knew I would never be the same. Afterward, I found a local branch of Sufis who follow the teachings of Sheikh Muhammad Bashir, and I studied with them. The Sheikh said that only those who are ready to approach the truth find him. In the centuries since his death, many have been drawn to his teachings of peace, universal love, and spiritual fulfillment."

"It sounds like an Islamic version of the 'peace and love generation.'"

"And you'd rather have the alternatives—war, hatred, greed?"

"Homeland Security's concerned that the Islamic groups you met with are using you and your music as a tool to recruit young people for Islamic terrorist organizations."

"Islamic. Terrorist. Why are those two words so linked in the minds of Westerners? As if Muslims are the only people in the world who have ever picked up a weapon and fought for what they believe in. Why is it that when the United States military rains down 'shock and awe' in Iraq that kills tens of thousands of innocent civilians it's called 'liberation,' but when a resistance fighter sacrifices himself and kills ten people it's called terrorism. I don't condone violence. But I also don't condone stigmatizing Muslims as the purveyors of violence in the world, when this country," he pointed down to the floor, "has committed terrorism on a much grander scale. War, Mr. Shannon, is a form of terrorism, in case you've forgotten."

"I think the point is that the United States is acting to prevent that resistance fighter from blowing himself up on the streets of New York City or Boston or San Francisco."

"And decimating a country like Iraq accomplishes that?"

"Bringing democracy to the country might."

"Funny brand of democracy. Destroy the country. Turn the people who once looked toward America as a beacon of hope into insurgents willing to sacrifice their lives against America's occupation. You can't believe that's the way to quell violence and bring about peace."

"What I believe isn't important. I wasn't the one found visiting the top ten countries on the State Department's terrorism list. I'm here to assess whether your sympathies and your conversion to Islam makes you a security risk to this country."

Al-Salaam closed his eyes and swayed round and round as he sat. He opened his eyes suddenly. "Sufism teaches peace. If advocating for peace is threatening, then I'm a security risk. Sufism is against violence. If calling for an end to the war in Iraq and the removal of all US forces is threatening, then I'm a security risk. Sufism proposes the brotherhood and sisterhood of all people. If asking for America to join the world community on issues like the Kyoto Treaty, the International Criminal Court, and the Convention for the Removal of Land Mines is threatening, then I'm a security risk. I—"

Suddenly, Biggy appeared as if from nowhere, hulking over al-Salaam. He leaned down and whispered in the rapper's ear. Al-Salaam stood.

"Excuse me for a minute, please. I have some business to attend to."

Al-Salaam glided across the carpet, white robes fluttering, and disappeared with Biggy through another door.

A gangsta rapper turned man of peace. A miraculous conversion. Idealistic? Yes. Committed to his beliefs? Yes. Caught up in the theatrics of his conversion? Yes. A threat to the security of this country? I doubted it.

At first I thought the loud muffled voice emanating from an adjoining room belonged to Biggy. But the more I listened I realized it belonged to al-Salaam. He sounded agitated, upset.

"Fuck you. What do you mean you won't? I'm Yousef al-Salaam. No . . . no . . . you have to . . . it's mine . . . I own it. Man, you threatening me? Who the hell you think you are? Fuck you." Then silence.

"I want this taken care of, you understand?" Al-Salaam raised his voice again.

"Yo," Biggy said.

"Time to end this once and for all."

"Yo."

A moment later, the door at the back of the parlor swung open and al-Salaam flowed in, robes trailing behind him. A forced smile smothered his face. He didn't sit. His gaze darted around the room. I rose to meet him.

"Trouble?" I asked.

"Bid'ness," he said. For the first time since meeting him I heard the gangsta in his voice.

"Man, can we continue this conversation at another time?"

"We can," I said, "although there is a favor I'd like to ask of you."

"Shoot."

"My son's a huge fan of yours, and—"

Al-Salaam laughed. "Wait here."

He disappeared through the parlor door again. When he returned he was holding an eight-by-ten glossy color photo of him onstage, dressed in white.

"What's his name?" Al-Salaam asked.

"JJ," I said.

Al-Salaam's felt-tip pen squeaked as he autographed the photo, "To JJ—Peace and Love. Al-Salaam."

# THREE

I PUSHED MY APARTMENT's front door buzzer and cringed, waiting for the tiny computerized trumpets to begin. But instead of John Philip Sousa, the computer's rendition of "Maria, Maria" by Carlos Santana came on. JJ must be home from school. I opened the door and found him sitting cross-legged on the floor. A wire stretched from his computer to a plug underneath the building access system's monitor. He looked up.

"Simple," he said. "USB connection from the computer to your access console. And a website where you can download ringtones and load them into your doorbell's computer. Probably a couple of hundred ringtones." He pointed to the monitor screen. I closed the door and bent down to have a look. "Thought you'd like Santana. You know, something old, something new, something we can both agree on."

I smiled and placed a hand on JJ's shoulder. "Any ringtones by Yousef al-Salaam?"

"C'mon, dad. He's a little too hip for you. Maybe we should stick with Santana. He's more your age anyway."

I gently shoved JJ. "Wait a minute. Are you trying to tell me that your ol' man's not hip?"

"Well, you know . . . like someday when I get old I won't be hip to the music that the kids are listening to."

"So let's see . . . I'm old and I'm not hip."

"C'mon dad. You know what I mean."

"Then tell me, what's an unhip, old man like me doing with an autographed color photograph of Yousef al-Salaam, the rapper formerly known as Deuce F?"

I whipped the photo from the file folder I carried and dangled it above JJ's head. His eyes widened.

"Hey, lemme see that," he said.

I held it in front of him long enough so he could see the picture and the signature. JJ reached for it. I pulled it back.

"Lemme see. You got that for me? Where'd you find it?"

"I didn't find it."

JJ was on his feet now, lunging for the photo. I backpedaled into the living room, keeping it just out of his reach.

"What do you mean, you didn't find it?"

He barreled at me with his hands out. I palmed his head, then straight-armed him to keep him at bay. He struggled against me.

"I went over to al-Salaam's house and asked him for it."

JJ batted my arm away. "Sure you did. Now lemme have it."

I planted a hand on the back of the couch and vaulted over to the other side. I crouched and faced JJ, who crouched and faced me. With the couch between us, he feigned moving right, then left, trying to decide the best way to get to me.

"Lemme see it," he said.

I held the photo over my head. "Not until you say that your ol' man's a hip young dude."

He slid to his right. I slid right too. JJ laughed. "Can't do that."

"Why?"

"'Cause you taught me never to lie."

I laughed. "Okay. Okay. Then say, 'My ol' man's a cool dude.'"

JJ chuckled. "How about I say 'I love my ol' man 'cause he got me an autographed photo of one of my favorite rap artists'?"

"You win."

I handed the photo to JJ and pulled him around to my side of the couch. We sat, and I put my arm around him. He stared at al-Salaam's photo and traced the rap star's signature over and over with his finger. I told him about visiting al-Salaam at his home, and I also told him why.

JJ winced. "The State Department thinks that al-Salaam's a terrorist? That won't go over big."

"Won't go over big with his fans?" I asked.

JJ shook his head. "See, that's why I couldn't lie and say you were hip. No, dad, it won't go over big with the rapper T-Mo, al-Salaam's homeboy and former running buddy."

"Yep, I'm not hip. Tell me why?"

"It's simple. You see, T-Mo's still cranking out gangsta rap. Means he's stylin' himself as the meanest, baddest rapper. King of the Streets. T-Mo dissed al-Salaam for converting to Islam and turning to that 'peace and love' stuff." JJ flashed me a *V* with his fingers. "But it meant that T-Mo had one less rapper to compete with. Now the State Department's put al-Salaam on a terrorist list. That means he just leapfrogged over T-Mo as a mean, bad rapper."

I held up my hands. "Wait, I don't get it." I tapped on the photograph. "But al-Salaam's still doing 'peace and love' raps. So how does that make him the meanest, baddest dude?"

JJ sighed and shook his head. "It's not his rap, it's his rep. You can rap about anything you want, but if you get the baddest rep, then you the baddest dude. And the State Department just handed al-Salaam the baddest rep. Get it now?"

I grimaced. "I think so."

For the rest of the evening I couldn't do anything wrong. Homework and dishes got done. JJ's bedtime came without a complaint.

\* \* \*

"Dad!"

JJ's scream shattered my dreams. I bolted from the lumpy futon Nora lent me and raced into the living room. JJ sat in front of the television, whimpering. I checked the kitchen clock. Five a.m. I turned on a light. JJ held al-Salaam's photograph close to his chest, while the tears streaming down his cheeks caught light flashes from the flickering television.

"What are you doing up so early."

He sniffed back tears.

"I couldn't sleep," he said. "So I got up and turned on MTV. Sometimes in the early morning they play oldies. I thought maybe I'd catch one of al-Salaam's gangsta raps." He clutched the photograph tighter. "But he's dead, Dad."

"What?"

28

I took a seat on the couch next to my son. JJ wept.

"He's dead. Al-Salaam's dead. Someone shot him and his bodyguard in front of a hip-hop nightclub late last night."

"You're kidding?"

"There." JJ pointed. "It's all over MTV."

JJ buried his body into mine and cried. I watched the television, where a younger version of al-Salaam, dressed in black, swaggered across the stage with his baseball hat turned ninety degrees and cocked at a sharp angle. I grabbed the remote control and switched to an all-news station. At the bottom of the screen a headline scrolled by, "RAPPER DEUCE F SHOT TO DEATH . . ." A few minutes later the young female news anchor said, "And now for our breaking story: Rap artist Deuce F, who recently converted to Islam and took the name Yousef al-Salaam, was shot to death in a drive-by shooting earlier this morning as he exited Hip-Hot-A-Mus, a hip-hop nightclub on the Lower Westside. Police are calling this a musicland feud within a violent hip-hop subculture. As al-Salaam stepped into his black Cadillac Escalante, another car came barreling down the street. Apparently, al-Salaam's bodyguard, Willis Johnson, exchanged a few shots with the assailants but both he and al-Salaam were pronounced dead at the scene. Action News Network will keep you informed as we learn more about this latest death in the violent hip-hop world."

The anchor's voice trailed off. A news camera panned the scene of two stretchers moving toward an ambulance. A black plastic body bag rested on top of each. One bulged at the seams.

I turned to JJ.

"I'm sorry this happened to al-Salaam," I said. "It seemed like he was trying to change his life for the better."

JJ said nothing. He just cried softly. I pulled him closer.

Later, I made him his favorite breakfast—pancakes, eggs, and bacon—but he said nothing as we ate. He also remained silent as we walked to school. I noticed he'd tucked the photograph of al-Salaam inside a plastic page protector, which he stuck into his loose-leaf notebook. I remembered when Marvin Gaye's father shot him to death. I walked around in anger and disbelief for days.

\* \* \*

On the subway down to Tucker's office, headline after headline blared the news. "RAPPER LIVES AND DIES BY HIS LYRICS," one read. "CONVERSION TO ISLAM DOESN'T SAVE A RAPPER'S LIFE," another read, then added, "BUT WILL IT SAVE HIS SOUL?"

When I walked into Tucker's office, Charlene gave me a subdued smile. She didn't have children. She didn't look like a hip-hop fan.

"Nephew?" I said.

She bit her lower lip and slowly shook her head. "Niece," she said. "She called me this morning crying so hard she could barely speak."

"Same with my son," I said.

Charlene shook her head. "I don't understand why they love the music, but it broke my heart to hear my niece so upset." She motioned toward Tucker's door. "He's there," she said. "Just walk in."

I did.

From his wide grin, Ken Tucker apparently didn't have young children or relatives affected by al-Salaam's death. Tucker motioned to his soft, high-back leather chair. I declined the offer.

"Shortest investigation you'll ever be on, huh?" he said.

"Short and tragic," I said.

"Tragic? Hell, one terror suspect out of the way. One foul mouth rapper off the streets. Net plus if you ask me."

"He'd changed his raps."

"What? From singing in English to singing in Arabic?"

"He'd converted to Sufism, a sect that promotes peace."

Tucker winced. "I thought you were more hip than that." He chuckled to himself. "Boy, he sure reeled you in."

"How?"

"Come, have a look for yourself." Tucker waved me over to his side of the desk.

Out Tucker's window, an orange-brown smog had settled over the city. He pushed aside his vase of fresh yellow roses and plopped a laptop down. He flipped open the top and the disk drive whirred.

"I just got these from Washington last night. Not that they matter now."

He tapped a button and a black-and-white photograph popped onto the screen. In it, a thin man, unmistakably al-Salaam, sat at an outside cafe, a cup of coffee raised to his lips, talking with two other men dressed in Western suits.

31

"This was taken in Tunis," Tucker said.

He moved the cursor arrow over one of the men. "Ibrahim bin Fatah, an Iranian agent also known as 'Al Jabbar.' The other man's identity we don't know." He pushed a button and brought up a new slide. "But here he is two weeks later in Karachi." He hit the button again. "And here, a week after that in Istanbul." Another slide flashed onto the screen. "And here only days later in Kabul. He disappeared after that."

"And that's supposed to prove that al-Salaam was a terrorist?"

"No, but this helps . . ." He hit the button again and another black-and-white photo of al-Salaam appeared, this time onstage looking like he'd just finished performing. A group of men with white beards and tightly fitting white skullcaps sat behind him, caught by the camera in the midst of clapping. "A Syrian, a Sudanese national, two Saudis, a Pakistani, another Iranian. Whaddya think? Maybe they're al-Salaam's backup singers."

"Here." Tucker pointed to a new photo. "Here's half of the Supremes in Jordan, trying to get on a flight to Baghdad. Fortunately, Jordanian intelligence stopped them. Two of the group were on a list the Jordanians maintained of known members of an al-Qaeda splinter group operating inside Iraq. You want more?"

I waved Tucker off. "No. But it still doesn't prove anything about al-Salaam." I walked around to the other side of the desk and faced Tucker.

"Yeah, it doesn't connect the dots. You were supposed to do that. I guess I should be thankful al-Salaam made a hit list other than the top forty." He chortled. "Guy must have been a real smooth talker if he talked his way around you."

"He didn't have to talk his way around me. Everything he said sounded logical. It made sense."

Tucker grimaced. "What made sense?"

"His desire for peace. His reasons for wanting the United States out of Iraq. His call for America not to 'go it alone' in the world."

Tucker slammed a hand on his desk. "You believe all that crap or did he convert you? What next? Are you going to change your name to Muhammad?"

"What I believe isn't important."

"It damn sure is when you work for me and the Office of Municipal Security. If your personal beliefs place you in conflict with the mission of this office to protect the lives of the citizens of New York, tell me now and let's get this over with."

"I do my job regardless of my personal beliefs. Since when is there a litmus test of personal beliefs that qualify you to be an effective law enforcement officer?"

"Agent Shango." Tucker ordinarily used my code-name to mask his anger. He stood up and jabbed a finger my way. "Maybe you've forgotten that you're not a law enforcement officer anymore. You gave that up when the NYPD charged you with murder and sent you to jail. You're an intelligence officer now, and your personal beliefs color the world you see, color the information you report on. That's why they matter to me. Let me say that again. If you have any personal beliefs or feelings that are in conflict with the mission of this office, I need to know now."

I pushed the chair back and leapt to my feet, leaning over the desk toward Tucker. "Yeah, right now 'dismay' is the belief that's in conflict with this office, and 'anger' is the feeling that's rising."

"Then it's just a well that al-Salaam's dead. Neither dismay nor anger would have served you well on this case."

Tucker sat down and lowered his head to some papers on his desk. He brushed me off with a flick of his hand. "You're on contract. I'll call you if I need you."

I turned and walked toward the door. I'd just grabbed the doorknob when Tucker called out. "JJ's fourteen, isn't he?"

I spun around. "Yeah," I said.

"You have my sympathies," Tucker said. "He's probably taking al-Salaam's death pretty hard."

I nodded, but I didn't answer. Then I pivoted again, yanked Tucker's door open and steamed through the office.

"Good luck with your son," Charlene said in a pleasant voice.

I had my head down. When I raised it, a snide comment waited on the tip of my tongue. But I held back. I managed to mumble "Thanks" to Charlene.

Outside the office, I pummeled the elevator button with the side of my fist.

# FOUR

AL-SALAAM'S MURDER AND Ken Tucker's intransigence effectively rendered me temporarily unemployed. So, upon exiting City Hall, I turned north and walked up to SoHo. With a bare apartment, and nearly four hours before JJ got out of school, I decided to indulge in a time-tested method of therapy for pent-up emotions: shopping. It worked like a charm. I outfitted my bedroom with a low-rise Scandinavian bed, and a mattress with 6,000 springs the saleswoman claimed would trick me into believing I floated. For the living room, I got an eggshell-colored woolen carpet that accented the dark brown leather sofa, loveseat, and recliner. Come football season, I knew I'd enjoy watching games on the 52-inch wide-screen that would fit perfectly on one side of the fireplace.

When Charles Promise and I walked around the prison yard, I'd rail about being convicted on trumped-up charges of murdering a fellow police officer. Promise would listen, nod his head, and then say softly, "John, anger is a beautiful emotion, you just have to know how to use it; like a carpenter's tool—a chisel or a hammer. You pull it out of your tool pouch when you need it, and you put it back when you're through. But if you let anger use you it turns into the deadliest of emotions. All the while you think you're getting back at someone who aggrieved you, anger's dripping away like bottle of acid with a hole in it. Drop by drop eating you up from inside."

After the furnishings, I headed over to the Museum of African Art, where I picked up several pieces of wooden sculpture, and one oil painting of a Masai warrior with the snow-capped peak of Mount Kilimanjaro in the background. When I got through, I'd racked up a bill of nearly fifty thousand dollars and eaten up three hours. Fortunately, I'd also managed to keep my credit cards in my pocket. My only actual purchases took place in my mind.

When I got back home to Harlem, I pushed my front door buzzer just to hear Santana. But Carlos never arrived onstage. Instead, the doorbell system played something with a funky, hip-hop beat. I pull out my key and opened the door. JJ sat on the floor with his computer tied in to the doorbell system again.

"Hey, what's up?" I said.

"Not much," he said. His voice sounded subdued.

"Did you change the doorbell ringtone?"

"Uh huh."

I pointed to monitor. "Who is it?"

"Deuce F . . . al-Salaam," he said. "One of his first big hits."

"It's just the music, not the words," I said.

"And the rhythm," JJ said. "That's what I liked about him most. His beat."

I walked into the kitchen and grabbed a glass of water. JJ pulled out the cord from the doorbell system, folded his laptop closed, and came into the kitchen to join me. We sat across from each other at the small table. He rested his elbows on the table, his chin in his hands.

"Water?" I asked.

"Nah."

"Milk? Soda?"

"Nah."

"What then? What do you need?"

He took a deep breath, then sighed. "A favor."

"Name it," I said.

When he looked at me, I could see puffiness under his eyes. He took another deep breath, sighed again, then folded his hands and rested them on the table. He stared at me without flinching.

"You were supposed to investigate al-Salaam, right?"

"Right."

"Well, now that he's been murdered, would you find out who really killed him and why?"

It was my turn to take a deep breath and sigh. "The man I work for pulled me off of al-Salaam's case today."

"Why?"

"Al-Salaam no longer mattered to him once he was dead."

"Well, he still matters to me," JJ said. "And knowing who killed him and why would help me a lot. It'd also help lots of other kids who are sad because of his death."

"NYPD's investigating right now," I said.

JJ's voice rose. His eyes widened. "After what they did to you, you trust them to find out the truth? Al-Salaam's just another rapper in their eyes."

I shook my head slowly. "I can't argue with you on that one, son. And I'm proud you could ask for what you need." I took a deep breath. "I'll see what I can find out." I held up a finger. "But on one condition."

"What's that?" JJ asked.

"You have to help me."

"Help you? How?"

"We both know that I know next to nothing about hip-hop and rap. If I'm going to investigate the murder of a hip-hop artist, I'll need your help with the culture and the lingo."

A smile broke over JJ's face. He nodded and pointed to me. "Bet," he said. "I can do that."

He stood up from the table and started to walk from the kitchen. He took one step, then turned around, his earnest expression still in place.

"Dad," he said, "thanks. And you know what? You're cool."

I scratched my head. "Does this mean that you're my client, and I'm now working for you?"

JJ pursed his lips and smiled. He nodded his head slowly at first, then more vigorously. "Yeah, I guess it does."

"Does this mean that you're going to pay me too?"

"Well . . . I hadn't . . . I guess . . ."

"Just kidding. But you can tell me the name of the nightclub where al-Salaam was shot."

"The Hip-Hot-A-Mus."

"And is there someone there you think I should talk to?"

"Rapper named T-Mo," JJ said. "He owns the place."

* * *

Tucked away on New York's Lower Westside between Ninth Avenue and the Hudson River, the "Meat Packing District" once made a name for itself as a rough-and-tumble area where animal carcasses hung in cold basement rooms, and men wielding long iron tongs grappled with ice-blocks from the back of vans. Now upscale lofts, fashionable boutiques, high-end eateries, and trendy nightclubs like the Hip-Hot-A-Mus lined the streets of the District.

When I exited the subway station and turned the corner from Ninth Avenue, I ran into a lineup of people and cars waiting to get to the Hip-Hot-A-Mus. A column of red brake lights receded several blocks down the street and I moved through a curtain of fumes from the idling engines. Cadillacs, Lincolns, Porsches, BMWs—most of them SUVs. With each breath, acrid exhaust stung the back of my throat.

The lineup of people and the hard-driving thump of bass began about a block before the club. Amidst the baggy pants and baseball caps tilted at rakish angles, I had difficulty discerning a fashion statement from among those waiting to get into the Hip-Hot-A-Mus Club. At least I recognized that skin was still in—or should I say out? Thighs, cleavage, and biceps stood out among those in line. A pungent smell, part marijuana, part dueling perfumes and aftershaves, wafted through the air.

A glass enclosure, erected over the former loading dock, pushed the dance floor out above the sidewalk. Red and green lights shimmered inside. Dancers vie for coveted spots on the floor where they could be seen by passers-by. One young man, dressed in a pink suit and short-brimmed pink hat, propped his hands against the glass, trapping his dance partner against the enclosure. She had on a very short, very tight, black outfit. She faced the street, alternately opening then closing her eyes slowly, smiling ecstatically, and moving her lips as though moaning, while her buttocks bumped and grinded against her partner's groin.

Apparently, a two-tiered admissions policy existed at the Hip-Hot-A-Mus. Men pulling up in overstuffed SUVs, slapped car keys into the hands of valets, then strolled into the club with sleek women hanging on to their arms. But a big man with long dreadlocks that danced like a troupe of marionettes patrolled the lineup on the street. He sized up those waiting to get in. Women twirled in place to give him a global view. One man pulled him close, whispered in his ears, then shook his hand with a bill.

By whatever criteria the big man used, every so often he'd point to a couple and motion with his head toward the club's entrance. The woman would squeal, and the man would step from the line, offering his arm back to her. Then they'd both strut slowly toward the club as though St. Peter had just selected them to enter the Pearly Gates. Some of the Chosen Ones smiled, exchanging a few words with those still in line who looked on with adulation and awe.

I, however, ran a gauntlet of scornful looks as I bypassed the line and walked up to club's door. When I pulled the door open, a beefy palm thrust into my chest, pushing me back a step.

"Yo, man, where you think you going?"

The voice belonged to a big man who could have doubled for St. Peter of the Sidewalk, except he wore sunglasses and didn't sport dreadlocks. I flashed my badge, but it didn't have the intended effect. The bouncer grabbed my wallet and stared at my credentials.

"Office . . . of . . . Municipal . . . Security." He mouthed the words slowly. "Never heard of it."

I snatched my wallet back. "I'm here about al-Salaam's death."

The bouncer grimaced. "You know how many times I heard that tonight? What, you think it's tonight's password to get in? Well, I'm here about al-Salaam's death too." He pointed himself and then to the black ribbon tied around his arm. "Fact, tonight's been declared al-Salaam night at the club in honor of a fallen homie. So you and your badge ain't nothing special." He put a hand on my shoulder and pointed outside. "Line starts at the back. Sly, the dude with the dreads, will let you know if you're gonna get in or not."

The bouncer spun me around and started to push me out of the Hip-Hot-A-Mus, when I reached up and grabbed his hand. In one smooth motion I pivoted, turned him with me, and brought his hand and arm up behind his back. He started to reach inside his jacket, but I flexed his hand toward his wrist, hard. He groaned, and his knees buckled slightly. Together we walked into the club.

I whispered in his ear. "Smile, so you don't look like a complete idiot in front of all these people. And here's what you're going to do. You're going to point me in the direction of T-Mo, and when I release your arm you're going to go back to guarding the front door. There are twenty or more armed law enforcement officers from different agencies in here tonight, so if you do anything stupid I'll give them the real password and this place'll be shut down before the DJ can put another scratch on that LP. You understand?"

The bouncer stiffened his body against me, but he said nothing. I ratcheted his arm higher. He winced.

"You understand?" I asked.

Still nothing. I flexed his wrist again. This time I heard it pop.

"You're about ten seconds away from a broken wrist," I said.

That seemed to get his attention.

"Stairs at the back of the place. Second floor. Ask the man at the top of the stairs for T-Mo."

I let the man's arm drop. He rubbed his shoulder and his wrist. He turned to go, then twisted around. He wagged a finger at me. "Man, you one crazy motherfucka, coming in here like this. I hope you do got a big posse wit' you, 'cause you gonna need one to get out."

# FIVE

I COULDN'T HELP BUT bob to the beat as I brushed past breasts and buttocks bouncing and bumping around me. Tiny flashes of red and blue light shot from the mirrored globe dangling in the center of the floor. At the far end of the dance hall, a stairway led up to a second-floor tier. The heat and smell of hundreds of gyrating bodies ascended with me as I climbed the stairs. I looked up. A tall man with muscles bulging from his wife-beater tee shirt, stood cross-armed, eyeing me. A black cord trailing from an earbud looped in front of his chest. A thin microphone hung down over the side of his face. He stepped out to block my way. He had an intricate tattoo of writhing snakes covering the dark skin of his right biceps. He stared impassively. "Yo, wrong way," he said.

I hiked my thumb over my shoulder. "Fella downstairs said I could find the club's owner up here."

"Yeah, you could find him up here, but you ain't," he said.

I pulled out my badge. The man pressed his earbud closer and looked away from me. "Got him," he said into the microphone. "Says he wants to see T-Mo." He twisted back and glared at me.

I flashed my badge. "I need to ask the owner some questions," I said.

The tattooed man grinned, and the red and blue lights sparkled off his shiny, white teeth. "Like that badge is 'posed to mean something? Roy said you gave him some problems downstairs."

He took a step down the stairs, closer to me. I heard footsteps coming up the stairs behind me. I glanced over my shoulder quickly. The bouncer who'd asked me to leave headed upstairs, a swagger to his step, a sly smile on his face.

"Yo, dog," the tattooed man said. "Now, Roy and I are gonna escort you to the door. And we don't wanna see yo' sorry ass around here again. Dig it?"

I took another step upstairs, and the tattooed man put his hand out to stop me, which is what I'd hoped he'd do. Fighting uphill places you at a distinct disadvantage with one exception: gravity and leverage are on your side. I grabbed the tattooed man's arm, bent down, twisted around, and gave a pull. He went flying over my shoulder downstairs, colliding with Roy like a bowling ball knocking down a single pin. While they tumbled to the bottom of the staircase, I jogged my way to the top.

I stepped out onto a plush carpet, and what looked like the glass-enclosed VIP lounge behind doors. Men in suits, and women in evening low-cut gowns sat on a U-shaped leather couch around a large glass coffee table, sipping drinks and talking. I opened the glass doors. Inside the lounge, only the murmur of music and a steady but dampened bass beat from the club trickled through. I walked up to the couch. Everyone sitting seemed to flinch.

"Can someone tell me where to find T-Mo?" I said.

"Depends on who's looking for him," a wiry man with thin sideburns and a narrow mustache said. He wore a white suit and a white Stetson hat.

"I—"

Two arms grabbed me from behind.

"Sorry, boss," the man with the tattoo said. "He got by us. We'll show him out now."

He jerked on my arm.

"Wait," the wiry man said. He squinted, and pointed his finger between the bouncer and the guy with the tattoo. "Got by both of you? What the fuck I pay you for? Dude made it this far on his own, shows he's got initiative, unlike you sorry motherfuckers." He waved them off. "Now go back and see if you can at least manage to guard me from some freaky bitch that wants to get a piece of T-Mo."

T-Mo tugged on his lapels as the two guards turned and slunk off.

"Chumps," T-Mo said. He turned to me and smiled. "Sit, man, and tell me what bid'ness you want with me."

I took a seat at the end of the couch, next to a thin woman in a vibrant red dress that stood in sharp contrast to her caramel-colored skin. She smiled demurely, then scooted over to make space.

"Something to drink?" T-Mo said.

"No, thanks."

"Reefer? Coke?"

I waved him off. "No, thanks."

"You one polite motherfucker," T-Mo said. "Yo' mama taught you good, didn't she?"

He laughed, to himself at first, but then he kept on until everyone around the table joined in laughing with him.

"I'm here about the murder of Yousef al-Salaam," I said.

The laughing stopped.

"You the law?" T-Mo said.

"Office of Municipal Security."

I reached for my wallet. T-Mo reached inside his jacket. By the time I stretched my arm across the table with my credentials, he had a semiautomatic Glock pointed in my face. The people around the table gasped and reared back in their seats. But they must have looked closer and realized the ridiculous nature of this standoff between leather and steel. Several women began laughing. The whole table joined in. T-Mo stared at me without flinching. I stared back. Finally, a wide grin broke out over his face. His upper front teeth were crooked.

"Can't be too careful nowadays," he said. He slid his gun back into his jacket and waved away my wallet. "What you wanna know I haven't already told the NYPD?"

I shrugged. "I don't know since I haven't spoken to the NYPD."

A woman walked by. T-Mo waved her over. He smiled. "Tashawna, baby, bring T-Mo another Johnny Walker." He turned to me. "Mr. Manners, you sho' you don't want something to drink?"

"No, thank you," I said again.

"Fucking polite dude." He pointed at me and shook his head.

Someone passed a joint around. T-Mo sucked in a lungful of smoke, then blew out a thin stream. "Means you wanna know it all. That right, Mr. Manners? Now who'd ya say you work for?"

"Office of Municipal Security," I said.

"The Mayor's Office of Municipal Security?"

"Uh-huh."

T-Mo broke out laughing. He tried to stop several times but he couldn't. Giggles traveled around the table. The woman next to me put her hand on my thigh, as if to say "Don't worry he's always like this." Then she called across the table.

"What's so funny, T-Mo? Man just told you where he works."

"What's so funny?" T-Mo asked. He glared at the woman until she looked away. "MOMS," he said. "Take the first letter of each word of where Mr. Manners works and it spells MOMS. That's what's so funny." T-Mo started laughing again. No one joined in this time.

"Seems you're the only one that finds it funny," I said.

That brought T-Mo back with a vengeance. He slammed the table. "You dissing me, Mr. Manners?"

I said nothing, just stared at him. He pointed at me.

"You be careful, Mr. Manners. You're here and you're alive because I want you to be here and alive." He straightened his lapels. "Now, where were we? That's right, you wanted to know what happened to my good friend the Deuce. Well, like I told the NYPD, Deuce and his entourage came into the club shortly after midnight. We talked a little bid'ness over a drink or two, then he

47

said he had to leave. Somethin' 'bout getting up early for morning prayers—not that I understand that shit. Anyway, man leaves, and as he's walking out apparently some dude comes barreling down the street and BLAM!BLAM!BLAM!"—T-Mo cocked his thumb and shot at me with his index finger—"next thing I know my place is crawling with cops and EMTs, and the Deuce is pronounced dead . . . Sad thing, you know? Seein' your homey go down like that."

T-Mo smiled, but I struggled to find even a glimmer of remorse in his words.

"My son's a huge fan of yours," I said.

T-Mo grinned. "Kid's got good taste."

"Maybe you can help me understand something he's been saying about an ongoing feud between Old Style and New Style hip-hop rappers. My fourteen-year-old son seemed to think that might have had something to do with al-Salaam's death."

A few chuckles whisked around the table. T-Mo grinned even more. "Maybe yo' kid should be here 'stead of you . . . Old Style . . . New Style. A hip-hop feud?" He shook his head. "Man it's like Bro' Marvin used to say, 'Believe half of what you see, son, and none of what you hear.' Sure, there's a feud in hip-hop, but it ain't between the Old and the New. It's a marketing feud between 'Us'"—he patted himself on the chest—"and yo' kid's money"—he pointed to me. "And all this hype about a 'feud' between older artists and newer artists just helps sell more CDs for everyone."

"And I suppose the fact that al-Salaam's from the west coast, and you're from the east coast doesn't mean anything, either?"

T-Mo blew me off with a wave of his hands. "Sure it mean something. The man had to travel farther than I did to get back to his 'hood."

"So rumors of a feud between east coast and west coast rappers are nothing but marketing hype too?"

"Holmes, you learn quick, don't you?"

"And the fact that al-Salaam referred to you in one of his songs as 'Slo Mo, who don't know and can't show.' That's more marketing hype as well, isn't it?"

T-Mo shifted in his seat, his grin turning into a glare. "That would be my assumption."

"So let me get this straight. Al-Salaam started as a gangsta rapper from a west coast gang with a history of rivalry with the New York City gang that you belong to—"

"Belonged to." He exaggerated the *B*.

"Belonged to," I said. "You two trades insults in songs, and sometimes in public. Then he converts to Islam and takes his rapping and his audience in a whole new direction, away from the direction you're headed. Shortly after he's back from overseas he's shot dead walking out of your nightclub. His death a marketing trick to boost sales too?"

T-Mo laughed. "It worked for Tupac."

"What?"

"Man's sold more since he was dead, then he did when he was alive."

"And you want me to—"

T-Mo pushed back from his chair. He walked over to me. I stood up. We eyed each other like two bull elk ready to lock antlers.

"Time's up," he said. "'Sides, I didn't like where this line of questioning was heading, Holmes. Like you trying to in . . . sin . . . u . . . ate that I had something to do with my man's death." He started out the door, then turned back. "Rosy, Chanelle." He pointed around the table. "You two take care of Holmes here, make sure he has a good time. I've got some bid'ness to attend to." T-Mo whipped the glass doors open and walked briskly toward the stairs.

I reached for the door handle to follow him, when the woman I'd been sitting next to popped up in front of me. Then slender arms wrapped around me from behind, and a pair of firm breasts jabbed into my back. I walked through the door, pushing one woman ahead of me and dragging one behind.

"Honey, where you off to in such a hurry," the woman in front of me cooed. "You ain't even gonna stay for a drink?"

"Some other time," I said.

The woman behind me went up on tiptoes, nibbled my ears, then whispered. "I love bald men." She ran her hand over my head. "And I love to touch that smooth skin on the top of their head 'cause it reminds me of some other smooth skin that I love to touch." She started to slide her hand down the front of my body.

I pried her arms away from me, then twisted around and faced both women. The woman who'd been standing behind me, wore skintight brown leather pants and a silky sleeveless white blouse cut so low that cleavage was too modest a word to describe what she revealed.

I smiled and held up both hands. "I'm sorry, ladies, I know you're following T-Mo's orders, but I really don't have time."

The slender woman in the red dress pouted. Her friend with the more ample figure waved her hand at me in disgust. Both women pivoted at the same time and walked back into the glass lounge. I headed for the staircase, and when I got there, I looked down to see four brawny men steaming up, the bouncer and the guard I'd flipped among them.

The guard pointed at me and sneered. "That's him."

The bouncer smirked malevolently. "Told you you'd need a posse to get out."

# SIX

I TURNED AND RAN the other way along the narrow walkway, past the lounge and toward the lighted exit sign. Below me a thumping bass sounded louder and faster, and my heart kept pace with the beat. Behind me, the bouncer and his posse crested the stairs, heading my way. Ten feet ahead, the door under the exit sign swung open suddenly. Two more beefy men came at me. I turned back toward the bouncer. He had a 'gotcha' smile on his face. I looked over the railing down to the dance floor. I thought about jumping, but there's no way I could have made it. By the time I turned back, the men had almost converged on me.

I faced the two men who exited the staircase. Everything moved to the driving, funky sounds that emanated from the dance floor—the men with their hard expressions bearing down on me, and me moving toward them—as though the music choreographed our actions and somewhere unseen a music video television camera rolled. The bigger of the two stepped forward. I swung at him but he blocked my punch. He must have been trained in martial arts, because he grasped my arm, twisted around, and tried to flip me onto the floor. But my height proved more than he could manage. He couldn't force me down. Then two men grabbed me from behind, pinning my arms to my sides, and my struggle was over. They bent me over the railing.

The bouncer punched me twice, hard, in my kidney. I winced.

"You thinking 'bout jumping? Huh, motherfucker? Just tell me," he said. "We'll help you over." He crashed his elbow into my back.

"Man, not here, Roy," a voice said. "Frisk the motherfucker, then we'll take him down to the basement."

The bouncer patted me down. "Dude's clean," he said. "You really are some stupid ass motherfucker, comin' in here talkin' trash, and you ain't even carrying. Well, I am."

He peeled me off the railing, and jammed the end of his pistol into my back.

"C'mon. We all gonna take a little walk, then make a little talk."

"Here," the bouncer said. He handed his gun to another man who jabbed it into my back again. Then the bouncer grabbed my arm, bent it, and ratcheted it behind my back. I stiffened against the pain.

"Payback's a bitch, ain't it?" the bouncer said. "Now you make sure you don't try any cowboy shit this time, 'cause we ready for you." The gunman thrust the pistol barrel harder into my back.

With two men in front of me and two men behind, the group hustled me toward the stairs, then pushed me down into the heat rising from the dancers and lights; down into some hell I could

53

only imagine the bouncer concocting in his mind. He kept my one arm painfully tight and high up my back.

When we hit the dance floor, we turned right and wove our way through the thinner crowd at the edge of the dancers. A DJ spun an old LP back and forth under a needle. The "whacka whacka" sound reverberated through the hall and sent the club's lights pulsing in rhythm to the beat. Up ahead, a young woman in a tight, almost sheer, white dress stood talking to a man. When we reached her, I swung my free arm out and hooked her around the waist. The men around me kept moving, pushing me with them. I dragged the woman along a few feet before my entourage stopped.

I said loudly, "You one fly bitch. Can we dance?"

I held on to her. Her eyes widened, but before she could say anything, her man was in my face. Shorter than me, he barked and jabbed his finger at me like a drill sergeant dressing down a recruit.

"Who the fuck you think you are motherfucker, talking to my woman like that? Let go of her."

The man holding the gun pressed it deeper into my back. The bouncer cranked my arm higher. Still, I held on to the woman, fighting off the pain. Her boyfriend, a guy of medium build, didn't speak again. He swung at me and I ducked. His blow glanced off the side of my face. I still held on to his girlfriend, which only infuriated him. One of the men escorting me stepped in front to push the boyfriend off, but the boyfriend landed a hard right into his stomach, doubling him over, then turned and ripped his girlfriend from me. He swung at me again and I managed to block him. The bouncer tried to jerk me away, but the boyfriend saw him make the move and he went after the bouncer instead, pummeling him with blow after blow, forcing him to make a decision about whom to go after.

The moment I felt the bouncer's grip lessen, I swung my free hand back and down hard into his groin. He yelped as he doubled over in pain. I dove to floor and kicked my leg out to sweep the man with the gun off of his feet. I stayed on the floor, but he jumped up and started swinging wildly. He hit a tall man standing near him, and the man swung back. Perhaps the gunman had mistaken the tall man for me. But by now it didn't matter. A melee engulfed the club.

The boyfriend had all but forgotten about me, and even his girlfriend. He and the bouncer danced above me, circling each other, trading punches. I slithered forward to one of the large round posts that supported the second tier, then I pulled myself up, hiding partially behind the post. Despite the fighting, the rap music kept on—a perfect, if not macabre, soundtrack for the brawl.

T-Mo's thugs wrestled the boyfriend from the club. His girlfriend strutted behind the throng, turning her head and smiling to the onlooking crowd as though enjoying the attention. The men hustled back inside and fanned out among the crowd. I crouched and made my way forward through the dancers, trying to get to the entrance. But nearing it, I saw a line of men guarding the door, eyeing everyone leaving.

Suddenly, the music ended. The speaker blared with the DJ's voice, "Everyone—hit the floor, now."

The drill must have been familiar. En masse people dove to the ground, men falling on top of women as though simply performing another funky dance move. I crouched low and moved away from the door. Absent the music, the red and green lights still pulsed off the mirrored ball in the middle of the dance floor. I crouched among a group of dancers on the riser underneath the glass enclosure, which protruded out into the street. On the dance floor below me, seven or eight men spread among the crowd, pointing guns at the heads of terrified sprawled-out dancers, demanding that they turn over for a better look.

Suddenly, the house lights flashed on, momentarily blinding me. I dove to the floor, squeezing between bodies, but when my eyes adjusted, I saw several people kneeling above pointing down at me.

"Here," a young woman said. "He's over here."

The DJ barked into the speaker. "Down. Everyone please remain down."

The people standing above me dropped to the floor. The men after me tiptoed over patrons. I got onto my hands and knees to crawl, but I soon came to the glass enclosure and had no place to go from there.

I stood up with my back against the glass and looked out over a sea of bodies.

"There," a man said, pointing to me.

Pistols came up. I dove back to the ground as a brief outburst of gunfire rattled. Bullets struck the glass with a sharp sound, creating a spider web of cracks. The men moved more quickly toward me. Sweat forced its way from my pores. I threw my shoulder against the glass at a spot where the fracture lines radiating from two bullet holes met. The glass creaked, but I bounced back. A man with a gun hopped up onto the riser. I flung myself at the glass again. It groaned, but it only buckled slightly. Two men were only ten feet away when I moved back slightly, mustered all the strength I had, and rammed the glass with my shoulder.

I popped a fragmented chunk of glass out into the street. I seemed to hang in the middle of the glass, most of my body inside the club, my shoulder and part of my arm outside. Finally, the enclosure let go, showering tiny glass fragments everywhere, and dumping me onto the street.

I didn't look back. Shots followed me as I raced down the block away from the club. Then I turned a corner and ran right into three men dressed in baggy pants and dark hooded sweatshirts. I couldn't see their faces well, but all of them held guns. They grabbed me, and threw me up against the brick side of a building. One man yelled.

"Hands above your head pressed up against the wall. Do it."

Another man kicked my feet apart. I turned my head slightly to see the men who'd pursued me in the club coming around the corner with their guns drawn, T-Mo among them. The moment they saw me they stopped. T-Mo held his hand up.

"It's taken care of," I heard him say. "Let's go back and see about the club."

"NYPD," one of the men behind me said. "Hands behind your back."

"I'm an agent with the Office of Municipal Security," I said.

"Shut up," a voice said.

Someone grabbed one arm, then the other, and jerked them down behind my back. A hand reached from behind me and patted me down.

"Inside jacket pocket on the left," I said. "You'll find a wallet there with my identification."

A pistol muzzle dug into the base of my skull. A hand came around from behind and snaked its way into my jacket pocket, tugging, wriggling my wallet until freeing it. I tried to turn around, but a man drove me back against the wall.

"Keep your face against the wall," a voice said.

Police sirens whooped as they came closer. Someone behind me said, "Keep him here while I check."

In the distance, I heard the sounds of static over a radio and someone talking, but I couldn't make out the conversation. A moment later, a voice and fine spray of spittle entered my ear. "What the fuck are you doing in this club?"

I tried turning around again.

"Stay facing the wall," a man said.

"Investigating the murder of Yousef al-Salaam," I said.

"Under whose authority?"

"I work for the Office of Municipal Security."

"Right, we got that. But this's our party. We've set this undercover operation up for six months, and now in one night you stroll in like some fucking lone wolf and nearly blow our cover."

I remained silent. I didn't think it mattered to them that I once worked as an undercover officer for the NYPD too. Out the corner of my eye, I saw a squad car pull up. A door opened and slammed shut. A uniformed officer walked up behind me.

"Wait 'til we've walked away," one of the undercover agents said to the uniformed officer, "then put him in the car and take him away from here. You'll need this to unlock his cuffs."

Footsteps moved away. A hand grabbed my shoulder, turned me around, and pushed me toward the squad car. I craned my head to see three dark, hooded figures swaggering like ego-puffed gangbangers down the street, before disappearing into the night.

# SEVEN

THE NEXT MORNING, I awoke to sunlight shooting through the slats in my window blinds. I rolled over and checked the clock. Nine. Damn. I hopped out of bed and hustled into the living room. A jumble of sheets and blankets lay on the couch. On top of the pile, a note from JJ read, "Tried to wake you, but I couldn't. Guess you enjoyed yourself at the Hip-Hot-A-Mus. Hope the investigation's going well. See you later."

I rubbed my eyes and stumbled into the kitchen to make a cup of coffee. I pulled open the cabinet doors. The shelves were nearly empty. I looked down. The only two cups I owned sat dirty in the sink, so I grabbed a glass and settled for water.

Sleep drained from me, carrying with it the fragments of a dream. I tried to hold on, but managed only to recover a few disjointed snippets. Something about confronting the bouncer last night on the club's staircase, but the bouncer morphed into my estranged wife Liz. Then when I burst through the club's front window, instead of running from the guys in pursuit, I ran after Liz, who fled down the block away from me.

After my release from prison, I thought Liz and I had a good chance of reconciling. The city and the federal government dropped all charges against me for murdering another law enforcement officer, removing the main reasons I believed she filed for a separation in the first place. Although I slept on Nora's living room couch, I often visited JJ and Liz in my former Striver's Row home. I even spent a few nights in my former bed with Liz. We laughed, and talked, even made love a couple of times. But our conversation always returned to one subject. Liz had this notion that somehow she'd lived her life according to everyone's expectations but her own—her parents, her teachers, me, JJ. And even though she was a well-respected gynecologist, she didn't know who she was. One night in bed, after we'd just made love, she started weeping.

"John," she said. "I just can't do this. I need time. I need to find myself. I need to discover what I should be doing with my life."

I snatched the catalog from the Sigma Center off the kitchen table, rolled it up, then thwacked the table with it. I'd spent two long years of soul-searching in prison, so I understood what it meant to look at yourself, to try to find some meaning and purpose in your life. I discovered that I'd let working as a detective consume me, pull me away from my child and my wife. I wanted more than anything to correct that when I got out. Liz discovered something quite the opposite. She took a leave from the hospital, started doing more yoga and meditation, and going to workshops like the two-week retreat at the Sigma Center.

I sipped some water and mindlessly thumbed through the catalog. Yoga workshops. Meditation workshops. Buddhism workshops. Hinduism workshops. Women's workshops. Men's workshops. Silent workshops. Workshops on how to give workshops. Funny how the description of every workshop sounded remarkably the same. "Self-exploration." "Self-discovery." "Self-help." "Self-growth." "Self-enlightenment." Then I scanned the prices. "Self" made pretty good money for the Sigma Center.

I turned a page to a color photograph of a dark-skinned older man with a shocking white beard, deep penetrating eyes, and an alluring smile, which seemed to me to say, "It's all a game. Don't take this 'self' stuff too seriously." I smacked my glass down on the table, reached for the phone, and called the Sigma Center. A woman with a dreamy voice answered.

"Hello, this is the Sigma Center. My name is Jaya. May I serve you?"

"I want to register for Sheikh Tariq Bashir's workshop on Sufism," I said. "But I'm wondering if I could speak to Mr. Bashir about the workshop first?"

"Can you hold a minute, please?" Jaya said. "Take a few deep breaths and I'll be right back with you."

Take a few deep breaths? I heard a click and then the angelic sounds of a harp, flute, and cello.

"I'm sorry but Sheikh Bashir does not allow for prospective workshop participants to contact him directly."

"Then how am I supposed to know what to expect?"

"You mean you don't know Tariq Bashir?"

She sounded incredulous, as though I'd asked a die-hard football fan if he knew who'd won the Super Bowl.

"I wouldn't be asking to contact him if I did."

"He's a seventh generation Sufi master. You know, the spiritual teacher to super stars like actors Brad Thomas and Melissa Coleman."

"And Yousef al-Salaam?"

"Who's that?" Jaya asked.

I mimicked her. "You mean you don't know Yousef al-Salaam?"

Her voice dropped. "Sorry," she said. "When you're here at Sigma most of the time you tend to believe the rest of the world lives like you and knows everyone you know. Tariq Bashir's Sufi center is in Brooklyn. Maybe you could get more information from them directly."

"Thanks," I said.

"Follow your bliss," Jaya said.

I did. I hung up.

\* \* \*

A quick "finger walk" through the Yellow Pages located Tariq Bashir's Sufi Center in Brooklyn, just off Seventh Avenue, not too far from Prospect Park.

Approaching the center on foot, a red heart with a yellow star and crescent in the middle and wings on both sides dominated the sign on the three-floor brick building. The bottom of the heart sat above a wave of Arabic letters. Beneath the sweep of letters a sign in English read, "Sufi Center of Brooklyn." Beneath that, more Arabic covered the bricks.

A cadre of young men dressed in white took aim at the brick with paintbrushes and rollers. I stared at the paint squad, trying to decipher its mission: repaint the Arabic messages, or cover them over in preparation for painting something new?

When I pulled the door to the Center open, the smell of frankincense greeted me. A cast-iron rack of shoes sat just inside the door. I slipped mine off and walked over the light blue carpet to a desk where a young, olive-skinned man in long white robes and a white skullcap sat, staring into his computer monitor. He raised his head.

"Salaam Alaikum," he said.

The greeting's often heard in prison where a large number of black inmates convert to Islam. Fortunately, I'd also heard the response.

"Walaikum Salaam," I said.

The receptionist grinned. "Yes, my dear brother. My name is Ali. How may I serve you."

I chuckled to myself. I didn't think Ali would appreciate a comparison with Jaya, probably a young, upper middle-class white woman from the suburbs, but they came across as remarkably similar to me.

"I'm here to speak with Mr. Bashir about Yousef al-Salaam."

Ali's smile broadened as though I'd made a joke.

"Yes, my dear brother," he said. "Master Bashir isn't available, but I can have you speak with his assistant, Brother Hamid."

Ali picked up his telephone handset, pressed some buttons, then uttered a few staccato phrases in Arabic. He appeared to argue with whomever he spoke to, but when he placed the headset down his smile returned.

"My dear brother," Ali said. "Have a seat." He motioned to some pillows against the wall behind me. "Brother Hamid will be with you shortly."

I walked over to the pillows, but I chose to stand. The light lavender walls of the reception area combined with the powder blue carpet to give the room an airy, spacey feeling. A set of portraits adorned the wall: some pen and ink drawings, some looked liked old daguerreotypes, some were photographs; all were of men with smiles like Ali's, and the last name Bashir. I recognized the photo of the man with the striking white beard, farthest to my right. The same picture of Tariq Bashir appeared in the Sigma Center catalog.

"Eight centuries of an unbroken lineage of Sufi masters."

The thin, wispy voice came at me from behind, and I spun around to a thin, wispy tall man with a scraggly beard facing me. He too had the Sufi smile. He didn't introduce himself. But I guessed I'd just met Brother Hamid.

He pointed to the leftmost portrait. "From Sheikh Muhammad Bashir, our founder"—he pointed to the only face I recognized—"to Sheikh Tariq Bashir, our present leader. Eight centuries. Twenty men. One ideal. Would you care to follow me?"

He swept his hand forward and pointed to a set of double glass doors with stained wooden frames. Hamid grabbed both crystal doorknobs, one in each hand, then pushed the doors open, revealing a large room with highly polished, varnished wooden floors. A stack of pillows sat at one end of the room.

"We dance in here," Hamid said.

I imagined Yousef al-Salaam twirling over the wooden dance floor, white robes trailing him, as I'd seen on TV. On the other side of the dance floor, Hamid pushed through another set of glass doors, which led to a carpeted hallway. I followed behind Hamid as we walked past several doors that lined one side of the hallway.

"Our *mureedin* live here."

"Mureedin?"

Hamid kept a brisk pace down the hallway. His white robe fluttered as he walked. He answered me without turning around. "Students who have received *bayat* and chose to live here to deepen their studies with Master Sheikh Bashir."

"Bayat?"

Hamid huffed. "Initiation into a Sufi order of self-discovery and enlightenment."

"Is there a dictionary for the undiscovered and the unenlightened to understand the terms used by the other half?"

Hamid didn't respond. Instead, he opened a door to a small room with a desk and a computer at the far end. Just inside the door, a few embroidered pillows lay around a low antique wooden hexagonal table. Handcrafted silverwork capped each corner of the table. A few dark Persian rugs covered the floor, the dark red, brown, and green of their weaves standing in sharp contrast with the ever-present light blue carpet. An antique, hand-tooled, silver teapot with a long curved spout sat on the low table, in the middle of four matching silver teacups on silver plates. Hamid pushed his white robe to one side, gracefully folded his legs under him, and sat at the table. I must have looked like an ungainly giraffe, but I managed to cross my legs under me and join Hamid at the table. Hamid lifted the teapot, and a tiny puff of steam exited the spout.

"Tea, Mr. . . . ?"

"Shannon," I said. "John Shannon."

"Tea, Mr. Shannon?"

"Yes," I said.

A thick, fragrant, sweet smell rose from the cup as Hamid poured the tea. I've never been to the Middle East, but the aroma and the rugs and the silver all conspired to transport me to a mythical clandestine room in the back of a business where men with beards sipped tea and whispered in hushed Arabic. I took a sip of tea and the fantasy crashed instantly, as the bitter, strong taste assaulted my tongue. I placed the teacup on its plate. Hamid smiled.

"Yousef al-Salaam was a student of Sheikh Bashir?" I asked.

"We are all *mureedin* of Sheikh Bashir," Hamid said. "What is your interest in our dear departed brother?"

I pulled out my badge. "I'm investigating his death."

Hamid didn't flinch. "Such a tragedy. A young man who had found the path, taken before he had proceeded very far. But it puzzles me why you are here and not among the—how do you say it?—hoodlums who were part of our dear brother's previous life."

"I've been among those in his previous life, but I wanted a fuller picture of whom Yousef al-Salaam had become. Had he received ba . . . yad?" I asked.

"Bayat," Hamid corrected me. A frown crossed his face, but a Sufi smile soon replaced it. "He had found the tariqah."

"He'd found the path."

Now I gave Hamid a Sufi smile. But he retreated behind his smile, which seemed a convenient place to hide. He appeared to be struggling for words, then suddenly picked up his teacup and took a delicate sip. After he set it down, he said, "Our young brother tried."

"Did anyone at the Center object to the way he tried?"

The corner of Hamid's lips wrinkled as though he fought to maintain his smile. "We are Sufis," he said. "Ours is a path of the heart . . . a path of truth . . . a path of enlightenment. Everyone travels at a different speed in a different way on this path. With so much work to be done on one's own tariqah, there's no room for objection to another's journey."

"Sounds idyllic. So did anyone object to the way al-Salaam went about finding his path?"

Hamid sipped more tea. "He had much to learn. He seemed to be in a hurry."

"In a hurry?" I asked. "In what way?"

"Our Sufi order has a lineage that goes back generations. One *murshid*—teacher—has passed a set of teaching to his students from which a teacher passed the same set of teachings to his students, and on and on . . ."

"Lemme guess. Al-Salaam didn't follow the rules?"

Hamid put his teacup down and stared at me. His penetrating eyes reminded me of Promise's. "Not rules, Mr. Shannon. Teachings. Guiding principles. Insights. All gathered by learned masters throughout the ages."

"Did someone object to the way al-Salaam followed the teachings?"

"Sufism attracts the objections of others, Mr. Shannon. It's called *malama*, the Path of Blame by the outside world."

I'd had enough. I slapped both hands on the table. Hamid flinched. I stared at him and made a circle in the air with my finger. "Could we skip the spiritual double-talk? My question was simple. Would someone inside this organization, this Center, this order—or whatever you call it—dislike Yousef al-Salaam enough to kill him?"

Hamid regained his composure quickly, and though he smiled, his eyes said plainly, "You cannot shake me." After his next long, drawn-out sip of tea, he nodded and said, "You should ask our young mureedin this question."

"The ones painting Arabic messages on the building?"

"They are not painting messages, Mr. Shannon. They're removing a message."

"And what message are they removing?"

"A message that says, 'Death to the Sufi Infidels.'"

"And who'd paint that message on your walls?"

"All who object to our way."

"No." I shook my head. "Not all. Only those who object and know Arabic. Like other Muslims."

Hamid's smile remained firm. "You see, Mr. Shannon, you have arrived at your own truth. Sufism is the mystical order of Islam, and mystical truths are never arrived at easily or directly."

I guess not.

# EIGHT

ONLY THE GODS ENJOYED the sun, leaving us mortals struggling beneath the layer of clouds and haze over the city. I walked briskly from the subway station. I wouldn't make it home before JJ, but I still wanted to be there not long after he arrived from school. I needed to talk with him about my investigation into Yousef al-Salaam's death.

I could take the easy way out and tell him that I guessed that al-Salaam's murder *was* the result of a feud with gangsta rappers who didn't like him trying to bring a new, less violent ethic into hip-hop music. If JJ insisted that I needed to find out exactly who pulled the trigger, I could also tell him everything that happened the night I visited the Hip-Hot-A-Mus Club—that might satisfy him enough to allow me to drop the investigation.

On the other hand, I could tell him the truth: that I really didn't know who killed al-Salaam or why, and that the deeper I got into the investigation, the more the different possibilities seem to emerge: a feud between rappers, a feud among different factions of Islam, or a feud within the Sufi community. Of course, for the latter to be true you'd have to believe that Sufis could be violent. It's not what they profess, but the Sufis I'd met smiled a lot and hid a lot behind those smiles.

I turned the corner on my block. When I got to my brownstone, I took the stairs two at a time. I shoved my key into the front door lock and shouldered open the door. I walked more slowly up to my second-floor apartment. Each step brought me closer to facing the fact that I doubted I should continue investigating al-Salaam's death. Each step also brought me closer to facing the disappointment in the eyes of my son.

I pressed the doorbell just to see if JJ had changed the ringtone, but the same al-Salaam ditty still played. Before I could get my key in the door lock, JJ swung the door open. I looked at him. He was dressed to go jogging. I walked in, and he tossed a pair of running shoes at me.

"Here," he said. "Let's go for a run in the park and you can bring me up to date on your investigation."

It left me about as speechless as him calling Nora my 'ho. I couldn't count all the times over the years that I'd asked JJ to go jogging with me. He always found a reason not to go.

"You're on," I said. "Lemme change into my running outfit."

I closed the door behind me and headed for my bedroom. It's the kind of offer no sane parent of a teenager refuses. They say that somewhere between thirteen and sixteen, glimmers of an adult begin to breakthrough the veil of childhood, like the sun breaking through a layer of haze. Maybe, today, sun was in the forecast for us mortals after all.

To most people, JJ and I look alike. Same broad shoulders. Same high cheekbones. Same wide nose. Same strong chin. Same chocolate skin. JJ, however, had not figured out what he wanted to do with his hair: let it go dread, straighten it gangsta style, sprout short, curly braids. I'd made up my mind right after leaving prison: cut it all off and go bald. The two of us, dressed in black running pants and jackets, must have looked like a pair of those stackable dolls—African-American rather than Russian— as we jogged across Cathedral Parkway and headed into Central Park. I held up at the first bench we came to inside the park and put a hand on JJ's shoulder.

"Stretch," I said.

He frowned. "But dad . . ."

I planted a foot against the bench and leaned over my outstretched leg.

"Stretch," I said again.

"But—"

"Stretch."

"Okay . . ."

JJ bent over and made a half-hearted attempt at stretching. I smiled to myself. After all, it was only a glimmer of adulthood that supposedly shone through these teenage years, not a full-on sunny day. I finished stretching and we jogged over to a well-trod path and fell in behind a young woman running with a leashed St. Bernard. Both the woman's hips and her dog's switched back and forth with the same loping rhythm. JJ elbowed me and pointed.

"That's cute," he said.

"What's cute?"

"The way that bit . . . I mean, that woman's butt moves just like her dog's."

"Thanks," I said. "It is cute."

After we stopped laughing, JJ asked, "So what's the 4-1-1 on your investigation?"

And the weight of a role reversal crashed onto my shoulders as though JJ had stepped into the role of parent and I'd become a child who needed to 'fess up.

"I'm not sure," I said.

And I proceeded to tell him everything I knew. What happened at the Hip-Hot-A-Mus Club. My meeting with the Sufi group. I laid out the possibilities of who killed al-Salaam. JJ sighed. He stopped running and walked over to a bench. I followed him and we sat down. He took a deep breath, then turned to face me.

"Dad, listen. I wanted you to find out who killed al-Salaam because it would help me and a lot of kids I know come to grips with his death. But the last thing I'd ever want is for you to get hurt, or even worse, to get killed trying to discover the truth. I want you to back off of the investigation now."

Another moment of sunlight just broke through.

"Thanks, son," I said. "I kinda feel the same way."

I put my arm around JJ's shoulder and pulled him in to me, but his body stiffened and I didn't insist. I reminded myself to enjoy the moments of sunlight I'm given and not to push for more.

"You wanna go down near the reservoir, do a lap and come back?" I asked.

JJ jumped up. "Yeah, let's go."

73

We came to a roadway that meanders inside the western perimeter of the park. While waiting at the red light, we jogged in place with a group of runners. Once the light changed, the group headed across and each of us sidestepped a pile of horse dung in the middle of the black dirt of a horse trail. The pack of runners separated out, many taking off before us. JJ and I brought up the rear. I'm sure he'd have loved to break into a sprint, but I wasn't in shape.

Ahead of us, two tall, muscle-bound men dressed in matching deep purple running suits jogged at a leisurely pace. Their bright red sweatbands looked like devilish halos. From their lackadaisical gait, frequent exchange of conversation, and roving eyes, I guessed they were out trolling for women. They reminded me of the bouncers at the Hip-Hot-A-Mus Club, though it wasn't them.

Suddenly, I heard the brakes of a car squeal to a stop on the roadway we'd just crossed. I spun my head around but I didn't see anything. Still, after fifteen years as a police officer and detective, my nerves hover on the brink of alertness whenever I'm on the streets. JJ jogged by my side in oblivion. After a bend, the running path took us past an area with a small stand of pine trees on one side and a grassy area on the other. No other runners were around. I'd lost sight of the two men who'd been jogging before us, and the needle of my internal alarm meter jiggled toward red. They hadn't been running fast enough to disappear that quickly. I turned my head again, and as I turned back I heard two cracks, then the dull thud of a bullet lodging into a tree trunk.

I rammed my shoulder into JJ, pushing him off the path onto the grass.

"Dad, what the—"

"Run. Someone's shooting at us."

JJ's eyes flashed wide open. We both picked up our pace. I looked behind me, but I only saw a thin man in an iridescent blue jogging suit running up the path.

"Are you sure someone shot at us?" JJ asked.

"Keep running," I said.

When I looked behind me again, the man in the blue jogging suit had veered off the path onto the grass, heading our way. A gunman wouldn't risk shooting while running, which meant he wanted to get closer. I pushed JJ forward. He breathed hard.

"Faster," I said.

I looked behind us. The man in the blue running suit seemed in no particular hurry. Even though JJ and I widened the gap between us, the man maintained a steady pace in our direction. Evening had settled over the park and orange sodium lamps buzzed and hissed as they flickered on. JJ and I came to a path that led west out of the park. We took it. The path dipped down to a tunnel underneath a stone traffic overpass. The brake lights of rush hour traffic glowed red above us as we entered the tunnel.

But something didn't feel right. I yanked JJ back from the tunnel. That's when I saw the two large men who'd been ahead of us before coming at us from the other side of the tunnel. I looked back. The man in the blue running suit still headed our way. No wonder he ran so leisurely. He intended to herd us, not to catch us.

"Up the side," I said to JJ.

I pushed him up the embankment. We scrambled in the dirt to the top of the overpass where a line of rush hour traffic crawled in both directions. The two men also made it to the top of the embankment. From the other side of the overpass, they ran our way. I looked down. The man in the blue jogging suit headed up the embankment as well.

"What now?" JJ's breathy voice telegraphed his fear.

"Across the traffic," I said.

I grabbed JJ's hand and pulled him between two cars rolling slowly west. I held my other hand out, but the driver laid on his horn and kept moving. I slammed my fist on his hood. He stuck his head out his window and cursed us. The eastbound lane of traffic sat without moving. Behind us, the three men also made their way across the traffic. Ahead of us, a yellow taxicab pulled so close to the car in front that JJ and I couldn't squeeze through the gap, so I rolled myself over the hood of the taxi. JJ followed. The taxicab driver also blew his horn, rolled down his window and hurled obscenities our way.

We found no footpath on the other side of the traffic. The man in the blue running suit hadn't made it across the first lane of traffic. The two big guys stood in the middle of the two lanes. I pulled JJ down behind the taxicab, and whipped my keys from my pocket.

"Nora's apartment is close to here. Do you remember where she lives?"

JJ said nothing, but he nodded rapidly.

I thumbed through the keys until I got to Nora's. I slipped her key off. "This is hers." I handed the key to JJ. "Stay down. Crawl in that direction," I jabbed my finger west, "and go to her apartment. Don't let anyone follow you. I'll meet you there later."

JJ pointed. "But Dad, the guys are coming that way."

"They won't be for long," I said.

"What about you?"

"You go to Nora's. I'll meet you there later."

"I don't want to leave you."

"You don't have a choice." I hugged him quickly, then pushed him away. "Now go."

The moment JJ took off, I bobbed up from the side of the taxi. The two big men saw me, and instead of crossing the eastbound lane, they swam between the two lanes of traffic heading my way. The man in the blue running suit was also between lanes, coming at me from the other direction. I decided to play "chicken" with him. I ran at him as he ran toward me. It must have surprised him at first. He hesitated for an instant and reared back. When he did, I rolled over the hood of a car moving west, dove for the embankment and tumbled down to the path below.

I must have hit a rock or a piece of glass on the way down. When I stood, a searing pain shot up my leg. I looked down to see a gash in my running suit. I limped as I started to run, and when I grasped my thigh, my hand felt a warm, sticky wetness. It didn't matter. I had to keep going. The man in the blue running suit headed down the embankment, and closer to the tunnel one of the big men headed down the embankment as well, which meant, I feared, that the other big man had gone after JJ.

I made my way down the path JJ and I had taken before, trying to run, but the pain in my leg kept me from moving quickly. I looked behind me. Both men headed toward me. The man in the blue running suit now picked up his pace, putting him well ahead of the big man. The path made a short jog to the right, and after the turn I leaped for a low-hanging tree limb. I pulled myself up onto the branch and waited.

In this dim light, I hoped the first man behind me wouldn't see me. His footsteps kept up their pace. I sucked in a breath as he rounded the corner, and when he was below me I leaped from the tree onto his shoulders. He crumpled, and I slammed his head into the ground several times. His body went limp. I reached into his pocket and pulled out his pistol, then I turned to fire once at the big man as he came around the corner. I missed, but the big man must have thought twice about having a shootout with me because he pivoted and quickly disappeared around the corner.

I stuck my hands into the pockets of the man on the ground again. Nothing. No wallet or identification. He appeared to be unconscious. I shoved his gun into his pocket and limped away as fast as I could. Someone would find him and call the police. Right now, I didn't care about him. I cared about JJ's safety.

# NINE

SOME ANIMALS WILL FAKE a broken limb to distract predators from their young. I hobbled north through Central Park, away from where I'd last seen JJ just in case either of the two big men came across me while looking for him.

Once inside my apartment, I lunged for the telephone and called Nora's number. JJ didn't pick up. I slammed my fist on the kitchen table, then went into the bathroom to hurriedly bandage my leg. A six-inch gash ran down the middle of my right thigh. I winced as I dabbed it with an antibacterial cream, then I wrapped a gauze bandage around it, changed clothes, and raced back outside. I flagged down a taxi.

When we got to the El Dorado, Nora's massive twin tower apartment building at 88th Street and Central Park West, Uri, a doorman dressed in a gray uniform, swung the door open. I hopped out. Uri smiled.

"Ms. Daniels told me you now had your own place," he said.

"Have you seen my son, JJ?"

Uri shook his head. "Not since I came on duty at four."

I thought about heading back into the park, but something told me to go upstairs and wait.

"I gave him the keys to Nora's apartment," I said. "I told him to meet me here."

Uri waved his hand. "No problem. I'll let you in."

We rode the elevator to the tenth floor. Uri unlocked Nora's door, then pushed it open, but the door jammed against the chain.

I called out. "JJ?"

"Dad?" A voice came from behind the door.

JJ slid the chain back.

"Thanks," I said to Uri.

Uri smiled and so did I.

JJ still had a determined look. He wielded a broom handle. I put my hands out.

"It's okay, son," I said.

I closed the door behind me. JJ collapsed into my arms, sobbing.

"I called 911," he said. "I thought those men killed you."

"That's good," I said. "We'll call them back and tell them I'm allright."

The 911 dispatcher thanked us for calling back. I walked into Nora's kitchen, grabbed a soda for each of us, and we plopped down on her plush white couch.

"What happened?" I asked.

JJ took a few sips of soda, then wiped his mouth with the back of his hand. His breath was still rapid, shallow. "One of the men started after you, then he must have seen that I wasn't with you because he turned and came in my direction. I had trouble getting through the line of cars. I ran as fast as I could. I thought about running down the street, but I came to a subway station and heard a train pulling into the station. I ran downstairs, jumped over the turnstile, and hopped onto a downtown local. I don't know if the man followed me, but I got off at 72nd Street, switched back to an uptown local, and rode it two stops past Nora's. Then I got out and circled the block twice. I didn't see anyone behind me, so I walked to Nora's. When the doorman walked out to help an older woman from a taxicab, I slipped inside. I didn't take the elevator; I walked up to Nora's floor. And I didn't answer the doorbell or the telephone."

I put my arm around JJ's shoulders and pulled him into me. This time he didn't resist. Instead, he melted into my side. "I'm proud of you," I said. "You did just fine."

"Do you know who tried to shoot us?" JJ asked.

"No," I said. "But I intend to find out who, and why."

"Think it has something to do with al-Salaam's murder?"

"That'd be my guess. But let's not worry about that now. We'll order pizza and stay here tonight. I'll take you to school in a taxi. We'll stop by the apartment first."

"Dad," JJ said. "I know you wanted to back off this investigation, but it looks like you might not have a choice because the investigation doesn't want to back off of you."

I hugged my son tighter and basked in the sunshine of yet another adult moment. "JJ, sometimes what you say amazes me," I said.

* * *

The next morning we stopped by the house to pick up clothes and JJ's schoolbooks. Since I wasn't sure who'd taken shots at us, and how much they knew about JJ, I decided it was best for us to stay at Nora's until she returned from her conference.

I'd just left JJ at school and started walking back to my apartment when my cell phone rang. The slow, controlled cadence and low rumble of Ken Tucker's voice added up to one thing—anger. I showered, changed clothes, and jumped on a downtown subway.

Charlene sat facing her computer. She swung around as I entered Tucker's office and the smile on her face wilted.

"He's not in a good mood."

I managed a smile. "So what else's new?"

I knocked on Tucker's door.

"Yeah." A muffled voice came through the thick oak.

I opened the door to Tucker sitting behind his desk, tapping his palm with the blunt end of a silver, stiletto letter opener. He put down the letter opener, propped his elbows on his desk, and leaned forward. The consummate chessplayer. Tucker made slow, deliberate, studied movements. I slid into a leather chair in front of his desk. He eyed me until I'd settled in.

"FBI called me yesterday," Tucker said. "I like Bill Jenkins. We've worked together in the past. Don't mind his temper. It flares quickly. It's a weakness, but I still like him."

He picked up the letter opener and studied it. Then he raised his head.

"NYPD called me this morning. I don't like Art McCluskey." He paused and tapped his palm a few times with the letter opener. "It's not that I don't like him. Let's say I don't like it when he calls me about one of my agents."

Tucker pointed at me with the business end of the letter opener.

"A hip-hop club trashed. An undercover investigation compromised. An unconscious man in Central Park. Your fingerprints on his gun. What the hell is all this about?"

I stared back across Tucker's desk. "Yousef al-Salaam," I said.

Tucker's jaw flexed. The letter opener hit his palm a few more times.

"Deuce F? Deuce F's a goddamn corpse, or have you forgotten that? You're investigating his death?"

"I am."

"For a client?"

"Yes."

"Whom, may I ask?"

"My son."

Tucker's jaw flexed again. "You're kidding?"

"No."

"Why?"

"JJ doesn't believe that al-Salaam was killed in a hip-hop feud."

"So you're destroying property and leaving people lying in Central Park to prove something your son probably heard on MTV?"

"Guy in the park came after me unsolicited."

"Hell, you've already stirred up a hornet's nest. No wonder someone came after you." Tucker shook his head. "Look, I run a security and intelligence agency, not a gumshoe squad, and certainly not a goddamn teenage rumor mill." He pointed the letter opener at me again. "What you do on your own time is your business. But understand this: as far as I'm concerned, you're officially off the investigation of Deuce F. You get into trouble with the bureau or with the NYPD from here out, don't expect a helping hand from me."

"That it?" I asked.

"Yeah," Tucker said.

I got up to leave, but the moment I grabbed the doorknob, Tucker called out in a low, slow rumble. "Are you sure you want to get involved in this just for your son's sake?"

I turned around and leaned my back against the door.

"The way I see it, I'm involved now whether I like it or not. Someone didn't like it when I started asking questions. They came after JJ and me with their claws out. I don't suspect they'll stop unless I stop them."

"Watch your six," Tucker said.

I could feel my six pressed into the back of his door. I shook my head, stepped away from the door, and pointed at Tucker.

"I'm touched," I said. "You sound concerned. Or is it that you want someone investigating al-Salaam's death, only you don't want the investigation connected to you? What's that called again?" I snapped my fingers. "Plausible—"

"Deniability," Tucker said.

He pinched the letter opener between both index fingers, then he spun around in his chair to look out the window. A layer of orange-brown smog blanketed the city. I pivoted, yanked the door open, and closed it hard behind me as I walked out.

\* \* \*

In the foyer of my building, a folded sheet of paper stuck from the slot of my shiny metal mailbox. I pounded my thigh with my fist. Damn. Was my furniture due for delivery this morning? No telling how long I'd have to wait now for a bed and living room set. But when I snatched the paper and opened it, my breathing paused and my heart skipped a beat. I couldn't read a word. All I saw were three lines of hand-written Arabic. I flashed on the threats scrawled on the side of the Sufi Center in Brooklyn, and then I remembered the sign outside of the building that said introductory Sufi classes were held each evening at seven o'clock. I folded the sheet of paper and slipped it into my shirt pocket. I didn't know if I'd just received an invitation to attend tonight's class, but I decided I'd take it that way.

Once inside my apartment, I threw some of JJ's clothes and mine into a bag and called JJ's school. I left a message that he should take a cab directly to Nora's apartment and that I'd be there when he got home from school.

Before I left for Nora's, I ran to a nearby hardware store and got a few cheap timers. I programmed my television and some lights in the apartment to turn on and off at various intervals, just in case anyone staked out my place. And on my way out for the last time, I didn't leave through the front door. Instead, I went down into the basement of the brownstone where I'd stored a few boxes. I swept away a few spider webs. It didn't take much to pick the lock holding the cast-iron flaps of an old cellar door together. They swung up and out with a creak. I threw my bag outside, then pulled myself up into the garden of the brownstone. After closing the doors, I hopped a few fences until I found an alleyway between two buildings that lead to the street next to mine. And I was on my way.

\* \* \*

Shoes sat in neatly arranged pairs everywhere I looked in the hallway of the Sufi Center. I slipped mine off and walked across the powder blue carpet.

"My brother, Salaam Alaikum."

I heard Ali's voice behind me and turned to see that Sufi smile spread over his face.

"I'm so pleased that you've come back for class," he said.

"Walaikum Salaam," I said. I think it came out sounding more like a tepid mumble, which matched my enthusiasm for being here.

"Please, follow me," Ali said.

When he opened the doors to the large room next to the reception area, a wave of heat swept out and smacked me in the face. There must have been more than 150 people crammed inside the room. A light blue carpet had been rolled across most of the wooden floor. Everyone sat cross-legged on lavender and black cushions. A low hum of conversation wafted through the air, so it seemed suspended in the dense, sweet aroma of frankincense.

A riser had been placed at the long end of the room, and the crowd faced that way. Several bouquets of red and yellow roses stood it tall vases on each side of the platform. In the middle, a wide, plush, high-back chair had been draped with a white satin cloth. A pitcher and a glass of water rested atop a similarly draped table next to the chair.

On tiptoes, I threaded my way along the wall toward the rear of the crowd where I'd spied a few unoccupied cushions. I turned down a row toward the empty seats, only to find myself hemmed in by a clutch of people sitting in a circle, talking. One woman gently nudged the woman next to her in order to give me room to pass. The second woman raised her head toward me. Our eyes met. I felt an electric zing make a round-trip between us. It caught me by surprise. I lingered for an instant. She smiled. And then I made my way past her toward my seat. I sat and folded my legs under me as comfortably as I could. While slipping out of my jacket, I caught a glimpse of the woman staring at me discreetly. It brought back memories of being the new kid in a high-school class.

Suddenly, a hush washed over the room. A door at the front opened, and a small brown man dressed in a satiny white robe strolled in. Slowly, meticulously, he climbed the few steps up to the riser, then, with deliberate intention, he sat, gracefully pulling one leg, then the other, under him. Ali pulled a microphone closer to the small man. Around the room, all gazes riveted on the man. A few women had their hands clasped to their chests, a look of teary admiration in their eyes for Sheikh Tariq Bashir.

From out of nowhere, the room burst forth with the haunting, tremulous sounds of a human voice—part Muslim crier calling the faithful to prayer, part operatic soprano filling the voids of a concert hall. I didn't understand the language, but the effect was unmistakable. My body vibrated with each note the Sheikh held as his voice quaked through the room.

Men and women around me closed their eyes and swayed back and forth as the sheikh's voice held them in a trance. The sheikh's chanting continued for at least fifteen minutes. I found myself blinking my eyes to keep them open, squeezing my fists hard closed, focusing on the remembered pain of a prison guard's baton jammed into my rib cage, distracting myself in whatever way possible to keep from being swept under by the hypnotic pull of the sheikh's voice. When he stopped chanting the room seemed to exhale in a collective sigh of exhausted exaltation.

Finally, the sheikh spoke. His voice trilled up and down like a bird's call with a breathy British and East Indian accent that was hard to understand. He talked about finding God, and being unable to do so in any book, the Bible, Koran, or the Torah.

He pointed up. "There . . . No." He pointed out toward the window. "There . . . No." He pointed down, and laughed. "No." Then his face lit up with that Sufi smile. He tapped his chest. "Here . . . Yes. Only find the God here. Only find the God here." He laughed and laughed like a child who'd made and understood his first joke. And the more he laughed, the more the room joined him in laughing, until the entire place shook as though the building, too, laughed from an overheard cosmic joke.

And that seemed to be the sheikh's message. He tapped his chest repeatedly. "Only find the God here. Only find the peace here. Only find the love here. Only find the wisdom here. Only find the self here."

I laughed too, but not so much at the sheikh as at the thought of Liz spending lots of money, lots of time, and traveling more than one hundred miles upstate to the Sigma Center when she could have taken a train to Brooklyn to find herself. "Only find the self here . . ." I heard in my mind.

After nearly an hour, the sheikh abruptly ended his talk with another outburst of chanting. This time many people in the audience joined in with him, and wave after wave of Islamic words washed over the room. Again, I didn't understand what was being said, but I did hear "Salaam . . . Salaam . . . Salaam" woven into the chants, which brought to mind the last music video of Yousef al-Salaam. It was not hard to imagine the pull a scene like this must have had on an entertainer who made his living enchanting people through his music and his words.

When Sheikh Bashir stopped chanting, the audience stopped as well. Seated at his podium, he then bowed deeply to us and most in the room bowed back. He stood up with grace and precision, then walked like a king from the dais and disappeared through a side door.

A buzz restarted in the crowd. Some people stretched their legs out. I rubbed my knees first then unfolded them slowly. They cracked as I stood.

"It's your first time here, isn't it?" a woman's voice said.

I turned to see the woman who'd eyed me when I entered. The top of her head reached only to my chest. She looked up at me and smiled. She wore a long dark-blue skirt and white blouse. It looked like she'd stepped from an office to come here. I placed her in her early thirties. Her skin, a few shades lighter than mine, glowed with a subtle reddish hue. She'd wrapped the braid of her long, thick, black hair into a bun at the back of her head.

"Samantha Adams," she said.

Samantha extended her hand to me and we shook.

"John Shannon," I said.

"Mr. Shannon, a group of us meet after the sheikh's talk at Java 'n Jazz, a coffeehouse a few doors down from here on Seventh Avenue. Perhaps you'd like to join us?"

She flashed me a Sufi smile, and I started to feel there might be some benefits from becoming a convert.

"Love to," I said, "but first I have to talk with Ali."

"I understand," Samantha said. "We'll be at the coffeehouse for at least an hour. See you there."

Samantha made her way back toward her friends, and I wormed through the crowd toward the front of the room, looking for Ali. I found him holding one of the rose vases, so tall it covered his face as he walked.

"Ali," I said.

He peeked from behind the vase and his face lit up. He stopped walking.

"My dear brother. Did you enjoy the Sheikh's talk?"

"Interesting," I said.

My lack of enthusiasm didn't seem to dampen Ali's.

"Great message," Ali said. "Great message."

"All in here." I tapped on my chest. "Pretty simple message."

"Simple," Ali said, "but not an easy message to live by."

"Do you speak Arabic?" I asked.

Ali smiled. "Does the sun shine?"

I pulled the sheet of paper from my pocket and unfolded it. Then I held it up to him. "What does this say?"

Instantly the smile drained from Ali's face. He set the vase down and took the paper from my hand. He studied it slowly.

"Where did you get this?" he asked.

"Someone left it in my mailbox."

He looked at me, then at the letter, then at me again. He shook his head. "Very bad . . . very bad."

"What does it say?" I asked again.

"It says, 'Death to the Infidel. Death to him who defames Allah.'"

I took a deep breath and stared at Ali. He reached down to pick up the rose vase, but I yanked him aside and pushed him up against a wall.

"Let's see," I said. "The only Muslim group I've had any connection with in the last several days has been this Sufi group here, so maybe you can tell me why I'd get such a charming note stuck in my mailbox."

Ali smiled. He looked over my shoulder and jerked his head slightly as though motioning to someone behind me, but before I could turn for a look, the hard, blunt barrel of a pistol rammed into my back.

So much for finding peace and love "in here."

# TEN

AT SIX-FOOT-TWO, I'm tall, but the two men at my arms rose above my head. They hustled me toward the side door through which the sheikh exited. I didn't resist. With people still milling around from his talk, it didn't seem like a good time to scuffle with armed men. One of the men pushed me into the back hall-way. Another man ratcheted my arm high up my back while holding the pistol into my ribs. I squeezed my hand into a fist, which crumpled the piece of paper I held. Then I twisted to move away from the gun barrel, but the man only jabbed it deeper into my body. I winced.

A door opened and I recognized the man that stepped out— Brother Hamid. One of the men stretched an arm out and handed Hamid the paper with the Arabic on it. Hamid ducked back into his office, and a moment later a man threw me inside with him.

The two men then stationed themselves in the hallway, like bookends on either side of the door. A muscular hand reached out and yanked the door shut. I caught a quick glance of my escorts. One of the men had skin darker than mine. His strong nose, thick lips, and deeply set eyes suggested African origins. The other man had high cheekbones, fair skin, and smooth jet-black hair. Egypt, Algeria, Tunisia all came to mind. But then I guess that'd make him African too.

When I turned to Hamid, he looked up from his desk with a scowl. No silver teapot and cups this time. He didn't offer me a seat, and I didn't take one.

"Tea?" I asked.

It didn't garner the Sufi smile.

"Mr. Shannon, why did you come back here?"

"To hear the sheikh speak, and to find out who left this message for me, and why?" I unfolded the sheet of paper and pointed to it.

"Do you speak Arabic?" Hamid asked.

"No."

Hamid uttered something to me in Arabic. I raised my shoulders and shook my head. He laughed.

"No," he said, "I guess you don't."

And I guessed that Hamid had just cursed my mother.

I tossed the piece of paper onto his desk. "Look, someone left that in my mailbox." I pointed again.

He hit the sheet with a light, glancing blow. "So why bring this filth here?"

"First, because I didn't know until a few minutes ago what it said. And, second, because this Center is the only contact I've had with Islam in the past several days."

"I thought you said you interviewed Yousef al-Salaam?"

"I did."

"Well, did it occur to you that someone may have objected to his practice of Islam?"

"Someone like whom?"

"Someone who considered al-Salaam an Infidel."

"Which is all the more reason to come back here."

Hamid rose. He placed both hands on the table and sneered. "You think—"

"I think that Yousef al-Salaam learned about Sufi Islam from this Center," I pointed to the floor, "and I think that whoever painted that Arabic graffiti on your outside walls doesn't like the form of Islam you practice." I pointed at Hamid. "Therefore, they didn't like al-Salaam's form of Islam, either, since the two were the same. And furthermore, I think they knew I went to al-Salaam's house, and then came here, which somehow connected me to Sufism and you."

"You think this. You think that. You think. You think. You think. But you know nothing." Hamid's laugh sounded more like a cackle of derision. "Take some advice, Mr. Shannon. Since you know nothing about Islam, step away from this whole investigation. For you've already stepped into the middle of matters much older and more complex than you could ever imagine."

I put my hands on Hamid's desk and leaned across to meet him face to face.

"Good advice," I said, "but maybe too late. This investigation has stepped in front of me, and I won't step away until I find out who's behind that note."

"Then I would be prepared for much trouble," Hamid said.

"I am."

I turned and walked toward Hamid's door. When I jerked it open, both bookends craned their necks and stuck their heads in. Hamid barked something to them in Arabic, and they parted like the waters of the Red Sea to let me pass. The big guy who could have been from Northern Africa kept his hand in his pocket. I paused in front of him before I left.

"Remember," I said, "it's all in here." I tapped my chest. "Not in here." I patted his pocket.

Hamid's voice boomed from inside his office. "They don't speak English well."

I stuck my head back into his doorway. "If it's all in here," I said, "what's the point of Sufis with guns?"

Hamid snorted. "Mr. Shannon, spirituality is no protection against depravity."

I winked at him and pointed. "Now that might be the most important lesson of the night."

* * *

Around the corner from the Sufi Center, and midway down the block, lights sputtered out in the Java 'n Jazz Coffeehouse. I pulled the door open to a wild saxophone blaring over the speakers, as if the player had been hopped up on too much caffeine or some other drug. I paused inside the doorway and let the raucous torrent of notes wash over me, then I raised my head to the bearded man behind the counter and snapped my fingers.

"Charlie Parker," I said.

He looked at me, expressionless, and I lowered my head to listen further. The man was right. Too much tonality in the riff for Bird. Then the piano took over, and I recognized the tune. I raised my head again and smiled.

"'Lights Out.' Jackie McLean. Original 1956 recording."

The man behind the counter nodded. "All right, my man," he said. "Enter."

Parker, Coltrane, Monk, McLean, Mingus. Old album covers lined the exposed brick walls inside Java 'n Jazz. I walked over to the counter.

"Might as well call this place Beans 'n Bebop," I said.

The man behind the counter pointed at me and laughed. His salt and pepper hair and beard framed his dark face. His laughter accentuated well-worn smile lines on either side of his eyes and lips. "Hey, that's a good name for a coffee shop. When I open my next one, I'll use it. Look we're officially closed, but for anyone who recognized Jackie like you did I'll make an exception. Name is Mike. Mike Saunders." Mike put down the rag he'd been using to wipe off his espresso machine and extended a hand to me over the counter.

I extended my hand to him. "John Shannon," I said.

Mike's eyes lit up as though he knew me.

"Just get out of the Sufi Center?" he asked.

"I did."

"Hell, I don't know all that they preach over there, but I'm sure glad they attract as many people as they do. After 9/11 some folks in the neighborhood wanted the Center out. Claimed it was a potential gathering spot for terrorists and all. I say, they're quiet, they don't bother anyone, they're damn good for my business. And best of all, the fellow that runs things over there, Sheikh Bashir, he's a huge jazz fan. Comes in here during the day sometimes when no one else is around and loves to tell stories of recordings he made years ago of Dexter Gordon and Eric Dolphy playing in European cafes. You want a latte?"

"Sure," I said. "Did you know that rapper, Deuce F, who was shot a couple of nights ago? Used to come to the Center."

"Yousef al-Salaam," Mike said. "Sure. He came in here once or twice with some of the others. Funny you should ask."

"Oh, why's that?"

Mike bent down behind the counter, then popped with a folded slip of paper in his hand.

"A woman I'd always see with him whenever he'd come in left this for you."

Mike handed me the paper, then he turned to make my latte. The handwritten note read, "Sorry we missed you. Give me a call sometime. Sam Adams." At the bottom she left her number.

Mike turned to me with a latte in a heavy paper cup. "Seems like a nice woman. You know her?"

"I don't yet."

Mike smiled. "Thanks for stopping by," he said.

I reached into my pocket for my wallet. Mike held up his hand.

"Latte's on me," he said, smiling. "It's the least I can do to repay you for the name of my new shop: Beans 'n Bebop . . . Like it."

* * *

I sipped my latte as I walked toward the subway station, the cup's warmth a buttress to the crisp night air. The automatic turnstile ate my ticket, then spit it out. I pushed past the metal gates and took a seat on a wooden bench toward the front of the station, the only person on the desolate station. I sipped more coffee, then stood up and walked gingerly toward the edge of the platform. I nudged my foot partway over the yellow line and looked left. Way in the distance, beyond the lights of this station, the lights of another station twinkled in the darkness, but I didn't see the headlights of a train. I retook my seat. Though hard to believe, six or seven hours from now, this station would be packed with rush-hour commuters clamoring to get to work.

Several voices echoed through the station. I twisted around toward the turnstiles in time to see three men hopping over, which meant they hadn't paid. They lingered together in front of the turnstiles while one of the men leaned out over the tracks and looked left. Then, en masse, they turned and walked my way. Each man had one hand in a pocket and the other free. I looked around for a transit cop, but I didn't see one, and I hadn't brought my weapon with me.

I didn't take my eyes off the men as they came closer. Now, I've been at the wrong end of "racial profiling" more than once, so I know how dangerous it is to prejudge a person based on appearances. All of the men heading toward me had dark complexions, but none of their bodies moved with the swagger and sway of the streets. The most I'd venture to say is that they came from a foreign country, but where, I couldn't say. Their relentless movement toward me and the cold stare in their eyes sent a chill running up my spine. I left my coffee cup on the bench and stood to face them, then one man pulled a pistol from his pocket and my worse fears were confirmed.

I jumped forward, ducking behind one of the large, riveted steel posts supporting the arched dome of the station, just as a bullet whistled through the air. I looked left. I didn't see any headlights. So with barely a second thought, I jumped between the tracks and starting running. Several shots followed me into the darkness beyond the station.

Two great dangers lurk along the darkness of the New York City subway tracks. Trains are obviously one of them. The ever-present third rail is the other. I hustled along the tracks, looking over my shoulder for headlights and gunmen, sensing the presence of the third rail to my left. Several bullets pinged off the walls around me. I jumped up onto the catwalk above the tracks.

I didn't know how much these men knew about the anatomy of subways. A rite of passage in my high school days entailed walking the catwalk from one station to the next, timing it so I'd get there before a train and to avoid apprehension by a cop. The men behind me seemed to hesitate at the end of the station. I heard them talking, though I couldn't make out what they said. Shooting and walking on the narrow catwalk would be difficult at best. I moved swiftly, feeling my way by hand along the soot-caked railing that ran the length of the catwalk. Overhead, an occasional incandescent lamp provided only dim illumination.

Suddenly, the walls shook and a deafening thunder rumbled through the darkness. I turned behind me, but I still saw no lights, which meant the train raced forward toward me but on the other side of these tracks. An ear-piercing screech of metal on metal echoed around me as the train slid to a stop at the station I'd just left. But when I looked behind me this time, a brilliant dot of light shimmered in the darkness before the station. I picked up my pace. I could no longer see the men pursuing me, but I could still hear their footsteps and their voices.

Lights from the station I headed toward grew brighter. I passed a metal ladder traveling upward and thought about taking it. But who knew where it led to—a heavy manhole cover to the streets above? A small crawl space crammed with electrical cables? Or simply a dead-end?

The voices of the men pursuing me grew louder, coming at me from both directions of the tunnel as though I'd just slipped on stereo headphones. Echoes can play tricks, I know. Still, the voices didn't make sense until I squinted. Against the backdrop of lights from the station ahead, a few human forms moved along the catwalk toward me. I glanced behind. The headlight from the oncoming train barreled my way.

I passed another ladder and started to make my way up. The roar of the train grew louder. Its light rocked from side to side. But I let go of the ladder, hit the floor of the catwalk, and pounced down onto the middle of the tracks. My knees buckled under me, and when I stood I saw the conductor's face at the head of the onrushing train. He must have seen me too. He blew his horn twice. Sparks flew as he slammed the brakes. Metal cried out. I hopped up on top of the wooden plank that covered the third rail. I pressed my body against the side of the tunnel as the train first pushed a wind devil my way that pinned me harder into the wall. Train cars whirled by, just a few feet in front of my face.

I slid back along the top of the third rail. The subway train finally ground to a halt. I passed lighted windows as I moved, peering into the world of late night riders. A man buried his head in a newspaper. A couple snuggled into each other. The eerie scene juxtaposed them sitting in safety and me coming within inches of certain death.

A scream rose from inside the car I passed. A young woman pointed my way. Suddenly, everyone in the car turned to look, and a momentary image flashed across my mind of a condemned man strapped in an electric chair, peering at the witnesses to his execution as they peered at him. More people pointed. Some people ran from the car. I came to an overhead light and an arched opening in the wall that separated the set of tracks moving in opposite directions. More voices called out in the tunnel now, and I heard the squawking of police radios.

I backed down from the third rail, but I knew to expect another for trains running on the opposite tracks. Standing underneath the arch, I pivoted slowly. To my right, I saw the headlight of a train coming from the opposite direction. Light from the train behind me barely allowed me to see my way. I lifted my foot high and stepped over the third rail. I pushed off, planted one foot in the middle of the tracks, then leapt for the catwalk railing on the other side.

The headlights of the oncoming train hadn't reached me. I felt my way along the catwalk until I came to a ladder. This one I climbed just to be out of view of the oncoming conductor, and I held on as winds from the train buffeted me from below. When the underground gales had blown over, I climbed down to the catwalk and raced back to the subway station I'd first entered.

I forced my way through the turnstile, took the stairs two at a time, and disappeared into the Brooklyn streets. Even under the streetlights, I could see the dirt covering my hands and my clothes. I ran a few blocks before stopping, then I paused under a streetlight. I whipped out my cell phone, yanked a crumpled sheet of paper from my pocket, and punched in Samantha Adams' number.

"Hello," she said.

I hesitated, still breathing heavily.

"Hello," she said again.

"It's John. John Shannon."

"Oh, Mr. Shannon. I see Mike gave you my message. I was hoping you'd call, but I hadn't expected a call so soon."

"I know it's late," I said.

"Are you all right?" she asked.

"No," I said. "I need to see you now."

"Oh . . . well . . . I . . ."

"About Yousef al-Salaam. I need to speak with you about him."

"At this hour?"

"Please . . . it's urgent."

"What makes you think I—"

"I'll meet you wherever you want, but I need to talk with you now."

"I'm not dressed to go out." She sighed. "You sound desperate. Are you in trouble?"

"Samantha, if you'd like someone else in the house with us, that's fine," I said. "I just want to ask you a few questions."

She sighed.

"Come over," she said, "but on one condition."

"What's that?"

"Call me Sam."

# ELEVEN

Sam Adams gave me an address in Greenwich Village, just off of Sheridan Square. It would have been a simple matter to hop on a subway, but I'd had enough underground excitement for one evening so I flagged down a cab. On the ride over to Manhattan from Brooklyn, I whipped out a handkerchief, moistened it with my tongue, and wiped some of the grime from my face and hands. Such primitive cleaning wouldn't help my clothes. Not a good way to make a first impression.

The taxi left me in the middle of block. I jogged up the building's front stairs, then mashed the buzzer marked, "Sam Adams" with my thumb. She buzzed me in and I hiked up four floors to her apartment. When I rounded the corner from the staircase, Sam stood in the middle of her doorway, a bathrobe wrapped around her and slippers on her feet.

She started to smile. She also started to say something, but her bottom jaw unhinged slightly. She let out a gasp, then said, "What happened to you?"

"Sorry," I said, "but I know I must look a mess."

She stepped aside as I entered her apartment, then closed the door behind me.

"You're welcome to take a shower," she said. "There's a washcloth and towel in the bathroom."

"Thanks. Maybe not a shower, but at least I'll wash off some of the subway grit and grime."

"Subway?" she asked.

"Ever walk between stations?" I asked.

"Along those narrow walkways?"

"Uh-huh."

"No, but kids in my high school used to."

"You must be from the city."

"What makes you say that?"

"It's a ritual few others would know about."

"And you were out reliving high school days tonight?" she asked.

"Not because I wanted to."

"I don't understand."

"Let me clean up first, then I'll explain."

"Something to drink?" Sam asked.

I started to say, "I'll take a Sam Adams," but I wagered that she'd heard that too many times before, and the way Sam narrowed her eyes and looked at me I think she must have sensed my deliberations.

"How about a Guinness?"

She sighed as though relieved. "No Guinness. No Sam Adams." She winked. "Got an almost-Guinness."

"Almost Guinness?"

"Kaliber. It's a nonalcoholic beer they make."

At least Sam had a sense of humor.

"Kaliber it is," I said. "I'll be out shortly."

I filled the sink basin with hot water, and by the time I'd finished scrubbing with the washcloth and soap, the water had turned a dark shade of gray. I wrung out the towel and dusted my clothes off with it, which took off the surface layer of dirt. I walked down the long hallway of Sam's apartment. Her wooden floors squeaked under my weight.

Sam sat in a chair by the window, with an angular view of Sheridan Square. She held a cup of steaming liquid in her hands. Streetlights set her skin glowing a rich, dark shade of orange. Small starbursts of light gleamed in her eyes. With her hair still up in a bun, the streetlights illuminated her profile, accentuating the round contour of her head, her long neck, and the strong, statuesque features of her face. She had no makeup on at this hour of the night, but then Sam was the kind of woman for whom makeup dimmed her natural beauty.

Outside, a Department of Sanitation truck whirred and grinded as it went about picking up trash cans. Sam handed me a cold glass of the nonalcoholic brew, and I took a chair on the other side of the window. I gave her a quick rundown of what happened when I tried to catch the subway home.

"So, you work for this Office of Municipal Security and you're investigating Yas' death?" she asked.

"Yas?"

She smiled. "It's what Yousef liked to call himself," she said. "From the first letter of each of his Islamic names."

"I do work for OMS," I said. "But I'm not investigating his death for them."

She sipped her tea or coffee. "OMS." She laughed. "Who would have guessed a spiritual name for such an agency."

"Spiritual?"

"You know, like the chant om . . . om . . . om . . ."

"Some people put an *M* in front of it for Mayor's Office of Municipal Security, and come up with another interpretation completely."

"MOMS," Sam said. She took a long sip from her cup. "It could still be spiritual, I guess . . . if you're into the Goddess, feminine spirituality, and the like. But you said you're not working on this investigation for OMS, or MOMS. Then for whom?"

"For my son."

"You're kidding . . . your son?"

I filled her in on the general details of how I got involved in this case.

"Have you been involved at the Sufi Center for long?" I asked.

"About three years," Sam said.

"So you knew al-Salaam when he first started to visit the Center?"

"Who didn't? A music superstar begins attending classes at your spiritual center? Everyone takes notice."

"Did you have more than a passing interest in al-Salaam . . . Yas?"

She took a reflective sip and answered while staring out the window. "Do I have to answer that?"

"No."

"What makes you ask?"

"You have an engaging, outgoing personality. You seem unafraid to introduce yourself to new people who come to class. You also knew a name that few others knew him by."

Sam kept staring out the window as though searching for something. "You know what it's like to be thirty and single in the city?"

I smiled. "I'm a bit older than thirty, but I'm learning."

"Well then add to that, do you know what it's like if you're a woman, you don't drink, you hate bars, sports bore you to tears, and your idea of a good time is listening to a talk by a spiritual master?"

"Kinda limits your choices in men, huh?"

"What choices? Did you notice the composition of the audience at the sheikh's talk tonight?"

"You mean seventy percent were women?"

"And of the men that made up the remaining thirty percent, fifty percent were gay, forty percent didn't speak English, and five percent were married or in a relationship."

"Okay, math isn't my strong suit. Where's that leave us? I mean you?"

"Five percent of thirty percent," she said. "Little more than one percent of the guys that come through the Center's doors."

"You must work with numbers," I said. "What, an accountant? A statistician?"

"Computer programmer," Sam said.

"Anyway, I get that that means there aren't a lot of available, interesting guys. What about Yas?"

She lowered the cup from her lips and shook her head slowly. "Musicians are in a category by themselves."

I thought I saw a half-smile cross her lips.

Sam continued without being asked. "Truth is, I was interested in Yas. We'd hang out at Java 'n Jazz after lectures. Talk a lot. He had an ephemeral mind."

"Ephemeral?"

"Like a bird flitting from one branch to the next. He could talk about his days as a gangsta rapper, then in the next breath talk about his deep commitment to Islam, then in the next talk about why he needed to buy an expensive SUV. It never seemed to matter to Yas that his thoughts and actions were inconsistent. He seemed to live in the moment, as if all moments that preceded the current moment didn't exist." She sighed.

"Including you?" I asked.

"Including me what?"

"Including you if you were a part of a previous moment."

"You're perceptive, Mr. Shannon."

"Was he a ladies' man?"

"Yes and no. Despite his MTV persona, he didn't sleep around as far as I know. But women were always around him. Especially women at the Center. He could have had his pick."

"And he chose you?"

"Maybe I was just more persistent, or more stubborn, than the rest. But it didn't last long. I think we were together for a whirlwind two months. Then Yas left for his Middle East trip . . . He came back a changed man."

"How so?"

"More serious and dedicated to Sufi Islam than I'd ever seen him. Said he was ready to commit his life and his music to promoting Sufism and peace." She laughed. "He used to call himself the hip-hop Rumi."

"Rumi?"

"Jalal al-din Rumi, the thirteenth-century Sufi poet. The whirling dervishes, whose brand of Islam began in honor of Rumi's verse, intrigued Yas. 'Poetry and motion,' Yas used to say. 'That's what Rumi and I are all about.' I think Yas found something on his trip that lifted him beyond the narrow confines of his past. He began organizing whirling sessions with a few selected people from the Center who met at his house. He also seemed obsessed with his latest recording, which had yet to be released on an album. He kept saying it would lay out the truth for everyone to see. But he was also afraid that his label wouldn't want to release it."

"Did he say why?"

"No, and when I'd ask, he'd smile and say, 'Just wait until you hear it.'"

"Is this the piece with him whirling and chanting 'Salaam Alaikum' at the end?"

"No," Sam said. "A recording he made after that. Yas only told me he'd found a place to record at outside of the city, where he had total control over his music. He felt he'd gained enough stature in the industry that people would have to listen to this next piece 'even if they choke on my words,' he said."

"But nothing more about what those words were?"

Sam sighed. "Nothing more."

"How'd the sheikh take Yas' newfound zeal for Sufism?"

"At first, Sheikh Bashir seemed to embrace him like a son, much to the chagrin of Hamid, I might add. But then people began clamoring for Yas to lead whirling sessions at the Center."

"I take it the sheikh didn't appreciate that?"

"One evening, Hamid, not the sheikh, gave a lecture on the dangers of polluting traditional Sufism with western ways and western values. Not long after that talk the whirling sessions at Yas' house stopped. He also stopped coming to the Center. Then one night after a lecture, the sheikh was attacked."

"By someone in attendance?"

"It's not clear. On his way home from the Center, a car drove up and opened fire on the sheikh's car. The sheikh's driver was killed and the sheikh's car then crashed into a utility pole, toppling it over. The commotion probably caused the gunman to flee, and the sheikh escaped unhurt."

"And people blamed it on a disgruntled rapper."

"Some did." Sam sucked her teeth. "And some blamed it on another Brooklyn mosque, whose mullah considered Sufism the scourge of Islam."

"You sound like you don't believe either version."

"I wouldn't have put it past Hamid to orchestrate the whole thing to make it look like Yas did it."

"That way it'd discredit him once and for all."

"Yeah, and if the sheikh was killed, Hamid would step into his place."

"Do you know the name of this other mosque, or its leader?"

"I don't," Sam said. "But I've heard it's a traditional form of Shiite Islam."

"Thanks," I said. "You've been most helpful."

"It surprised me that the police never came to question me after Yas' death."

"Talk was that he was killed by another rapper to settle old scores."

"And the NYPD bought that without investigating?" Sam asked.

"Sure makes their job a lot easier," I said.

Sam shook her head. "The world according to MTV." She set her cup down on the floor beside her chair, then she leaned forward toward me. "Are you interested in Sufism at all," she asked, "or did you just come to learn more about Yas?"

"Hoping that I was in that 1 percent?"

Sam smiled. "Frankly, yes."

I spread my hands apart. "You might have to widen your field."

"Sufism teaches us to be open." She winked. "But whatever you do, I'd be careful."

"Of whom, what?"

"Stepping into the middle of a conflict between different interpretations of Islam."

"Or different styles of hip-hop," I said.

"Yes," Sam said. "They do have a certain similarity."

"In both fields people believe zealously in what they do."

"And in both fields people are ready to kill for those beliefs."

"Kinda like walking between two tracks, close to the third rail," I said.

Sam nodded.

# TWELVE

A KISS ON THE forehead awoke me the next morning, and for an instant I thought it was Liz. But when my eyes finally managed to open I realized it was JJ.

He whispered. "Dad. It's late and I'm heading off to school." He flashed some money at me. "Don't worry, I have enough from yesterday to take a cab."

I mumbled, "I love you," then turned over for a little more sleep. I awoke again at noon. I sat on the edge of the bed, massaging the remaining sleep from my eyes.

I thought about Sam last night. Nice woman. Very direct. A little intense. But overall a really nice woman. Funny. I suggested that she needed to widen her field in order to find romance. Truth is, she'd already widened mine trying to find a killer. A squabble amongst Sufis? A conflict between Muslims? A feud amongst gangsters? I didn't know the answer, but I did know that Hamid and Sam were right about one thing: I had little knowledge of Islam, in general, and Sufism in particular. So I picked up the telephone, called upstate, and made arrangements to visit someone who did: Charles Promise.

A tremor rippled through me whenever I called the prison where I'd been an inmate for two years. I had to hold myself back from saying something snide, like, "You didn't get me. You didn't trap me. Although I know you tried." The switchboard operator put me on hold. I checked my watch while I waited. If I left immediately after the call, I could make it to the prison just before dinner. When the operator got back on the line, I used OMS's special privileges to arrange for a meeting with Promise. That would probably piss Ken Tucker off, but then it'd probably be a few days before he found out. After I hung up with the prison, I called JJ's school to let him know I wouldn't be back at Nora's until late.

A wave of guilt washed over me. Elizabeth's voice stormed into my mind in its wake. "John, you always had a reason why you weren't home for JJ and me. Working late. Big case. Couldn't let it go. Had to travel. On a stakeout. All legitimate reasons, but you still weren't around . . . and we wanted you around."

Damn. I slapped the side of the bed. I wanted to walk away from the entire investigation, yet a force inside compelled me on. Someone had shot at JJ and me. that Ken Tucker had made fun of my attempts to help my son overcome his grief at the loss of a hero, however flawed. And al-Salaam was being portrayed as a terrorist or a gangster, when I thought I'd met a young man trying to change. A few years ago, I'd been painted as a rogue cop who killed another officer—the scum of the NYPD. I knew what it felt like to be castigated, even locked away, because of the system's failure to dig long and hard enough for the truth. Damn Liz. I *couldn't* let some things go.

I swallowed my guilt, bounced up from bed, hopped in the shower, then slipped into my clothes. I made myself a protein smoothie, which I gulped down, then I headed out the door. Nora parked her car in a garage between Amsterdam and Columbus Avenues. Henrico, the garage attendant, a young Puerto Rican fellow in oil-stained denim coveralls, knew me from having taken Nora's car out before. He disappeared up a short ramp, and a moment later I heard engines rev to a start, then tires and brakes squeal. I walked partway up the ramp. Henrico zoomed cars backward and forward in and out of tight spaces, moving them around like a kid playing with a Rubiks cube until he freed Nora's car. He drove her car down the ramp and held the door open as I slipped behind the wheel.

"Must be going out of town today," Henrico said.

"To prison," I said.

"Bad place." He pointed to his chest. "Was there for eighteen months."

I pointed to my chest. "Two years," I said.

His jaw fell. "But I thought . . . you are . . ."

"It's a long story," I said. "Someday, I'll tell you all about it."

In the rearview mirror, as I pulled out of the garage, I saw Henrico watching me, shaking his head.

Having a car in New York City makes no sense, and I hadn't owned one for years, but I still loved to drive, especially away from the city on a clear spring day like this. It's easy to forget that Manhattan is an island until you get on the George Washington or Tappan Zee Bridge and cross the Hudson River. I took the Tappan

Zee. Below me the gentle wind rippled the water's surface, giving the river a herringbone texture. In my rearview mirror, the tallest of the city's skyscrapers disappeared. Inside of me, a newfound sense of freedom emerged.

I flipped open my cell phone and said, "Nora."

The cell phone dialed her number and a moment later Nora answered.

"John? Is that you?" She laughed softly, then put on the voice she used when talking to Madame Meow. "What's the matter are you lonely?"

I laughed. "No. Just called to tell you that JJ and I are staying in your apartment and I'm driving your car."

"I see." She sounded serious. "It's worse than I thought. You have severe separation anxiety."

"No, nothing like that—"

"Truth is, I'm lonely," Nora said. "I'm bored with the seminars and I'm tired of getting hit on. Yes, darling,"—she put on that cooing voice again—"I'll come home early to be with you and the kid."

After I gave her a rundown of what had happened, she dropped the playfulness.

"Seriously, I thought about leaving two days early anyway. I'll leave tomorrow and help out with JJ when I get back . . . And don't worry, you guys can stay at the apartment when I get back."

We said goodbye and hung up.

In the distance, off to my left, rolling hills tinged with green dominated the view. I've often thought that the hard lines and edges of city buildings confine and trap the mind, while the irregular curves found in nature let it wander. I wandered back to the first time I'd met Charles Promise, my second day in prison, in the exercise yard. It turned into an ex-detective's worse nightmare: an inmate I'd busted years earlier for drug-trafficking, a burly guy with long hair who looked like the leader of a Hell's Angels troop, sauntered over to me with a line of cons behind him. I'd long since forgotten his name. Sunlight sparkled off the homemade prison knife he palmed. I crouched low, turning from side to side, wondering from which side the attack would come. The big guy looked into my eyes and sneered.

"Fucking cop," he said. "You busted me. Now it turns out you were dirty too."

The line of men behind him fanned out around us, blocking the view of any nearby guards. My muscles tensed, waiting for him to lunge at me. He took a few steps toward me. I backed up, but I ran into another inmate now behind me who shoved me forward toward the big guy. I thought I'd have to fight my way through prison, but I had no idea the challenge would come so soon. I searched the big guy's eyes for any telltale sign that might alert me to his first move.

Then, just when I thought the big guy was about to thrust the jagged blade toward me, someone pushed through the crowd. I looked down to see a short, older black man standing between my would-be assailant and me.

"Rome." That's all the old man said.

I couldn't see the old man's eyes, but the big guy must have seen something there because his ice-cold gaze melted. He stared at the old man for a long while, then he and his entourage turned en masse and walked away, and when the old man turned, what I saw disarmed me as well. Soft. That's the way I'd describe the old man's eyes. So soft they stripped away your tough outer shell—that "game face" you put on to keep yourself safe in prison—and left you naked, facing the vulnerability of your humanness. That old man was Charles Promise, and in the two years I spent in prison I saw him disarm many inmates and even guards in the same way.

Nestled in a valley of rolling hills just five hours north of the city, spring had not graced the land surrounding the prison yet. Sunlight hit the rolls of razor wire coiled atop the perimeter fences. The complex of tan brick buildings looked smaller than I remembered. I parked in the visitor's parking lot, then reported to a special area for law enforcement inside. I recognized Paul Murphy, the guard at the duty desk. Murphy bridled when he saw me.

"Fuck you doin' back here?" he asked.

"Here to visit an inmate."

"Fuck you doin' comin' in this entrance? Visitor's entrance is out the door and around the corner. But it's closed until"—he checked the clock on the wall behind him—"three-thirty. So come back in an hour and a half." He chuckled to himself.

"I think you know I'm here on official business."

"Yeah. Right. Fuckin' official business. Never figured out why they went easy on a cop killer like you."

My body flinched. "Promise's eyes . . . Promise's eyes . . ." I kept telling myself. I pulled my gun from my shoulder holster. Murphy went for his. I flipped mine around and slapped it on the table. Murphy jumped, then he laughed malevolently.

"Maybe I should just shoot you and claim I saw you go for your gun first," he said.

"Promise's eyes . . ." I told myself again.

"Maybe you should sign me in to see Charles Promise."

Murphy swept my gun off the counter into a basket. "Fuckin' voodoo old man," he said. "Belongs in a ward for the criminally insane."

"Be careful what you wish," I said.

"Oh yeah, why's that?"

I stared at Murphy. "'Cause they might transfer one criminally insane guard I know from here with him." Okay, I couldn't help myself.

Murphy glowered at me, but he buzzed me through a large steel door. A guard I didn't know met me on the other side.

"He's a former resident," Murphy said to the other guard.

The other guard shot Murphy a sideways glance. Murphy laughed.

"But he's here to see Charles Promise in a law enforcement room," Murphy said.

The other guard squinted.

"Go figure," Murphy said. "Never know what trash they'll recycle."

The second guard hesitated. The clean-shaven young man dressed in an olive-green uniform appeared to sport a military buzz cut under his cap. He also appeared unsure whether to shove me forward or escort me. He ended up pointing forward with his baton.

"Down this corridor, turn—"

"Left at the end, second door on the right," I said.

The young guard reared back. "Know the place, huh?" he said.

"From both sides," I said.

I started walking down the barren concrete corridor with tracks of florescent lights overhead. The young guard walked beside me. Suddenly, he put a hand on my arm and stopped.

"Wait a minute." The guard squinted at me, then he pointed his baton at my chest. "You're that cop . . . in for life for killing another officer . . . some smart skirt got you out."

"That the *Reader's Digest* version of my life?"

I continued walking.

"It's the scuttlebutt around here. Rumor is you got a full-cell salute the day you left . . . inmates standing silently when you walked your 'long mile.'"

I patted him on the shoulder as we walked. "You make it sound so glamorous, like I walked down the red carpet for an Oscar. Let me tell you, there's nothing glamorous about spending two years behind bars for a crime you didn't commit."

"So what? You get a new trial and an acquittal?'

"New York City and the Feds chose not to retry."

After we turned the corner, we came to a hall lined with metal doors. The guard slipped in front of me and pushed one open. I stepped inside the tiny conference room. While pulling the door shut, he said, "Never acquitted means you still might be guilty." His malicious laugh sounded more like an old witch's cackle. "Means we might still see you in here on the other side someday."

He slammed the door shut.

A single metal table stood in the middle of the room underneath a single overhead light. I walked around the table and took a seat in the metal chair that faced the door. I touched the cinderblock wall behind me. It held a damp chill. Over one shoulder and above, the ventilation system whirred softly, pushing air through a grated duct. Over the other shoulder, the tiny eye of a video camera glowed red.

Suddenly, the door to the room opened and Promise shuffled in, slightly stooped, chains clinking from his ankles and his wrists. The guard closed the door quickly.

I yelled, "Wait!"

Promise raised his shackled arms. "It's okay, John," he said.

But it wasn't.

The young guard stuck his head back in the room.

"Remove this man's shackles," I said.

"Prison regs," the guard said.

"Bullshit."

"Anyway, I'm new. I'd check with my superiors, but unfortunately I can't leave my post until after you've finished your interview with the prisoner."

Promise smiled. "It's okay, John," he said.

Promise shuffled forward and slid a chair back, then he took a seat to face me across the table. He nodded to the door.

"Young guy, just started. Army. Back from the Middle East. Likes to play psychological games with the inmates. You know, tell you he'll do something considerate, then turn around and do something cruel." Promise shook his head slowly. "Feel sorry for him. He must really be hurting inside. Something he'd seen or done while in the service would be my guess."

"Why do you say that?" I asked.

"You know I work in the library," Promise said, "and I have the privilege of walking to my job unescorted. On my way there a couple of weeks ago I heard someone crying and talking. I thought it was an inmate under attack by another inmate or by guards, but when I peeked around the corner, I saw Jason crying and muttering to himself. 'Sorry,' he kept saying. 'Sorry.' I stamped my foot down hard as I walked around the corner. Kid looked at me red-faced, turned, and hurried away."

"You still don't deserve to be in irons," I said.

"Hell, John, you know what I always say."

I smiled. "We're all prisoners of our minds."

Promise chuckled. "Least you didn't forget that."

Promise looked as old—or as young—as when I left prison almost a year ago. He always refused to tell me exactly how old he was. It became a standing joke between us. I'd asked and he'd say, "As old as Methuselah." He never seemed to age in the years I'd known him and I came to believe that when you looked at Promise you didn't see his wrinkled skin, or his whitish gray hair at first. You saw the sparkle in his eyes and the glow of his dark skin. By the time you'd finished marveling to yourself about how a man in prison for life could look so happy and content, you'd forgotten about his age and started wondering what he knew about living that you didn't. And when Promise looked at you with a soft gaze in his eyes, you felt he could see right into the core of your being and that in an instant he'd already discovered what you needed to know that kept you from the tranquility he'd found in his life.

Promise grunted softly, then lifted his manacled arms up from his lap and rested his hands on the metal table in a prayer-like gesture. He leaned forward and focused those soft eyes on me.

"What's going on?" he asked.

"Islam," I said. "I don't know as much about it as I need to."

"Deep subject," he said. "Important subject in today's world."

I told Promise about al-Salaam and the Sufis and the death threat I'd received. He nodded as I spoke, and when I finished he kept looking at me with his penetrating, soft eyes. I knew what was coming next.

"So, John," he said softly. "I know you want to know something about Islam, but what's really going on?"

I took a deep breath, leaned back in my chair, and sighed.

# THIRTEEN

"Elizabeth," I said. "She wants to go through with the divorce, and she's on this kick of 'finding herself,' which apparently excludes me."

"And that's bad?" Promise asked.

"It feels bad," I said.

"What? That she wants the divorce? That she wants to go off 'finding herself'? Or that you're excluded?"

"All of the above."

"Really?" Promise sounded unconvinced. "Or is it that you don't understand why she feels this urge to 'find herself' and you think if she'd just get rid of that she'd want you back in her life?"

"Could be," I said.

"Well, you keep that thought in the back of your mind while we talk," Promise said. "Where do we start?"

I started by telling Promise about Yousef al-Salaam's death and the events that had taken place since then. I ended by saying, "I don't understand what the hell Sufism has to do with Islam."

Promise chuckled. "You and a lot of Muslims."

He leaned back in his chair. I thought I saw his hands lift from the table as though trying to place them behind his head. The chain links on his wrist cuffs tinged softly as they tightened. For a moment I imagined Promise and I sitting in the living room of his home somewhere overlooking the ocean. A fire burned in a stone fireplace. Promise wore a sweater and blue jeans. He propped his feet on a stool and interlaced his fingers behind his head. He leaned back in his easy chair and held forth on a question I'd asked him, while I sat in a chair opposite him, hanging on his every word.

The buzz, then flutter, of the overhead florescent light startled me. It brought me back to the cinderblock room with Promise in drab olive prison garb, hands and feet bound in chains. It didn't matter. I still sat across from the old man, transfixed.

"*Tassawwuf.*" It sounded like a grunt, or an animal call.

I squinted. "What?"

"Tassawwuf," Promise said again.

The word floated in the cool air of the room.

"Tassawwuf," Promise said.

The echo reverberated off the walls, burrowing into my mind in such a way I knew I would not forget that sound again.

"Tassawwuf . . . the Arabic name for Sufism," Promise said.

He paused. We stared at each other for what seemed eternity.

"Some people claim that Sufism is a branch of Islam," Promise said. "Others believe that Sufism is the core of Islam. And still others maintain that it has nothing to do with Islam at all." He nodded, then gave me a knowing smile. "And therein lies the paradox, the conflict, and the truth."

I wanted to ask Promise what he meant, but Promise enjoyed warming up with some unfathomable utterance that kept his listeners spellbound, so I leaned back in my chair and settled in.

"Islam, the word, simply means faith. But the question is, faith in what?" Promise lowered his head, dropping into a moment's deep thought. Then he snapped up. "Some people think it's faith in what you do—prayers, fasting, living according to the word of the Koran and the Prophet Mohammed. And, yes, the Koran says if you do only those things—pray, fast, live by the Word—you're guaranteed a spot in heaven. But that's the outer Islam. Like the outer Christianity. You know—"

"Christians who feel that all you need to do is go to church, pray, and believe in the Word of the Bible and Christ," I said.

"Or the outer Judaism of those who go to synagogue, keep Sabbath, and believe in the Word of the Torah . . . or the Hindu who walks bead after bead from his prayer necklace through his fingers, while repeating a mantra . . . or the outer form of any religion when taken no further than these rites, rituals, and rules.

"But every religious tradition also breeds men and women who have turned inward . . . turned here," Promise raised his shackled hands from the table, fingers interlaced, and thumped his chest lightly in what reminded me of an eastern prayer gesture," Where they've discovered a truth deeper than simple adherence to the organized rules of their faith." He looked up. The florescent light still flickered as though nearing the end of its life. "Like a caterpillar that sheds the outer trappings of its cocoon to emerge as a beautiful winged butterfly seeking the light, these men and women have shed the outer garments of their faith to discover their winged spirits inside. The Sufis are those men and women who turn inward with Islam."

I laughed. "Now you're starting to sound like Liz," I said. "Self-discovery. Turning inward. Looking for inner truth."

"Nothing wrong with it," Promise said. "My guess is we all yearn for it. We all want to find meaning and purpose in our lives."

"And religion's supposed to help us do that."

"Yes," Promise said, "religion—from the Latin *religare* . . . 'to bind again'—not to bind us to a set of rules. An institution. A dogma. A mullah. A rabbi. A priest. But to bind us again to the deepest truth about who we are."

"Which is?"

Promise chuckled. "We don't have much time. You want the Cliffs Notes version of spirituality?"

"I guess I just want to understand what's so goddamn compelling about finding the truth of who we are. Why it can lead to the breakup of a perfectly good marriage, or perhaps the murder of a young man?"

Promise continued chuckling. "Look at you," he said. "You've come here to ask me about Islam in order to help you solve the murder of a young man. You didn't even know al-Salaam. You're not assigned to this case. You could walk away from it. And yet you're here asking questions. Why? Why are you after the truth?"

I liked it when Promise engaged me in a game of mental chess that forced me to dig deep and think. I ran my hand over the smooth skin of my head. "I can't rest until I know the truth about who killed al-Salaam. I don't believe what I'm being told— that he was killed because of a long-standing hip-hop feud. I sense there's more that I don't see and understand yet."

Promised nodded. "Can't rest . . . don't believe the surface truths . . . sense there's something more . . . I'd say that's the same reasons that Sufis and others turn inward to look for spiritual truths."

"Yeah, but you still haven't told me what they find."

"There's a saying that goes something like this: The first most important things we have no words for. The second most important things are the words we use to try to describe the first most important things. And after that, everything else in ordinary conversation. What do you find when you look inside? It's a hard question to answer in words. I think mainly because you don't really find something like a child finds an Easter egg during a hunt. You have an experience of the truth, of God . . . call it what you want. But what I can say is that Sufis and the men and women of other spiritual traditions do agree, in large part, on what the effects of an inner experience of God or the truth is. A piercing of the veil, Sufis will say. A realization of a deeper unity and oneness behind the apparent separation and fragmentation we see in the outer world."

"And other forms of Islam—say Shiite or Sunni Islam—don't like this realization of a deeper unity and oneness because . . ."

"Because it places the authority for truth or for God within the hands of each individual, and therefore takes authority away from the mosque, the synagogue, the church, the group. You name the religion, and throughout the years people who have professed their own experience of spiritual truth have been labeled heretics, burned at the stakes, or had an imam issue a fatwa for their death . . . organized religion does not like freedom of spiritual thought."

"So a Shiite considers a Sufi an infidel because the Sufi feels free to experience the truth as he or she sees it."

Promise nodded.

"Could one Sufi also consider another Sufi an infidel because he doesn't experience the truth the way the first Sufi sees it?"

"It also wouldn't be the first time someone was persecuted for professing a belief different from the group." Promise smiled and a twinkle lit his eyes. "I was a Muslim once," he said.

"I remember something about that, but I don't remember the details."

"In prison, two years is barely enough time to know someone."

"Shiite? Sunni? Sufi?"

I stared at Promise. He just smiled. I pointed.

"Sufi," I said.

He shook his head.

"Then what?"

"Nation of Islam," Promise said. "Black Muslim."

"Louis Farrakhan and that group?"

Promise chuckled. "Before Farrakhan's time. I joined the Nation in the early '60s when Malcolm was coming up in the ranks. They had an active prison-recruiting program. Wasn't long before I headed the FOI in this prison."

"FOI?"

"Fruit of Islam," Promise said. "It's what they called the most dedicated brothers."

"And how does the Nation fit into all we've been saying about Sufism and Islam?"

Promise sighed. "Long story," he said. "But the Cliffs Notes version is that initially it didn't. After Malcolm made his hajj to

Mecca it looked like the Nation was headed toward closer ties with the Muslim world. Then Malcolm was assassinated. A sad day indeed."

"People say he was killed by other members of the Nation. What do you think?"

Promise sighed. "Malcolm penetrated the veil. He was at odds with Elijah Muhammad, the Nation's founder. At odds with minister Farrakhan, its rising star. Any way you cut it, a feud within Islam set the stages for Malcolm's death regardless of who pulled the trigger."

"But you didn't stay with the Nation?"

"Couldn't," Promise said. "Eventually, a group within the Nation split off and did align itself with more traditional Islam. But I started believing something different from the rest of the group—"

"Penetrated the veil?"

Promise smiled softly.

"It's tough when you stand outside the group," I said.

"Dangerous too," Promise said.

We talked until the guard knocked on the door. Promise shuffled from the room, and a part of me wished I could sit with him at dinner in the prison mess hall and continue our conversation like we used to.

\* \* \*

I got back to New York City at nearly midnight. I parked Nora's car several blocks away from my apartment, walked into my place, turned a few lights on and turned others off, then slipped out. I drove down to the garage, parked, then walked back to Nora's apartment. JJ slept curled up on the couch, a schoolbook cradled in his arms the way he used to sleep with his teddy bear. I crashed into Nora's bed.

Sunlight streaming through the window awoke me the following morning. A note on the nightstand from JJ read, "Off to school. Can we have pizza together tonight?"

My heart panged. I'd spent the first part of our two weeks together running after and from disaffected Muslims and rap artists. I remembered what Promise said about my inability to give up until I'd found the truth, and how spiritual seekers on the quest for truth sacrifice much that others hold dear. Now, I'm not saying that I'm a spiritual seeker. And I'm also not saying that trying to find al-Salaam's killer justified leaving my son alone. But this feeling of sacrificing something so important for something so compelling did help me understand what Promise meant. And in some strange way it also helped me understand Liz. Maybe she felt driven to "find herself" even if that meant giving up something as important as our fifteen-year marriage.

I stumbled into Nora's kitchen and made myself some coffee, then I went into the living room and pulled out JJ's case of CDs. I thumbed through them until I came to one by Deuce F. I slipped it from its sleeve. I checked the record label: H&M records in New York City. I hoisted the thick Manhattan telephone book from a shelf below a small end table. It showed H&M records on 54th

Street and Third Avenue. Nora also had a thick Brooklyn phone-book nearby, which listed three mosques—two Shiite and one Sunni—in the vicinity of the Bashir Sufi Center.

As a child, JJ loved those cars and trucks that you wound up, then let loose on the floor. They'd whir and run until they hit a wall or an obstacle, which they'd bounce into several times before slowly turning in a direction that would allow them to move freely again until running up against the next obstacle. I chuckled to myself. It reminded me of being a detective intentionally running up against obstacle after obstacle in search of the truth.

Friday's a holy day for Muslims. I figured that might be a good time for me to run up against the walls of a mosque. Before that, perhaps bouncing into the walls of H&M records might turn up something about the last song al-Salaam wrote; a song that Sam Adams said his record company might have a problem releasing because of what it revealed.

\* \* \*

Third Avenue south of 59th Street reminds me of a concrete canyon with tall glass and steel palisades on each side. Smog lingered in the air, and the sun still hadn't risen over top of the looming behemoth buildings, which made it hard for me to tell whether to expect a nice day or not. I'd missed the morning rush hour, but people still swarmed the streets. After spinning through the revolving doors at the bottom of one of the tall buildings, I passed through a metal detector, signed in, and walked over to a bank of elevators. A guard asked me what floor I wanted, and when I said twenty, he directed me to a set of shiny metal doors with a sign over them that read, "Local."

A crowd of people spilled out of the car when the doors opened, and a crowd took their place inside along with me. Floral scents of perfume and cologne dueled in the small, cramped car. A few people reached around bodies to tap the oval floor buttons. Nothing happened. They tapped the buttons again. When the car stopped at each of the first four floors, regardless of whether anyone got on or off, sighs arose before everyone seemed to settle in for the long "Local" ride. I've always found it amazing how in crowded subways and elevators, New Yorkers, men and women alike, have their bodies pressed close against each other like lovers, and yet they dare not say a word.

It took almost ten minutes for the Local to reach the twentieth floor. I stepped out, along with an attractive young woman dressed in a blue skirt and a white blouse with a frilly front. Her hair was done in a wavy bun at the back of her head. A smell with a hint of spice wafted my way.

"Excuse me," I said to her.

She spun around and looked up. I'd hoped for a smile but I got a bland "so what" look.

"H&M records?" I asked.

She pointed down the hall to her right, then pivoted and walked left. When I looked down the hall I saw "H&M" in three-dimensional letters that must have been two feet high affixed to the light, wood-grained wall. A silver LP hung beneath the H and the M. The record company occupied one half of the floor.

When I got to the floor-to-ceiling front doors, I reached out, then smiled at the silver door handles fashioned in the shape of tone arms. It recalled days of lying on my stomach, tone arm perched delicately on my index finger as I tried to drop the needle in the smooth space before the grooves of one record track without scratching the entire vinyl surface. Ah, what skills today's youth missed out on.

A hip-hop tune thumped from the speakers in the reception area. In the middle of the room, a young woman with walnut brown skin and cornrows in her hair sat behind a shiny steel desk. Her body swayed to the beat as she poked at keys on the computer in front of her. I walked up to her desk. I don't think she noticed.

"Good morning," I said.

She flinched and her hand flew to her heart, then she sighed and went back to swaying, though she stared at me with a flirtatious sparkle in her eyes.

"Sorry," I said.

I saw her reach underneath her desk, and the music suddenly dropped several notches in volume.

"Sorry," she said. "It doesn't usually get busy here, until the afternoon."

"Main man in?"

"Phil?"

"Uh-huh."

"Is he expecting you?"

"No." I pulled out my badge. "I'm here investigating al-Salaam's murder."

She sighed. "You're a little late for that, aren't you? NYPD. FBI. DHS. Seems like they've all been here." She smiled, which accentuated her high cheekbones. "Want some advice?" She didn't let me answer. "Don't call him al-Salaam. Phil hates the name. Call him Deuce F."

"I'll try to remember that," I said.

"Have a seat," she said. "I'll tell Phil you're here."

I sat down next to a large window across from the reception-ist, which at twenty floors up didn't give much of a view except to the windows of other tall buildings along Third Avenue. From the floor up for three feet, a light wood covered the walls of the reception area, but from there up and across the ceiling, I saw white perforated panels, like you'd find in a sound booth. Music and video magazines cascaded over the table in front of me. I picked up a recent issue of *Hip Hopster* with al-Salaam and T-Mo head-to-head on the cover, looking mean, under a title that read, "Battle of the Groove: Who's Really Winning the Hip-Hop Wars."

I'd barely opened the magazine when I raised my head to a commotion down the hallway.

A man screamed, "I needed those contracts yesterday. What kind of stupid bitch are you, anyway?"

A woman whimpered, "I'm sorry."

Footsteps came closer, and I fully expected to see a buff rapper in gold chains swaggering into the reception area. But, instead, a short man with stringy gray hair down to his shoulders strolled in.

# FOURTEEN

"Who'd you say was here?" the short man hollered at the receptionist.

"This man." She pointed to me.

"Who're you?" the short man barked across the room.

"Someone with excellent hearing," I said.

"Hah. Least you got a damn good sense of humor, unlike most people that work for me." He strutted over to me, arm outstretched before him. "Phil Harmon," he said. "The *H* of H&M. But then Manny Steinberg's been dead for ten years, so I guess that makes me the *H* and the *M*." He laughed, but I didn't join him. I did shake his hand. "You're here about what?" Harmon said.

"Yousef al-Salaam."

Out of the corner of my eye I saw the receptionist shaking her head vigorously.

"Who the fuck's that?" Harmon asked.

"Hip-hop artist signed to your label."

"Hell it is. Never had anyone by that name working for me."

"Deuce F?" I asked.

A sly, subtle smile cracked Harmon's lips.

"Two-bit rapper," he said. "Dime a dozen. Make and break 'em every day. You know much about the music business?"

"No." I shook my head.

"Figures," Harmon said. He made a fist and rapped his chest. Harmon wore a shiny polyester shirt opened enough to show his gray-haired chest and gold chain. "Been in the business since the late '50s," he said. "Signed 'em all, big and small. I can smell talent when it walks into the room. So who d'ya work for?"

"Office of Municipal Security." I reached for my identification.

"Hell, don't bother," Harmon said. "If I can't size up a rap artist or a con artist by now, I oughta be in my grave along with poor ol' Manny." Harmon eyed me up and down. "'Sides you look about as outta place in here as a fish flopping around a desert." He waved me forward. "C'mon. We'll go back to my office to talk."

I followed Harmon as we stepped from the reception area into a hallway where the carpet changed from beige to red. Gold and platinum records lined the walls. A door opened abruptly and a woman in her twenties with red eyes shoved a manila enveloped into Harmon's slightly protruding gut. She sniffled. "Contracts, Mr. Harmon."

Harmon stopped, pulled her out into the hallway, and reached around her shoulders. "Desiree, you're one of my best employees," he said. "I'm sorry if I got sideways with you earlier. It's just that I hate to see anyone as competent as you underperforming."

"Yes, Mr. Harmon," she said.

Harmon made a point of checking his watch. "Lemme make it up to you," he said. "Take an hour and a half lunch today."

"Yes, Mr. Harmon," Desiree said.

She shrunk back into her office.

Harmon skipped a few feet farther down the hallway and yanked a door open. I stepped into his office behind him and he pushed the door shut.

"Fuckin' help," he said. "Damn kids can barely read or write. Only reason I hire 'em is because they know the music, and artists like to be around people that understand 'em."

"Must have a pretty high turnover in staff," I said.

"Whaddya mean?"

"Tastes change, artists change, staff changes."

Harmon let out a belly laugh. "Thought you said you didn't know squat about the music industry."

"I don't."

"Yeah, well at least you know rule number one: Everything changes."

Promise's voice played in my mind. "Everything changes. Sounds like Buddhism," I said.

"Whaddya do next?" Harmon asked. "Close your eyes and start chanting?"

"Depends upon how you answer my questions."

Harmon slapped me playfully on the arm. "I like you," he said. "You don't seem to take life too seriously."

I smiled. "Everything changes."

The huge desk Harmon slipped behind dwarfed him. I counted four large windows in what appeared to be a corner suite, but Harmon kept the blinds closed, which only let in suffuse light from outside. Overhead, track lights lined three of the four sides of the ceiling, shining tiny spotlights down on two dozen or more photographs of Harmon shaking hands or kissing the cheeks of the greats in the music industry. Sammy Davis, Jr. Harry Belafonte. Ray Charles. Aretha Franklin. Barry White. Tupac. Apparently, Harmon's taste in music skewed toward black artists, or maybe that's where his outstretched palm had always found the money.

The last picture of the series showed him standing between Yousef al-Salaam and T-Mo. Harmon wore a white suit and white tie. The rappers had on baggy pants and baseball caps, twisted to opposite sides of their heads. Both of them made fists that they tapped on top of Harmon's.

Harmon had no other chairs in the office except his, so I sat down on one of the two long couches that lined opposing walls. I pointed to the picture of al-Salaam and T-Mo.

"Looks pretty friendly," I said.

Harmon craned his neck to see which picture I pointed to. "Yeah, well that was an award ceremony where they both won something or other. Looks can be deceiving, you know?" He twisted his arm to check his watch. "Now, I ain't got all day, so let's get to it. Anyway, you're kinda a copycat act, aren't you?"

"Copycat act?"

"You know, like all them damn Elvis impersonators. Musta been half a dozen agencies in here asking questions the day after the Deuce was shot. Let's see. You wanna know if the Deuce had any enemies," he hiked a thumb toward the picture, "if T-Mo and the Deuce had broken the truce between them; and if the Deuce had been contacted by any foreign nationals—Muslims, that is—who might be terrorists? And when I answer 'No' or 'I don't know' to all of the above questions, you'll get up, shake my hand and say, 'Thank you for your time, Mr. Harmon.' That about right?"

"No."

Harmon's face blanched, but he recovered his smile quickly.

"Fresh act," he said. "I like that. Lay it on me."

I held up a finger. "One question," I said. "I'd like a copy of al-Salaam's last song."

Harmon sneered. "Then why the hell are you wasting my time? Go to a fuckin' music store and buy his damn CD."

"Not that last song," I said. "The last one he recorded but you refused to release."

Harmon's face turned beet red. "What'd you say your name was?"

"I didn't. But now that you finally asked, Shannon . . . John Shannon."

Harmon chuckled. "Sounds like some cowboy in a fuckin' Western." He massaged his brow. "Look, here's a crash course on hip-hop." He leaned back in his chair and folded his hands behind his head. "Used to be that I did everything. Found the talent. Found the songs. Ran the recording studio. Did the demos. Pressed the records. Distributed 'em . . . Times have changed. Now any fuckin' kid with a Mac and a synthesizer can make a pretty damn good demo. Sound studio's not that important to me. It was always a loss leader. Real money's in the distribution of an album and the promotion of an artist—takes talent for that." He rapped on his chest. "That's where I come in.

"Bottom line is all these rappers have their own studios. They do their own recordings, hire their own soundmen, backup groups, etc. I just wanna see the final product . . . something I can run with, something I can sell. So I have no fuckin' idea what these guys are doing in their studios. You wanna find out what happened to the Deuce's last recorded song, maybe you should ask T-Mo."

"T-Mo?"

Harmon let his chair spring forward. "Yeah, T-Mo. T-Mo's supposedly got this kick-ass new sound studio. The Deuce said he was working on his next release at a new studio. I assumed it was his homeboy's."

"And where's T-Mo's studio?"

"How the fuck am I suppose to know? For all I know, it could be in the back of his limousine. Somewhere in Brooklyn, I think. Look, if that's all you wanted to know, I got a meeting in ten minutes."

I held up my finger again. "One last question. Had al-Salaam's conversion to Islam helped or hurt his career?"

Harmon pounded the desk. His face went red again. This time he stood up, though he still looked small behind his desk. He muttered. "Harmon. Harmon." He raised his voice and pursed his fingers. "My grandfather was a Jew from Poland. You know what his name was? Przemysl Halusaynskyi. Some fuckin' bureaucrat at Ellis Island heard his name, stamped a paper, and

said, 'Welcome to America. You're now Emil Harmon.' Poof."
Harmon raised his hand toward the ceiling. "Stripped his identity from him just like that. And along comes some kid from the streets who can hardly speak English but knows how to make words rhyme with 'ho, bitch, and ass. So he changes his name to Deuce F and makes millions.

"Then he decides he doesn't like the very country, the very capitalism that put him into clothes, cars, and women, so he changes his name again to Islamic babble. Meanwhile, these same fuckers hate Jews and are trying to eliminate us from the face of the earth. Give me a fuckin' break." Harmon pounded the table. "May Manny rest in peace. Of course converting to Islam hurt his fuckin' career." Harmon sighed and sunk down in his seat.

"Kids still seemed to like him," I said.

"Fuck." Spittle flew from Harmon's lips like an aerosol spray. "Kids'll like whatever we tell 'em to like."

"Meaning al-Salaam remained popular with his fans, but not with the insiders of the music industry?"

Harmon flew out of his chair again. He leaned on his desk and glowered at me. "Meaning this fuckin' interview is over, buddy."

"Thanks for answering my questions."

When I left Harmon's office, I ran into Desiree in the hallway. Tears smeared her mascara. She looked at me, then turned away. I touched her arm lightly.

"Eat lunch quickly," I said, "then take that extra time to start working on finding a better job."

I winked. She smiled weakly.

The lights above the elevator doors indicated two cars headed my way, one dropping down from the twenty-fifth floor, the other rising from the fifteenth. Both arrived at the twentieth floor almost simultaneously, but the first bell declared the descending elevator the winner. As I stepped toward the open door, the other elevator bell rang. I walked toward the back of an empty car, and when I turned around I saw T-Mo with two beefy bodyguards walking past my car. I lunged for the "CLOSE" button and mashed it with my thumb, but the door didn't respond. I took a deep breath.

T-Mo turned toward me. Our eyes made contact, and for an instant neither of us moved. I think it took him that long to recognize me, but when he did he sneered and pointed. The elevator doors began to close as he pushed one of his bodyguards toward me. The last thing I saw was the man reaching into his jacket pocket and T-Mo leaping toward the closing doors. The doors to the car moved apart slightly, as if he tried to pry them open with his hands. Metal, perhaps from the butt of a pistol, pounded on the doors. The car started to descend. I exhaled, then I heard a muffled yell, "Take the stairs and get that motherfucker."

My stomach dropped as the elevator bounced to a stop at the nineteenth floor. The doors slid back and I peeked both ways. Whoever T-Mo sent after me hadn't made it down to this floor yet. The doors swung closed, and I let out a breath, but then my body stiffened. If I were racing after an elevator that I knew stopped at every floor, I'd run down several flights and wait for the car to come to me.

When the doors opened at the next floor, a young woman holding a stack of manila file folders stepped on. She pushed the "LOBBY" button, eyed me, then shrank into a front corner of the car. I smelled the sweet aroma of her perfume, but I also smelled her fear as she looked at me. But right now, it worried me more that this woman might become an innocent victim of T-Mo's goons.

At the next stop, the young woman looked out expectantly, hoping, I'm sure, that someone would step on to dampen her fears of continuing the ride alone with a tall black man. I looked out expectantly too, but T-Mo's boys hadn't stopped at this floor either. The doors opened to an empty hall two more times. The young woman kept her head down, staring aimlessly at the floor, her foot tapping furiously between elevator stops.

Then the doors opened at the fifteenth floor. The young woman looked up and gasped. Two more tall, imposing black men blocked her way.

"Excuse me," she said, "this is my stop." She elbowed her way between T-Mo's henchmen.

"Mine too," I said.

I elbowed my way between the two men as well, only I really threw my elbow hard into the solar plexus of the man on my right. He doubled over and sank to the floor. When the other man reached into his jacket pocket, I elbowed him at the base of his throat. He coughed violently.

The young woman started screaming, "Call the police. Call the police."

The elevator doors started to close. I jammed the down button with the heel of my hand and they parted again, then I peeled the first man off the floor and threw him into the car. His head hit the back wall and he moaned. The elevator doors closed.

The young woman's screams rang in my ears. Around the corner from the elevator, a door crashed open and a voice said, "Call the police; it sounds like a woman's being attacked."

The second man, bent over, struggled to recover his breath. I slammed my fist and forearm down on his back and he crumpled to the floor. Just then, a second set of elevator doors opened. I stepped into another empty car and looked back at the young woman, who stood trembling in the hallway.

"Miss," I said. "It might be wise if you took this elevator down with me."

"But . . . I . . ."

She had trouble speaking. The elevator doors started to close and I thrust my hand between them. They snapped back open. The man on the floor groaned. The young woman looked at him, then at me. I watched her do some rapid risk calculation in her head, then the man on the floor started to move. She sidestepped him and leaped into the car with me. I let the doors swing closed.

The young woman tried to disappear into the front wall of the elevator car. Her body trembled. She said nothing for the next several stops. No one got on the elevator with us for the remainder of the ride down to the lobby. Security guards swarmed around the one bodyguard I'd sent down on a car alone. The young woman walked toward one of the guards. I hurried toward the revolving doors when someone tugged on my arm. I spun around expecting to see a uniform, but instead I saw the young woman from the elevator car.

"I'm sorry," she said.

"For what?"

"You were trying to protect me back there, weren't you?"

"I was trying to protect both of us."

"Thanks," she said. Then she walked off toward a stand selling sandwiches and soup at the back of the lobby.

# FIFTEEN

A RUSH OF COOL air met me when I entered Nora's apartment, which meant an open window. The whiff of lavender and rose carried on the breeze meant that Nora had returned, but from the absence of claws scraping across the hardwood hallway floors Madame Meow had not arrived yet. The suitcases parked at the end of the hallway confirmed the diagnosis. I called out.

"Hello."

I didn't get an answer, but I did hear the muffled flush of a toilet followed by the downpour of a shower. I knocked on the bathroom door and cracked it open. A wave of steam swirled around my face.

"Nora."

"That you, John? Come in, and tell me what the hell's going on."

"I'll wait for you to finish," I said.

"Don't be silly," Nora said. "Come in and pull up a seat."

I wriggled my arms out of my jacket, tossed it onto the couch, and walked into the bathroom, where I pulled the cover of the toilet down and took a seat. Nora stuck her head from around the corner of the shower curtain. The water slicked her auburn hair back so it clung to the sides of her neck. She smiled.

"I didn't know you'd be coming in so soon," I said.

"I got an early morning flight from Phoenix," she said. "Five days of being with thousands of lawyers is enough. But what about you? What's all this about a rapper's death and Islam?"

The bathroom had begun to feel like a Turkish bath. "Hard to talk in all this steam," I said.

Nora stuck her head around the shower curtain again, then her arm. "Wanna hand me a towel?"

I did, and a moment later she stepped from the shower with the towel neatly wrapped around her from the chest down. She shook out her hair and a spray of water flew across the room. I ducked, but it still hit me.

"I'd hug you, but I'm wet," Nora said.

I pointed to the door.

"I'll wait outside," I said.

I plopped onto the couch and picked up a book by Noam Chomsky. In the background a blow dryer whirred behind the bathroom door. Chomsky leaped into a dense argument about American imperial power. I didn't make it through two pages before the bathroom door opened and Nora popped out with her hair and body dry but the towel still wrapped around her. She glided past me into her bedroom, closed the door, then opened it again. She pointed to the book.

"I started it on the plane. Do you know Chomsky?" she asked.

"No," I said. "But I know this much—he'd give Ken Tucker an upset stomach."

"Why's that?" Nora asked.

I ran my finger across a line I'd just read, then paraphrased it for Nora. "The United States has done more to sow the seeds of terrorism throughout the Islamic world than a hundred Osama bin Ladens. Tucker'd probably call in a hit on the professor."

"And what do you think?" Nora asked.

"Seem to remember there weren't any terrorists in Iraq before we went in, but tens of thousands afterward. How do you lawyers say it? Ipso facto."

"Better phrase would be, *ipse loquitur*."

"Which means?"

"The thing speaks for itself."

"Ipse loquitur," I said.

"You see what wonderful trivia hanging around lawyers brings? Have you eaten lunch yet?" Nora asked.

"No."

"Feeling adventurous?"

"About what?"

Nora laughed. "About lunch."

"Depends."

"Give me a few minutes to get dressed and I'll tell you what I have in mind."

I went back to slogging my way through a few more pages of Chomsky, talking about something called "blowback" and how America's foreign policy in the 1950s was "blowing back" to haunt us now. The piece about the British in Iraq really amazed me. Seemed like the Brits tried to do the same thing as we did—

invade the country, pacify it, recreate it in their own image—but in the end it didn't work. Who was it that said, "Those who do not learn from history are doomed to repeat it?" Aha. A few paragraphs later, Chomsky said the same thing. The quote apparently came from a philosopher named George Santayana.

Nora's bedroom door opened and she burst out in jeans and a sweater, chanting, "Raw food."

"Sushi?" I asked.

"Raw food," she said. "I went out for dinner in Arizona to a raw foods restaurant."

"Alone?" I asked.

"Yes, that's all they serve, raw foods."

"No, I mean did you go out to dinner alone?"

Nora smiled. "Jealous?"

She pulled her leather jacket off of a chair back and slipped it on.

"Curious."

I put my jacket on.

She huffed. "If you must know, I went out with a friend."

"Love interest?"

"Wait a minute, buddy. I just got through being with thousands of lawyers whose idea of conversation is cross-examination. I didn't come home expecting more of the same."

I laughed. "I'll take your evasion as a yes."

Nora pulled open her front door and held it for me as I walked out. I pushed the elevator's down button. She tapped her chest lightly.

"That's why I'm the lawyer, and you're the investigator," she said. "I went out to dinner with Celeste Youngblood, my roommate in law school. And if I didn't know better, I'd say I do detect a little jealousy."

The elevator doors swept open and we stepped on.

"Curiosity," I said.

"Killed the cat," Nora said.

I tapped myself lightly on the chest. "Lot worse things after this cat."

"Like what?"

We walked out of the El Dorado and around the corner. I gave Nora a more detailed account of events than I'd given her over the phone when we talked two days earlier. I'd just gotten to the point of telling her about my meeting with Promise, when she had us heading into Quintessence, an eatery on Amsterdam Avenue. Inside the long and narrow restaurant, shades of lime green paint covered the wall. We had our pick of tables, which caused me to wonder, but then I checked the wall clock. Almost two. The waitress, a young woman with a sunshine smile, came over the moment we sat down.

"Uncooked, unpasteurized, unprocessed," the young woman said.

"Unsafe?" I asked.

Nora threw me a sideways glance.

The young woman went on to tell us how nothing was heated above seventy degrees, and how they served only the finest glacier water without ice.

"No ice?" I asked.

"Bad for digestion," she said.

I picked up a menu and scanned it. Virtual reality food. That's what they served. Burritos. Burgers. Loafs. Pasta. Sandwiches. All of the names recognizable, but none of the ingredients. Pasta made from squash? Meat loaf made from nuts? Burgers made from sunflower seeds? I kept thinking as I read the menu that real men don't eat raw food. Nora beamed with enthusiasm. She ordered the nut loaf with gravy, and my ears perked up at the sound of something real.

"Gravy?" I asked the waitress. "What's it made from?"

"Creamed mushrooms," she said. "But the cream of course doesn't come from dairy products."

"Oh, dare I ask from where?"

"It's a milk made from fermented cashews."

I pursed my lips, shook my head, and slapped the menu closed. "I'll have the burger on one condition." I held up a finger. "You don't go into the details of what it's made from."

The waitress smiled and took the menus from our hands.

By the time I'd finished telling Nora about my meeting with Promise, our food arrived with quite an artistic presentation. Nora's loaf dripped with a rich-looking white sauce. My burger stuck out from beneath a healthy piece of lettuce. Parsley and flowers garnished both plates. My burger looked edible, and I guessed the two thin slices of brown something that it sat on passed for a bun. The red sauce in the paper cup on the plate looked enough like ketchup to soothe my anxious palate. Nora's fork hovered before her lips as she awaited my all-important first bite. I picked up the burger and took a good-sized bite, chewing slowly for the effect.

"Well?" Nora said.

I kept chewing.

"Do you like it?"

I frowned.

"Sorry," Nora said. "I—"

I laughed. "No, seriously, truth is the bun's a little dry but the burger tastes . . . well . . . earthy . . . and good . . . in a curious sort of way."

Nora dug into her nut loaf. She let me try a piece, and it too didn't taste all that bad. Halfway through the meal, Nora set down her fork, took a small sip of water, leaned back in her chair, and asked, "Why are you on this case?"

I set aside my burger.

"Because JJ asked me to find out who killed Yousef al-Salaam."

Nora pointed to her chest. "C'mon, John. It's me you're talking to. JJ's still just a child. You could simply tell him it's grown too dangerous to continue."

I'm sure my smile looked weak. "He already told me it'd be okay with him if I quit."

Nora's eyes flashed wide, and she frowned. "So, why are you still on the case?"

I mumbled. "I'm not convinced that al-Salaam was shot by a rival rapper."

"And you're not getting paid to risk your life to discover the truth. And . . ." Nora picked up a fork and dove back into her nut loaf. She smiled. "You still really haven't told me why you're on this case."

I shot Nora a "back off" stare, and she shot back one that said, "Don't try it buster."

"Suppose I don't like the fact that a lot of people—Tucker, for example—seem convinced that al-Salaam's just another misguided young man, or even worse, a potential terrorist that we're better off without. I met with him."

"Did he get to you?"

"Get to me?"

"Convince you of his good intentions . . . his innocence."

"He didn't seem that concerned about what I thought."

"But you're still concerned about what others thought about al-Salaam? Hmmm." Nora's fork hovered just before her mouth, a piece of nut loaf perched on it. A drop of gravy hung beneath the fork before dropping to her plate. She slipped the nut loaf into her mouth, slid the fork out between her lips, then tapped the air a few times with the fork in my direction. "Know what I think?"

"Do I have a choice?"

She rested her fork beside her plate and smiled. "What are friends for if not to tell you the truth when it's right in front of you but you can't see it?"

"What?"

"I think this is all about you and your anger. You wanting to get back at a system that falsely convicted you of murder, didn't believe you, was perfectly content to lock you up for life. Forget JJ. I think you want to prove Tucker and everyone else wrong, and the more times, the better."

"Something wrong with that?"

"It's a noble intention. Remember Prometheus?"

"Stole fire from the Gods to give to humankind."

"Pretty noble. Remember his punishment?"

"Remind me."

"Zeus chained him to a rock and sent an eagle to peck out his liver, which grew back every day."

I got her point, but I asked her anyway. "And . . ."

"They—the people who wrongly convicted you and think al-Salaam is at best a foul-mouthed rapper or at worst a terrorist—will always be that way. There will always be people like you falsely convicted. Some even falsely executed. People like al-Salaam, whom our justice system will characterize as terrorists and therefore not give a damn about the truth or their rights. It makes me angry. Sometimes makes me want to give up. Or move to Canada. I represent people like this all the time. Just like I represented you when you were in jail.

"Truth is, you can't right every wrong, and if you try, you become chained to the system that produced those wrongs just as sure as Prometheus was chained to that rock. And your liver, your heart, your soul is pecked out over and over again. And each time you pray you can grow them back. I left that conference of lawyers in Phoenix because too many lawyers I once knew with livers, hearts, and souls had over the years failed to grow them back."

"But you can at least try to right the wrongs that come your way," I said.

Nora shook her head. "No. The best you can do is pick and choose which wrongs you really want to do battle with, then try your best. Are you sure this one's worth it?"

I took a deep breath. "No," I said.

"Well, that's a start," Nora said. "At least you're being honest with yourself."

Nora finished her nut loaf. I put away most of my burger. The young waitress appeared and reeled off a list of what she called "guiltless desserts." Berry carob mousse. Raw pecan pie. Electrolyte coconut crème pie. Maybe I was too attached to my guilt. I waved my hand and passed on them all.

# SIXTEEN

With the exception of the painted image of a star and crescent, and the Arabic writing beneath it, the outside of the Majid Musa Mohammed on Prospect Avenue in Brooklyn looked more like a church than a mosque. The tremulous sounds of a *muezzin* floated eerily above the rumble of traffic and distant ambulance sirens, calling the faithful to evening prayer. A line of men, many in knitted white skullcaps, waited to enter the building on the right; a line of women in white hoods, clothed from head to toe in dark dresses, stood waiting on the other side of the mosque.

Ambling forward with the line of silent men, the first thing that caught my attention was that every man around me appeared to be African American. I looked over to the women, and as near as I could tell the same held true with them. A sudden warmth flushed through me. I'd expected to see men and women from the Middle East at this mosque, not men and women who looked like me.

At the entrance to mosque, I took off my shoes and slipped them into one of many wooden cubbyholes. A large, burly, dark-skinned man intoned "Salaam Alaikum," before motioning me to raise my arms. He patted me down, spun me around, and patted me down again before motioning me along.

The muezzin's recorded voice echoed through the cavernous inside of the mosque. Like a huge moving machine, men filed successively into place among the rows of ruby-red pillows. On the other side of a blue carpet that ran the length of the hall, women did the same. A subtle hint of frankincense wafted through the hall. I found my place and my pillow. I kneeled on it and studied the floor, waiting. An array of light, square patches dotted the varnished wooden floor, a remnant of the anchor points of a church's pews.

The rows of pillows turned nearly 90 degrees away from what once must have been the church's pulpit. I guessed that we were all now facing toward Mecca. A snippet of Promise's remarks floated through my thoughts. "The history of Western religions is each denying the authenticity of the other." My knees touched the very ground of that history now.

Except for the muezzin's tremolo, a grave quiet reigned. How different this was from attending a Sufi service. Finally, the muezzin's voice fell silent and the commotion of men and women finding their seats stopped. Several men scurried down the center of the blue carpet, quickly erecting a line of wood and fabric partitions, preventing eye contact between the sexes.

Suddenly, the muezzin's voice pierced through the speakers. His torrent of words washed over the hall. "Allahu Akbar . . . Allahu Akbar . . . Allahu Akbar . . . Allahu Akbar . . ." And though I failed to understand most of the words, the quivering of the muezzin's voice brought to mind an ancient river carrying me back in place and time. The muezzin finished with two shorter rounds of "Allahu Akbar."

Each man then stood, raising his hands to his ears, then folding them right over left above his heart. I believe in that old saying about what to do when you're in Rome, so I followed along as best I could. The men then dropped to the floor, placing their palms atop their knees, bowing deeply. Lips moved, releasing whispered Arabic phrases, I'm sure from the Koran, into the religiously charged atmosphere of the mosque. After this period of standing then kneeling, the men prostrated, whole body, on the floor, sat up, then prostrated again. Finally, a man turned to me, as did all the men turn to another.

"As-Salaam Alaikum wa-Rahmatullah, my brother," he said.

"Walaikum Salaam," I said.

He smiled obliquely, though he stared at me. I knew I'd offered the wrong response. Around me, "As-Salaam Alaikum wa-Rahmatullah . . ." sounded like a mantra. I turned to a man on the other side and repeated the phrase as best as I could to him. He promptly smiled and repeated it back. Imitation appeared to be the first lesson on this spiritual adventure.

The whole prayer time lasted about a half hour. Afterward, the men stood and many scurried from the hall. As I started toward the exit, a hand grabbed my arm. I turned around to see the man who'd frisked me. His smiled seemed as wide as his body.

"As-Salaam Alaikum, brother. The meeting for the newly converted is downstairs."

He pointed toward a staircase at the back of the men's section of the hall. In truth, his words sounded less like a point of information and more like an order. He gathered several men this way and ushered us toward the stairs.

Sconces holding incandescent lights with flickering filaments lined the downstairs hallway, giving it the feel of a subterranean hideout or even a catacomb. Several doors fronted the downstairs hallway. A group of women filed through one door. Our group stepped into a room, where a thin dark man with intense beady eyes sat with his hands folded in a prayer position, fingers touching his lips. Behind the man, pictures of black men in beards and white skullcaps lined the wall. We all took seats and he stared at each of us silently as though assessing how much of a challenge we'd posed. When he got to me, our gazes locked onto each other for an extra long time.

"As-Salaam Alaikum, my brothers," the man said.

He waited, but no response came. Even though I knew the correct response, I remained quiet.

"Walaikum Salaam," the man said. "That is the correct response when greeted the way I've greeted you . . . As-Salaam Alaikum," he said, slowly this time. He stared at me while he spoke.

Most of the other men repeated what they were told. The edges of man's lip curled up slightly, before he looked away to the other men.

"My name is Minister Wali bin Khalil," he said. "You are all here because you wish to become servants of Allah, recruits of Islam," Wali said.

I raised my hand. "Actually, I'm here to ask some questions. I—"

Wali shot a heated glance my way. "Questions are good, my brother," he said. "You'll find all the answers you seek in the Holy Qur . . . an," he separated the word as though it were two, "but first we must begin your instruction in Islam." Wali looked around the room at us. His voice dropped as though delivering an esoteric truth few knew. He whispered, "Islam is the only true religion of people of African descent. Christianity was shoved down the throat of Africa, but Islam is the religion of our birthplace."

Now, I'd spent two years learning about Africa from Promise, and I'd just come back from learning about Islam from him as well. And somehow the minister's comments didn't square with all that Promise had said. My hand shot up.

"Wasn't Islam brought into Africa?"

Wali turned slowly toward me. "Yes," he said.

"Wasn't it forced onto Africans often at the point of a sword or a gun?"

Wali coughed. "Our early Muslim brothers wanted everyone to reap the blessings of the Prophet."

"What about the native religions that existed before the time of Islam?" I asked.

He sneered. "Animal worship. Ancestor worship. Fetish worship. It's not religion. It's the naïve worship of those who have not been shown the truth."

"So Islam is the only true religion?" I asked.

Wali sighed. "Are you Christian?"

"No."

"Jewish?"

161

"No."

"Buddhist?"

"No."

"Hindu?"

I paused before answering, and borrowed a line from Promise. "Undo, maybe."

A soft snickering raced through the group.

Wali shook his head. His voice raised. "Then, a godless man," he said, "but at least one who's been led to the truth. Now the question is whether you will drink from the trough or turn away and walk back out into your godless desert."

Okay, I'd needled the good minister enough, and decided I'd listen to the truth—as he told it. I heard how wonderful Islam had been for Africa, and how the first great empires in Ghana were Muslim, and how the great schools and libraries at Timbuktu were Muslim. How Muslim captains sailed with Columbus. How Estavanico, an early conquistador, was a Muslim from Africa. How many slaves were Muslim, included Kunta Kinte, Alex Haley's forbearer. Wali also traced the Islamic influence in Black Americans from slavery through leaders of the early Civil Rights movement, and even a Cherokee Indian chief of African descent named Chief Ramadan bin Wati.

Most of the men sat in rapt attention as the minister spoke. While I enjoyed the history lesson, as I'm sure Promise would have, too, I gagged at the statement the minister made at the end.

"This is just a brief introduction to Islam, my brothers," Wali said. "The more you study, the more you understand, the more you'll come to see that there is no other path to the truth than Islam."

Another of Promise's sayings popped into my mind. Truth is one, paths are many.

When Wali finished his spiel, he called for questions. One man asked why women were separated from men during the prayer times.

"Because women are a distraction to the faithful," Wali said, "and during prayer you have to keep your mind on Him," he pointed up, "and not her." He pointed in the general direction of the women's meeting room.

I bet Nora and Elizabeth would have something to say about women being a distraction to the faithful. I had another question for the minister. I raised my hand.

"What about all the different branches of Islam?" I said. "I'm especially interested in Sufism."

Wali stiffened. His eyes narrowed and he bored into me with his gaze.

"Sufism is not a part of true Islam," he said. "Sufis are like children who smile at everyone. They are liberals—freethinkers without morals, ready to interpret the words of the Prophet in their own terms. Sufis believe that anything goes as long as it's called a 'gift from God.'" Wali then pointed a finger at me and shook it. "Don't get involved with Sufism, my brother," he said. "It is a dangerous distraction from the true beauty of Islam."

"So women and freethinking are distractions?" I asked.

Wali smiled. "The more you progress in Islam, my brother, the more you'll understand why." He turned to the rest of the men. "But we've said enough for tonight. Grand Imam Aziz speaks live via cable television two nights from now. I hope everyone will come back. Thank you. You're free to go."

I rose to leave, but Wali's long, thin arm reached out, and his bony hand grabbed me.

"My brother," he said. "Please stay."

I took a seat as the others left.

"You have many questions, my brother. The flames of skepticism burn in your eyes."

Only now did I notice the small, dark, round hole in the gap between two of the pictures behind Wali. A smooth, rounded object protruded just beyond the hole. Wali caught me staring.

"We're on a closed-circuit feed?" I asked.

"Observant," Wali said. "A good quality for a true believer, but somehow I suspect you didn't come here tonight for conversion."

"Observant," I said.

"Brother . . ." Wali reached out to shake my hand.

"Shannon," I said. I shook his hand. "I came because I'm trying to understand more about Islam, and why a young man recently converted to Sufism would be gunned down in cold blood."

Wali's face wrinkled as though I'd just asked an off-the-wall question. "Brother Shannon, whatever are you talking about?"

"A young man named Yousef al-Salaam," I said.

"Tragic," he said. "But then glorifying the horror and filth of the streets through song is not the way to heaven."

"I visited the Sufi Center that al-Salaam attended," I said. "And I noticed graffiti on the outside wall in Arabic. Something about 'death to the Infidels.'"

"Islam calls forth strong believers," Wali said. "I'm sure it was just some young men concerned about protecting the faith from impure teachings."

"Like Sufism?"

"Yes, like Sufism and hip-hop and rap music."

"Funny, I would never have put them all in the same category."

"Al-Salaam did," Wali said.

I smiled. "That enough to cause him to be murdered?"

"Strong believers," Wali said, "not murderers. Are you the police?"

"No," I said. "Al-Salaam was a friend of the family."

"Well, then, I'm sorry for your loss. But don't let your questions lead you down the wrong path. We're a community of the faithful here. We love and respect our brothers, even if they have gone astray."

I pointed to the gap between the pictures. "That why everything that happens in this room is on camera? So you can record all that love and respect?"

"We're also prudent," Wali said. "My brother, please come back to visit the Majid Musa Mohammed when your heart is more open to the greatness of the Prophet and his teachings. Allahu Akbar. Have a safe trip home."

I got that my time to leave had come. Outside the door, two large, unsmiling bodyguards waited. They silently ushered me to the mosque's entrance, waited while I slipped on my shoes, then stood by the door as I walked out into the crisp night air. The door to the mosque closed with a resounding thud behind me.

Walking back to the subway station, I couldn't help but reflect on the saccharine hatred Wali lavished on Sufism. For a guy making millions singing music, al-Salaam certainly had many enemies. His old hip-hop buddies didn't like him cleaning up the airways. His new Sufi buddies didn't like him branching out on his own. And then there were the Islamic faithful, like Minister

Wali Khalil, who considered anything but his form of Islam lesser in the eyes of God.

The chill in the air worked its way through my jacket. I pulled the zipper up, raised the collar flaps around my neck, and hunkered down into the leather. Suddenly, I heard footsteps behind me. I didn't turn to look, but I counted maybe five or six different gaits. A storefront window reflected the distorted images of a group of young men bobbing and swaying.

I stopped, then turned to face them—six young men, all dressed in hooded sweatshirts and baggy pants that fluttered as they walked. I couldn't distinguish their faces, but the tallest of the young men stepped out of line, making a point of brushing roughly past me so that the barrel and handle of his pistol swept across my side. He turned and gave me a gap-tooth smile as he swaggered by. An electric current ran through my body, raising the hairs on the back of my neck. "Set-up," I heard my mind say. "Set-up." I turned. Two older, taller, bigger men now came at me from the same direction that the young men had. I turned again and continued walking toward the subway station, but the group of young men spun around and headed back my way.

# SEVENTEEN

I TURNED BACK FROM the boys and walked toward the men. Both wore suits and long coats. They looked like professionals heading home from a long day at the office, except the orange glow from the street lamps illuminated a flinty look in their eyes—and they didn't carry briefcases. I thought about stepping between two parked cars and dashing out into street, but traffic moved in both directions, blocking my way. I glanced over my shoulder. The gang of boys took their time sauntering back toward me, posturing like predators certain they'd cornered their prey. Six against one, or maybe two against one? I didn't have long to make up my mind.

I pivoted and started walking toward the boys. The tall one who'd brushed past me stepped in front of the others, and pulled his gun from the pouch of his sweatshirt. He held the pistol at a 90-degree angle to the ground, pointed it at me, and swayed it back and forth in front of him as though walking an invisible dog. I kept moving toward him, but I slowed my pace, listening for the footsteps of the men coming up behind me.

The gang of boys grew closer. But so did the men.

Twenty-feet away from the boys, I stopped suddenly. The boys stopped, and so did the men. I put my hands up and said, "If it's money you're after, take my wallet."

The lead boy took a step in my direction, but I twirled to my left and dove over the hood of a parked car, curling into a ball as I hit the street. I bounced up, crouched, and raced a few cars down, then sidestepped back onto the pavement. I was now behind the two men. They turned, and I saw one reach into his coat. I lunged at him, pinning his arm to his chest, wrapping my other arm around his throat in a chokehold that squeezed tighter.

The boys took off running. The other man pulled a gun from his jacket and leveled it at me, but I propped up the man I held between us. His body shook.

"Don't shoot, Jamil," he said.

"Shut up, asshole," Jamil said. Then he spoke to me. "You let him go, or I'll kill you."

"That's not how this plays out," I said. "You put down your weapon and walk away, or the three of us will be dancing in the streets until the police arrive."

"This ain't worth dying for," the man in my arms said.

"I told you to shut up," Jamil said.

Under the orange street lamps, beads of sweat broke out over Jamil's face. He licked his lips. Apparently, he'd not been in a standoff like this before.

I squeezed tighter with my chokehold and the man in my arms coughed.

"Who sent you?" I asked.

"Fuck you," he said.

I jerked the chokehold tighter. "Not the answer I was looking for."

"Don't say a word," Jamil said.

I looked over my shoulder. The gang of boys had disappeared, so I started backing down the street, dragging the man in my arms with me. The man holding the gun moved with us. With one hard squeeze and twist of my arm, I could render this man unconscious, but then I'd risk him slumping to the ground and providing Jamil with a clear shot at me.

I kept up the chokehold and the pressure. I whispered into his ear, "Tell me who sent you and maybe we can work this out."

"My patience is running out," Jamil said.

I jerked quickly. The man gasped for air. He tried to raise his other arm from his jacket to pry my chokehold from his neck.

Jamil's eyes never left me. They searched for a moment's inattention on my part, a moment in which he might get off a shot. I let the man's arm reach for mine, and when he grabbed my forearm I ratcheted my hold on his neck tighter. He had little strength. His arm flailed at mine, and as it did, I tightened my grip again and reached into his coat pocket, feeling for the crosshatched grip, then pulling out his semiautomatic pistol. I held it to the head of the man in my arms while looking at Jamil.

"Game's changed," I said. I whispered again. "You want to tell me who sent you now?"

He squirmed, trying to writhe his way from my grip.

I looked at Jamil and smiled. "One shot and you're dead," I said. "Maybe you should tell me who sent you."

"Fuck you," Jamil said.

Jamil raised his gun. A bright flash of light and short explosion followed. The man in my arms let out a combined groan and deep sigh. I took aim at Jamil. He dashed between two cars into the street. Blood gurgled from the man's mouth, spilling sticky and warm over my arm. I kneeled down with him as he slumped to the pavement, then I heard car brakes squeal and the dull thud of fiberglass and metal encountering an object. Suddenly, traffic had come to a standstill, and when I stepped out into the street, I saw Jamil's body sprawled on the ground.

I tucked the other man's pistol into my pocket and headed toward the subway station.

\* \* \*

When the shower first hit my body, the water ran pink down the drain. With Nora home and looking after JJ, I decided to spend the night at my apartment for a change. I called out for pizza and opened a bottle of Guinness.

Before I turned in, I pulled back the drapes over my bedroom window slightly. Across the street and down the block, I saw the dim outline of two men in a parked car. I ran through several rooms in the house, switching lights on and off, then I grabbed my gun and raced down the steps, into the basement, and out the back door into the garden. I made my way out to the adjacent block. I walked down the street and rounded the corner, crouching low beside parked cars as I inched toward the men.

I slipped between two cars and got back onto the sidewalk. Three cars away, it looked like the head of the man in the passenger's seat slumped back over the headrest. Like a tiny mushroom, the door button stood with its head raised. I grabbed the door handle, jerked the door open, and ripped the sleeping man from his seat. I whipped a chokehold around his neck and jammed the barrel of my pistol into his head.

His partner flew out of the other door. Pointed his gun at me across the roof of the car. And for the second time in less than two hours, I was facing off against a man with gun and another in my arms.

"Wait," the man with the gun said.

"Who the hell are you?" I said.

"Your code-name is Shango," the man with the gun said.

I shouted. "Who are you?"

I clenched tighter with my arm and the man I held groaned. The other man kept his gun on me, but slipped his hand in his pocket and pulled out a wallet. He flipped it open with one hand and flashed the badge and ID card at me.

"Office of Municipal Security," he said. "We work for Ken Tucker."

\* \* \*

The following morning I rammed my shoulder into the door of Tucker's outer office, bursting into the reception area. I barreled past Charlene. Somewhere in the back of my mind I vaguely heard her say, "He's busy," but I twisted the door knob and hit the door to Tucker's inner office with my shoulder and blew inside.

"What the hell's going on?"

Tucker sat with his back to me, feet on his windowsill, looking out toward the Verrazano-Narrows Bridge as it curved through wispy fog. He let his feet drop and slowly spun around in his chair.

"Yes," he said to the person on the other end of the call, "I like to . . ."

Tucker looked up at me and smiled, held up his hand, then spun back around to the window. I lunged for the telephone cradle and punched several buttons until the lighted one went out. He dropped his legs and swung around again, appearing unruffled, as though I were simply minor inconvenience.

"I understand that you're—"

"Fuck you," I said. "Cut the crap and tell me why you had me followed. What kind of game's going on here?"

He waved me down. "Have a seat."

"I don't sit when I'm angry."

"It'd probably do you well if you did."

"What would do me well is to know why two men from OMS were outside of my apartment at 1:30 this morning?"

"A matter of national security."

"My ass."

"Truth is that someone's after your ass."

"And suddenly I'm a matter of national security?"

"No. The people after you are."

"And you sent someone to protect me from them?"

"Actually, I sent someone to discover who they were."

"So you're using me as bait?"

"Don't have to." Tucker chuckled. "Seems you do a pretty good job of setting yourself out as bait."

"And you couldn't bring me in on it."

"You didn't need to know. Besides, the less you knew the more naturally you'd act."

I shook my head, waved my finger at Tucker. "Bastard."

Tucker sneered. "Sit down . . . there's more."

I didn't oblige him. "What more?"

"There's a credible threat on Sheikh Tariq Bashir's life."

"So when did OMS start caring about the head of a Sufi order?"

"Since the threat emanated from Ibrahim bin Fatah."

"The man al-Salaam was photographed with in Tunis?"

"Yes."

"And Fatah is in this country?"

"Either he is, or he's sent an assassin."

"Why's Bashir so important to Fatah? More importantly, why's Bashir important to you?"

Tucker paused for an instant. And that's all I needed to know. "He's an asset, isn't he?"

Tucker remained silent. I flopped down into one of the high-back leather chairs fronting his desk and let my head fall against the headrest. I caught a subtle whiff of stale cigar smoke.

Tucker mumbled. "Something like that."

"And you couldn't tell me this before?"

"You didn't need to know."

"But you want me to know now?"

"No. I want you to protect Bashir."

"Protect him?"

"Yes, from Fatah, or whoever's after him. The man's a leading Sufi cleric, educated in Britain, but his family has contacts throughout the Islamic world. He gets our people intelligence and access that we wouldn't have a chance of getting on our own."

"And most Muslims don't like Sufis, so he's got contacts with many opposition groups."

Tucker laughed. "You're a quick study on Sufism. Promise help out?"

"You—"

"I keep an eye on all my assets."

"Well, I'm a contract agent. I think I'll pass on this assignment."

I got up to leave, and Tucker stood up.

"Sit down, dammit," he said. "I'm not through."

I turned around. "I am," I said.

"Intel says the hit on Bashir is likely to take place in the next few days."

"Yeah? Where?"

"When Bashir is teaching a workshop at a place in upstate New York. The Sigma Center. Ever heard of it?"

I flopped back down into the chair and ran my hand over my head. "Liz is there at a workshop."

Tucker smiled, "So I've heard."

"So what's al-Salaam got to do with all this? Was he an asset too?"

Tucker sidestepped the question. "There is one other thing. The Majid Musa Mohammed. Mosque where you worshipped last night." Tucker snickered. "It's one of several Shiite mosques under the control of Grand Imam Sayd Aziz."

"Let me guess. Aziz is connected with Ibrahim bin Fatah."

"They grew up in Egypt together," Tucker said.

"Is that why a death threat in Arabic landed on my doorstep after I visited Bashir's Center? Why someone wanted to prevent me from catching a subway after I visited a mosque last night?" I put on a huge fake smile for Tucker. "Someone close to Aziz, who's close to bin Fatah, thought I was working for OMS and feared I'd get wind of the plot against Bashir."

"Maybe," Tucker said.

"Maybe? You don't sound convinced."

"Too many loose ends."

I sucked in a deep breath and stared out Tucker's window. At the far end of the Verrazano-Narrows Bridge fog had cleared from around Staten Island.

"What was al-Salaam's role in all of this?"

Tucker turned away. Now he stared out the window. "What do you mean?"

"I mean you're telling me that a Sufi sheikh works for U.S. intelligence. A terrorist suspect wants to kill him. And al-Salaam, a student of the sheikh who met with this terrorist suspect overseas, already has been murdered. Aren't you the one who always says he doesn't believe in coincidence? What's the connection?"

Tucker spun around and pounded a fist on the desk. "I don't know," he said.

"Well, let me try this," I said. "U.S. intelligence doesn't really care about a rapper. What they care about is a rapper blowing the cover of one of their sources who happens to be this rapper's spiritual teacher."

Tucker sucked in a breath. "So what? We kill al-Salaam to keep him quiet?"

I pointed to his phone. "You'd put that past them?"

"I don't know. I'm an intelligence chief, and I don't like it when I don't know."

"And that's why you had people watching me?"

"When I don't know, I press every lever I can think of until I do know. It's your call. You want to take the lead in protecting the sheikh or leave it to someone else? Maybe you'll find out more about al-Salaam if you do."

"Just me?" I asked.

"No," Tucker said. "We've been in touch with the Center already, three of our agents will register for workshops—you, Chen, and Cummins."

"Both women?"

"More women in these workshops than men, in case you hadn't realized. You're lead agent."

"With Elizabeth up there, you knew I'd be in."

"What I know is how to press levers," Tucker said. "Why's she there, anyway?"

"Self-discovery, self-enlightenment, self-realization."

"That add up to self-indulgence?" Tucker asked.

"I don't know."

"Well, maybe there's a bright spot for you in going there."

"What? Seeing Liz?"

"No. Maybe they also have workshops on self-discovery and anger management."

"You think I need one?"

"What do you think?"

I took a deep breath, then, in my most polite, refined, and calm voice, I said, "Mr. Tucker, in my humble opinion I think you should go to hell."

I got up to leave.

# EIGHTEEN

BACK AT MY APARTMENT, I called Natalie Chen and Barbara Cummins. We agreed to meet for dinner later. After I hung up, I pulled a suitcase from the closet and started packing. With the Sigma Center's brochure in one hand, I went down the checklist of the items to bring: warm clothes, rain gear, a flashlight, a sleeping bag, loose fitting garments.

After I packed, I called Nora at work. She couldn't stop laughing. "You're on your way to adult summer camp," she said. "Oh, how fun." She resumed laughing.

"Maybe I don't get the joke," I said.

"You will. But don't worry about JJ. He and I and Madame Meow are having a grand time."

Just before I walked out of my apartment to meet Cummins and Chen, the telephone rang. Sam Adams sounded worried.

"I need to talk with you," she said. Her voice quivered. "I got a call last night. Someone thinks I have Yousef's last tape or that I know where it is. The caller told me to leave it in a brown paper bag in the steel city trash can at the end of my block when I left for work today." She sighed. "I don't have that tape and I don't know where it is, so I had nothing to leave, but they said . . . they said . . ." She sniffled, then started to cry.

"What time do you get home tonight?" I asked.

"About nine," she said. "There's a meeting at the Sufi Center, then—"

"Don't go to Java 'n Jazz tonight," I said. "Come straight home. I'll meet you at the entrance to your apartment at nine."

"I won't," Sam said. "I mean I will . . ." Her voice brightened. "I mean, you know what I mean."

I laughed softly. "I do."

"Thanks," she said. "I feel better already."

"Give me your cell phone number," I said. "in case I need to call."

I scribbled Sam's cell number on the back of the phone book. When I hung up, I programmed it into my cell phone. Just as I'd finished, the telephone rang again.

"Barbara and I want to know if you're an adventurous eater," Natalie Chen said.

"Depends," I said.

"Well, Barbara heard of this new restaurant on the upper West Side that sounds kinda fun."

"Where is it?" I asked.

"Eighty-eighth and Amsterdam," she said.

"Wouldn't be Quintessence?" I asked. "All raw food."

Natalie Chen shrieked. "You've been there."

"I have."

"And?"

"Well, let's just say I wasn't planning on going back anytime soon."

Chen's voice dropped an octave. "Maybe we'd better stick to Italian."

"Maybe we'd better," I said.

I put on my shoulder holster and tucked my pistol in before I left for dinner. Sam Adams' quivering voice played through my mind.

* * *

Il Giardino is an Italian restaurant in Soho. I hadn't been there before, but Natalie Chen assured me they didn't serve raw foods. I got there before she and Barbara did.

Inside Il Giardino, deep crimson carpets butted up against cherrywood wainscot, and above that, dark pink walls ran up to ornately carved crown molding supported by fluted faux columns placed strategically around the room. The maitre d' found a reservation under Chen, and a waitress escorted me toward the rear of the restaurant, behind one of the large fluted columns. She pulled out a carved wooden chair with a crushed velour seat the color of the carpet. I held up my hand and moved around to the other side of the table, in order to face the entrance. I never sit with my back to the door.

I hadn't made it through the wine list when I looked up to see Natalie entering the restaurant. At first glance, Natalie reminded me of a mild-mannered librarian with her large black glasses and her jet-black hair rolled up in a bun. She looked to be in her mid-twenties, about five-five, fine-featured. She wore a wrap-around, ankle-length skirt that covered the tops of her leather boots. I stood. She stuck out her hand.

"Natalie Chen," she said.

We shook hands. Call it instinct—or training—but I stepped around to pull out Natalie's chair for her. She thrust her hand toward me. Okay, I guess she called it male chauvinism. I stepped back to my side of the table. She sat down and immediately waved the waitress over. Natalie handed the woman her glass of water.

"I'll have it without ice," she said. Then she turned to me.

"I never went in for study groups in college," Natalie said. "I preferred—prefer—to do things on my own. Tucker knows that. So I don't know why the hell he assigned me to this baby-sitting detail?"

Did I say "a mild-mannered librarian?"

"Maybe he thought you'd blend in well," I said.

"Why? Because I'm Asian?" Natalie asked.

"Don't know. I do know that—"

"Hi y'all. I'm Barbara Cummins."

The southern accent surprised me, as did the African American woman standing over us at the table who looked to be in her mid-forties. Barbara took a seat next to Natalie, across from me.

She huffed. "Used to be a woman would have someone here to pull out her chair for her."

I started to answer, but Natalie beat me to it.

"Those were the days when women were treated like, like queens." Her words rung with disdain.

Barbara turned to look at Natalie. She rolled her eyes. "Hell. I kinda like being treated as royalty."

Natalie let her glass fall to the table with a thud. "Not me."

Barbara Cummins could have easily passed for an executive in a Fortune 500 company. She wore a nicely tailored pants suit with a white blouse. Gold pendant earrings dangled from her ears. And from across the table, I detected a pleasing floral scent as she sat down. Spunk and style. I glanced at the two women as they buried themselves in their menus. I think I knew why Ken Tucker chose them for the assignment: neither of them had the feel of law enforcement or intelligence agents about them.

We placed our orders. While waiting, we agreed on a working plan for monitoring the sheikh. With Barbara and Natalie registered in his workshop, I'd register in another course at the Center to give me the freedom of moving around. We'd check in with each other every night before bedtime. We'd carry weapons with us, but not on us, while attending class.

Dinner seemed to go by quickly and it wasn't long before Natalie pushed back from the table. "I've got an engagement in an hour," she said, "and I like still haven't packed."

She stood up and blew out of the restaurant, leaving Barbara and I staring and half smiling at each other.

"Remember when you were that age?" Barbara asked.

"Like, I do," I said.

"How'd you get involved with OMS?" I asked.

Barbara took a sip of wine. "I worked as a state trooper in Alabama until I got sick of wearing those unflattering wide brim hats. The Secret Service was looking for female officers, so I took up the challenge and moved to D.C. I met Ken Tucker there," she said, "and he made me an offer I couldn't refuse when the mayor hired him to head OMS." She smiled. "My husband of twenty years got tired of making moves for my career. He stayed in D.C. We'd never had kids, so we tried a commuting relationship." She stared into her wine. "It lasted about a year. And you?"

I took a few sips of my red wine and gave Barbara a run down of being convicted of murdering DEA agent Danny Rodrigues and serving two years in prison before being let out.

"And you're not bitter?" she asked.

"I have my moments," I said.

I also told her about the breakup with Liz, but for whatever reason I left out the part about Liz being at the Sigma Center. A warm glow flushed through my chest and I couldn't tell if it was from the wine or being in the presence of a very classy lady whom I liked. Suddenly, it dawned on me to check my watch. Eight-thirty. I waved the waitress over and asked for a check.

"Hot date?" Barbara asked.

"No," I said. "An appointment with someone who needs my help."

"Well, she's very lucky she can count on you."

"What makes you think it's a she?" I asked.

Barbara smiled. "Female intuition. Anyway, it's none of my business. I'll see you upstate tomorrow."

Barbara stood up to leave. I watched her walk out the door. She carried herself with a self-assured but unpretentious gait that brought a smile to my face. Maybe female intuition told her I'd be looking, because as she stepped through the restaurant's front door, she turned back and flashed me a warm smile.

Standing in front of Il Giardino, I called Sam Adams. She didn't answer.

# NINETEEN

I SNAPPED MY CELL phone closed and stepped into the street to hail a cab. I'd just raised my hand when my cell phone rang. A taxi cab also pulled over. I pulled my phone out. The display flashed Sam's number. I waved the driver on. He tapped his horn sharply twice. It's a cabbie's way of giving you the finger.

"I just got out of the subway station and I'm walking to my apartment as we speak," she said.

"I'll meet you there in about twenty minutes," I said.

"Would you like to get some coffee first?" she asked.

Sam sounded relaxed, unlike she had earlier in the day. "Sure," I said. "Where?"

"A cozy place on Bleecker Street."

Sam gave me the address of Coffee Beings.

"I'll meet you there," I said.

"If we're both walking, you'll probably get there before me."

I did.

Inside, Coffee Beings had a retro look and feel, a throwback to the Village's avant-garde jazz and beat era of the '50s and '60s. Pictures of Charles Mingus, Thelonius Monk and Pharaoh Sanders hung at odd angles from the walls. I draped my jacket on the back of a chair at the only open table in the rear of the coffeehouse, then I walked to the counter and got at the end of a long line. I stared at the oversized photo of a big band hanging above the hissing espresso machines. A hand touched me softly between my shoulder blades. I turned to face Sam. She'd wrapped a yellow scarf around her head.

"Hi," she said.

She kept her hand in place. Her touch felt good.

"Hi," I said. I pointed to the picture. "That's Sun Ra leading his Arkestra isn't it?"

"Wow, I'm impressed. You're the first person I've ever come in here with who knew that was Sun Ra. Question is, do you like his music?"

The coffee line moved forward. "I never thought much about liking Sun Ra. I mean, the man claimed to be from Saturn; that he belonged to a race of angels. His music is complex and deep, discordant and yet delicately woven together. Liking Sun Ra's music never crossed my mind. Getting in to it, being comfortable with all you couldn't quite grasp, recognizing you were listening to a master even if you didn't understand all that he said . . . I think that's how I relate to Sun Ra."

Sam beamed. "Did you ever think about becoming a jazz critic?"

"No," I said. "It's funny, though, talking about Sun Ra reminds me of my experience listening to Sheikh Bashir."

We stepped up to the counter. "Single mocha, tall," I said.

"Decaf soy, short," Sam said.

I paid and we stepped to the side to wait for our drinks.

"Sheikh Bashir would be honored by the comparison to Sun Ra," Sam said.

"I heard the sheikh's a jazz buff."

We walked with our drinks over to the table. When Sam sat down, she pulled the yellow scarf from her head. The frizzy ends of tiny curls sprouted from where her cornrows had once been.

"Do you like them?" she said. "I just took them out this morning."

She ran her hand through her hair and shook her head. Her curls bounced.

"I do," I said.

They gave her a wild, untamed look, like a modern-day Medusa.

"Would you tell me more about the call you received this morning?" I asked.

Sam sighed. "A man called early. Before I left for work. He woke me up. He said he knew that Yas left a copy of his last recording session with me. He needed to have that tape. I told him I didn't know what he was talking about. He said if I didn't want any trouble I should place it in a plain brown paper bag and throw it in the city trash receptacle at the end of my block on my way to work. Or else . . ." Sam sucked in a breath. She reached for her coffee, took a sip. "Or else they said I'd be hurt. No, that's not the truth . . . They said they'd kill me." She sighed again. "I tried to tell the man again I didn't have the tape, but he hung up. I didn't know what to do, so later in the day I called you."

"The man's voice. What did it sound like?"

"Typical American male. Not foreign, if that's what you're asking. In fact, it reminded me of my boss. You know, just a subtle hint of arrogance to it." Sam looked at me. She touched my arm. Her hand trembled. "I'm scared," she said. "What's in that tape that someone would kill me over?"

"That was my next question. What can you tell me about Yousef around the time he was making the tape?"

"He'd just come back from the Middle East, and he'd changed."

"How?"

Sam sipped more coffee. "Serious. Yas was way more serious than when he left. He said he'd seen things over there that really bothered him, and that he had to tell the world what was going on."

"Did he say what he'd seen?"

"No. But he did say the only way he could tell people about these things was in his music. He said he wanted ordinary people to know the truth."

"Do you know where he worked on his final recording?"

"He never said. After he returned from the Middle East our relationship evaporated."

I hadn't touched my coffee. I finally took a sip. "Evaporated?"

Sam pointed to her cup. "Just like this steam," she said. "For Yas, it was as though the few weeks we'd been together before he left had never happened. Vanished into thin air. After he got back he'd call. Occasionally he'd drop by to talk. He'd become a man obsessed with this recording project. Nothing else seemed to matter." Sam dropped her head. "Certainly not me."

I touched Sam's hand. She raised her head. A weak smile graced her lips.

"Sorry," I said. "I know what it's like to feel abandoned by someone you love who's off in pursuit of a dream that no longer includes you."

"Would you walk me home now?" Sam asked.

Outside of the Coffee Beings, Sam hooked her arm in mine. She didn't say much as we wove our way through the streets of Greenwich Village. When we got to the steps of her apartment. "Would you like me to walk you upstairs?" I said.

Sam nodded.

After the winding trek up four flights of stairs, we rounded the corner of the staircase and headed for Sam's apartment door. It took me a few seconds to register what I saw. I whipped my gun from its holster, and with my other hand I shoved Sam against the wall. Her body went rigid. I pointed with my pistol barrel toward the staircase.

"Go back down a flight, and do not come up until I tell you to."

I crept toward her partially open door, kicked it open, then spun inside the darkened apartment. I found a light switch and jammed it on with my elbow. I forced my eyes to stay open even though the bright hallway light stung. I flattened my back against the wall beside the first doorway I came to. I reached over and twisted the doorknob, then I kicked the door open and groped along the wall until my fingers touched the light switch. I flipped it on. I waited a moment, then, crouching, I twirled into Sam's bathroom. I nudged her shower curtain back. Nobody there.

I stepped back into the hallway and moved slowly toward the next door, keeping my gaze fixed on the darkened living room at the end of the hall. I stopped beside the next door. Sweat dampened my brow. After reaching in for the light switch, I kicked it open and pivoted inside. I pointed my gun across Sam's bed toward a closed closet door. I hadn't quite made it to the closet when suddenly something crashed to the floor in a room that was deeper inside Sam's apartment.

I raced back into the hallway and down toward the living room, but when I passed the opening from the hallway into the kitchen, a blast of cool air hit me. I ran to the open kitchen window and stuck my head out. The fire escape swayed and rattled. Feet hit the ground below, and a dark human figure scurried into the night.

Just to be safe, I quickly cleared every other room in the apartment, then I stepped to the front door and called Sam in. She ran into her living room first, and gasped, "My god, who'd do this."

I double-locked her front door and slid the security chain into place. When I got back to Sam, she stood at the entrance to her living room, trembling. Books lay everywhere on the floor. Empty drawers from her desk sat stacked atop each other on the floor, their contents dumped into piles. Sam's computer monitor lay face down next to the drawers. Sam walked toward her desk and bent down. She started to pick up and straighten a pile of papers, then she started to cry, "I don't know anything. I don't know anything about Yas' tapes."

She dropped the pile of papers and ran into her bedroom. Her muffled wail echoed through the apartment. I walked over to her and put my arm around her. We both scanned the debris. Someone had yanked all the drawers from her bureau, spilling blouses, socks, panties, and bras on her bed and over the floor. Sam buried her head into my chest and cried.

I helped her pick up clothes, then I replaced her books on her bookshelves while she sorted through her papers. A spider crack ran through the glass face of her computer monitor. When we moved to the kitchen, we swept up shattered glass mixed with brown rice, spices, and the porcelain shards of plates. I checked the lock on the kitchen window. After we finished, we sat on her living room couch in the dark. Garbage trucks whined outside and orange sodium lights bathed the room in an eerie glow.

I checked my watch. Eleven forty-five. Too late to call Nora and ask if she had room for another person. Sam yawned.

"I need to get some sleep," she said.

"Keep your cell phone next to you," I said. "I'll call—"

Sam touched my arm. "I'm scared. I can't stay alone. Would you please stay here?"

"I will," I said. "I'll take the couch. I have to leave early in the morning to pack for a trip to upstate New York. I'll be there a few days."

"I'll be up early tomorrow to go for my usual morning jog," Sam said.

She got up, and a few minutes later she returned with a stack of sheets, blankets, a pillow, a towel, and a washcloth. She placed them on the couch. Then she walked over to me and placed a long kiss on my cheek.

"Thank you so much. I feel a lot better knowing you'll be here. You are one of the most kind and considerate men I've met in a long while."

Sam walked back into her bedroom. The wet, hot ring on my cheek glowed. I slipped out of my clothes, placed my gun on the floor beside me, and lay down on the couch. I pulled a blanket around me, then tossed and turned, wrestling with my confusion about who would ransack Sam's apartment and what could be so important on al-Salaam's recording.

I also wrestled with guilt over my pulsing erection. I didn't want to be sleeping alone on this couch. I wanted to be in bed with Sam. An hour later, neither my confusion nor my erection had subsided. I got up for a glass of water. Sam must have heard me in the kitchen. Her bedroom door creaked as it opened. She walked into the kitchen wearing an almost sheer blue negligee. I felt naked, even though I had on my boxers and my tee shirt.

"I couldn't sleep," I said.

Sam yawned. "Neither could I."

She opened a cabinet door, took out a glass, and filled it with water from the faucet. She stared at me as she drank, which didn't help with my feeling of being naked.

"After this is all over, could we . . . I mean, could I . . . I mean, would it be okay?" I said.

Sam smiled. "After this is all over, yes . . . yes . . . and yes. I'd like that too."

Sam left the kitchen for her bedroom. I headed back to the couch.

# TWENTY

FOR SOMEONE WHO LOVES living in New York City as much as I do, it's amazing how much I also love leaving. I'd be gone for a few days, and Nora needed her car so I rented one to drive upstate to the Sigma Center. Even though it'd only been a few days since I drove up to see Promise, heading over the Tappan Zee Bridge then up the New York State Thruway felt like a great getaway, though a getaway with a measured dose of guilt. I hadn't spent much time with JJ since Nora returned. I found myself really excited about spending more time with Sam Adams. And on top of all of this, I'd be seeing Liz in a few hours and spending time at the same facility with her for several days.

I tried calling Nora on her cell phone to ask if Sam could stay with her, but I didn't reach her so I left a message for her to call me. Then I called Sam on her cell phone, but I didn't reach her, either. The message I recorded sounded too gushy, so I hit a few buttons, listened to it again, then pressed a key to erase it. I'd talk to Sam in person.

The thruway ran inland from the west side of the Hudson River. The Sigma Center operated from facilities on the east side of the river about one hundred miles north of New York City. I took the turnoff for a small bridge that spanned the Hudson near Woodstock. Swinging off the highway, I continued staring north. Another hundred miles that way would bring me to prison and to Promise.

After I crossed the Hudson, I headed south on Route 9. I pulled out the directions to the Sigma Center and found myself winding and weaving through back roads, past small lakes and large estates. Finally, I saw a tiny sign with a single, hand-carved yellow Latin character "∑," and an arrow indicating a right turn. A light drizzle began as I took the turn and bounced along a rutted, washboard dirt road for another few miles. At the end of the road, a sign read, "The Sigma Center for Holistic Studies." Let's see, my Latin wasn't that good, but being at the end of the road, I think I would have named the place "Omega."

The dirt road ended at the entrance to the Sigma Center, and a paved road lead into the facility. Off to my left, woods lined the edges of a massive clearing easily as large as a football field, crammed with vehicles like sardines in a can. A parking attendant in a thin parka waved me down. I stopped and lowered my window.

"Welcome to Sigma," the young blonde woman said. "I'm Nadine." She smiled. "Is this your first time here?"

"It is."

"Well, then, like, you're in for a treat."

I thought about meeting Liz and guarding Sheikh Bashir. "I'm wondering what to expect," I said.

"Course?" Nadine asked.

I cut the engine. "Um . . . sacred . . . um . . . sacred something or other."

Nadine kept smiling. "Sacred Journeys and the Self," she said. "I know the names can be, like, confusing."

"That they can," I said.

"You'll love the course," Nadine said. "Phillip Epstein is one of our best teachers."

Nadine pulled a clipboard from beneath her parka, flipped through a few pages, then asked, "Name?"

"John Shannon," I said.

She ran her finger down the list. "Oh," she said, "you're a guest of the Center. Even better. Right over there." She pointed. "That's the parking section for instructors and the Center's guests. And, Mr. Shannon, I see the Center's director has asked to see you once you arrive. Tony's office is in the administration building." Nadine pointed down the road from the parking lot, then she looked at me and leaned on the door. "Are you an author?" she asked.

"No."

Nadine frowned. "A workshop leader?"

"No."

Her frown deepened. "A seeker?"

I smiled now. "Yes, in a manner of speaking."

Her smile returned. "Well, then, you really have come to the right place."

I wanted to park but Nadine wouldn't step back. She kept staring and smiling. I finally got it.

"Not a lot of people of color attend the Center, huh?" I asked.

Nadine sighed. "Like, diversity," she said. "It's one of our biggest challenges."

I turned the engine on again and Nadine finally stepped back from the car. Like, I wanted to get on with the reasons why I'd come to the Sigma Center.

\* \* \*

A paved path from the parking lot cut through the woods and ended at the administration building, a three-story brick and glass structure that looked newly built. A Range Rover, two Land Cruisers, and several late-model white Volvo station wagons sat next to each other in the small parking lot behind the building. Business at the Center must have been good.

From a hand-carved wooden marquee on the wall just inside the entrance, I read that Tony Matarazzo's office was on the third floor. I took the stairs, which ascended against a wall of glass and a rising view of the Sigma Center's campus. A lake bounded the property at one end. Back from the lake, dozens of buildings dotted the landscape. Four or five large white buildings with red roofs dwarfed the others. A group of colorful small domes—red, blue, yellow—sat in a large clearing just up from the lake. I stared at the domes, at first unsure what they were.

I heard footsteps coming up from behind and turned to see a man in blue jeans wearing a long, dark ponytail with streaks of gray. His tee shirt read in front, "Oh, no. I lost the key to the universe." He stopped to look with me.

"In the summer," he said, "at the height of our season, that field of tents is a kaleidoscope of colors. I love to watch them rippled by a gentle breeze."

He turned and continued walking up the stairs. The back of his T-shirt read, "Thank God the universe was never locked to begin with."

Once on the third floor, I found myself at one end of a long hallway, whose wooden floors sparkled from the light through a skylight that ran almost the entire length of the hall. Tony Matarazzo's office was at the other end. I passed wooden doors with hand-carved signs that read, "Registration," "Counseling Services," "Newsletter," "Information Services," "Financial Services." Conspicuously absent was anything that said, "Security." Remote. Woods all around. No perimeter fence. A cakewalk for an assassin here after the sheikh.

I knocked on the door marked, "Executive Director."

"Come in."

Whatever I expected, it wasn't to see the guy with the tee shirt about the missing keys to the universe sitting behind the director's desk. But there he sat.

"Tony Matarazzo," he said. "Please have a seat."

I took a seat in a sleek, ergonomic chair in front of his desk and leaned back. Now this is something that Tucker needed in his office. Matarazzo's large wooden desk sat in a corner of the room, angled between two large picture windows. One looked out to the lake, the other to the hills above the property. With the exception of his dress, and maybe the placement of his desk, Matarazzo could have passed for any busy executive. His desk was covered with piles of paper. The screen on his computer appeared full of e-mails.

Behind Matarazzo's desk hung two beautiful outdoor photographs, each with one word written below the image: "Self-discovery" was beneath an image that looked down on a lone climber without ropes hundreds of feet up a rock face. "Self-exploration" was under a photograph of a man standing in a river raft as it crashed into a monstrous wall of whitewater.

He slipped off a pair of reading glasses, which revealed more of his sun-tanned face and his dark brown, searching eyes.

"You're the fellow from the Department of Homeland Security?" he asked.

"No," I said. "Office of Municipal Security, New York City."

"This is Duchess County. Isn't it a little out of your jurisdiction?"

"Maybe you'd rather let the local police handle the matter."

He chuckled. "All three of them."

"How many people know we're here?"

"Just me and my administrative assistant, Vicki. And believe me, the last thing we want to do is alarm the other workshop participants. It was bad enough when word got around that we had deer ticks."

"Lyme disease?"

"Yes," Matarazzo said. "Can you imagine what would happen if word got out that our workshop leaders were being targeted by terrorists while they were here?"

"Let's see . . . terrorism and self-discovery," I said.

Matarazzo narrowed his eyes. "It's not funny." He checked his watch. "Lunch is in a few minutes. The registration for the workshops doesn't start until later this afternoon. I'd offer to take you to lunch, but you'd stand out that way, and your meal ticket doesn't start until after you've registered. We have a nice cafe. Serves food until ten at night. You're staying in Condo Row."

"Condo Row?"

He smiled. "It's the nicest, most expensive accommodations we have. Mostly reserved for our workshop leaders. Queen bed. Private bath. Heating and air-conditioning. You'll like it."

"And my colleagues?"

"They're staying with the other women in the workshop in one of our open dorms."

"Low rent district?"

"Sorry," Matarazzo said. "The call I got said they needed to fit in. The sheikh insists on no creature comforts for his students during the workshop."

"So where's he staying?"

Matarazzo smiled. "Condo Row. Next to you."

"Better to be a teacher than a creature, huh?"

"He's a well-known teacher. He brings in lots of students. So he gets what he wants."

I looked at the photographs behind Matarazzo, and in my mind I turned the *S* in "Self-exploration" and "Self-discovery" into a "$." Shannon, you devil.

* * *

Tofu. Sprouts. Veggie burgers. Carrot juice. Carob. Yogurt. Every other word on the chalkboard menu sitting above the cash register read "Organic." Finally, I spotted the word "chicken," and I sighed. Forget "Sigma" or "Omega." I was beginning to feel as though I'd just arrived at Camp Granola.

The heavy scent of lavender wafted through the air. Large and open, with a stone fireplace and big cut and varnished tree trunks for supports, the inside of the cafe reminded me of a lodge you might find out west.

"Chicken Seitan," I said to the young man behind the counter.

"Gravy?" he asked.

"And biscuits."

He wrinkled his face. "Whole-grain muffins?"

"Twist my arm."

"Salad?"

"Yes."

"With sprouts?"

"No."

The salad and the muffin looked fine, as did the steamed broccoli on the plate, but I'd expected the chicken to arrive on skewers. Inside, a dozen or so cubes of chicken swam in a lake of gravy. I took my tray over to a wood burl table that looked out at the woods behind the cafe, then I had a bite of chicken. I nearly gagged. It tasted like something between cardboard and sawdust. I rushed back up to the counter. I couldn't find the fellow who took my order. A woman in line lifted her eyes from a book and over her reading glasses.

"Something wrong with the chicken and gravy?" she asked.

"Tastes funny," I said. "Maybe it's undercooked."

"First time here?" she asked.

"Shows, doesn't it?"

"Think you were getting 'Chicken Satay' on skewers like you do in any Thai restaurant?"

I looked at my plate. "Uh-huh."

"Seitan," she said.

It sounded like "Satan."

"Seitan?" I asked.

"Yes," she said. "It's a meat substitute, made from wheat gluten."

"Sounds dangerous."

"They'll take it back. Try the split pea soup."

"Thanks," I said. "It's like being at Camp Granola."

She laughed, then winked. "Just wait."

I sat down with my bowl of soup. Bits of what looked like bacon swirled in the thick green soup. I laughed to myself. At the Sigma Center, it couldn't be bacon. I thought about asking, then decided against it. I braved a taste, which wasn't bad.

After lunch, I found my accommodations at one end of Condo Row. Essentially, I stayed in a renovated cabin that sat several feet above the ground on concrete pillars. Inside, the floor was carpeted in beige, the bed was made with light blue sheets turned down, and I smelled the fragrance from a small bouquet of flowers sitting in a vase next to the bed. A note on one of the pillows read, "Enjoy your stay. Housekeeping."

I began to unpack when my cell phone rang. I flipped it open.

"Shannon."

I could barely make out Tucker's voice above the static.

"Bad connection," I said.

"Well, it doesn't get any better," Tucker said.

"What?"

"Got some news I thought you'd like to know. Woman's body was found along the lower West Side Drive early this morning dressed in a jogging suit. The coroner identified her as Samantha Adams. One bullet to the back of her head. She's a longtime member of Bashir's group. And—"

"I know her . . . knew her," I said. My legs started to give out. I slumped down onto the bed.

"Yeah, I kinda figured that," Tucker said. "That's why I called."

"You figured that I knew Sam Adams?"

"Helluva name for a woman," Tucker said.

"Helluva woman."

Tiredness descended over me. I wanted to sleep.

"Anyway, yes, I figured you knew her because a slip of paper with your cell phone number was found in her purse—maybe the first kill for whoever's after the sheikh."

I struggled to focus on Tucker's words, but I didn't say anything.

"You okay?" Tucker asked.

"Yeah," I said.

Tucker hung up. I pounded the bed with my fist. I forced my mind to focus on why I'd come to the Sigma Center. There'd be time to mourn Sam Adams' death later.

I heard voices outside. I stood up, stepped over to the window, and turned a roller on the louvered blinds, angling them to get a better look. The sheikh had arrived with an entourage. I recognized Hamid and Ali. I turned back from the window.

"Bashir's here," I said to Tucker. "Gotta go."

I hung up, and a moment later heard a knock on the door. I peeked through the blinds again and saw Hamid. He'd backed away from the door to look up at the window. He looked agitated. He seemed to be pacing. I stood to one side of the door, twisted the doorknob, and pulled the door open. Hamid bounded up the steps into my cabin. He slammed the door behind him. He stood ramrod straight. His body shook.

"Why did not you tell me?" he asked.

"Tell you what?"

"That the Americans assigned you to protect Master Bashir."

"And when would I have told you?"

"That night at the Center. Why should the sheikh have to tell me that Americans have been assigned to protect him?"

I laughed. "You head up the sheikh's security detail, right?"

"Yes."

"You follow orders, right?"

Hamid narrowed his eyes and said nothing.

"Well, I follow orders, too," I said, "and I just found out yesterday that I was being assigned to guard the sheikh because there's a credible threat against him."

Hamid huffed. "You think you are better than we are? We are his brothers, his students. We have pledged to protect Sheikh Bashir's life. The sheikh does not need you. We do not need you to do our jobs."

"That's great," I said. "You do your job and I'll do mine, and that way we'll be sure the sheikh leaves here unhurt."

"The Sheikh said there would be several other agents here during this retreat. Who are the others?"

"N2K," I said.

Hamid squinted. "What?"

"Need to know," I said, "and right now, you do not need to know."

Hamid clenched his fist and move closer. Just then, a voice from outside called.

"Hamid . . ."

He loosened his index finger from his fist and shook it at me. "You stay out of my way. Understand? You stay out of my way or suffer the consequences."

"You do your job," I said, "and there'll be no need for our ways to cross."

Hamid turned abruptly from me, muttering something in Arabic under his breath, then he stormed from the cabin.

# TWENTY-ONE

I FELL ONTO THE bed on my back. I let my head sink into the pillow, trying to absorb the news of Sam Adams' death. Promise often said that upon death the soul does not immediately leave the body; particularly with a sudden, violent death, it often hangs around, confused, for days.

"You can talk to a soul," Promise said. "Doesn't matter about space and time. You can talk to it. Tell it what you need to tell it. Help usher it on its journey beyond this world. Wherever you are, that person's soul will sense you, hear you."

I closed my eyes. "Sam, I'm so sorry this happened." Tears welled in my eyes. "I feel like I let you down. I should have stayed with you until I knew that you were safe."

I sucked in a breath. "After this was over, I wanted more than just last night with you."

I slammed my fist into the bed. "I will not let your murder pass unredeemed. I will find out who did this. And they will be brought to justice."

I couldn't stay in bed, so I unpacked and threw my clothes into drawers. Then I slipped into jeans and my jogging shoes for an unguided tour of the campus. I jogged down the length of the entryway thoroughfare, which ran right through the Sigma Center to connect with a small county road on the other side.

Spring had not arrived as fully here in upstate New York as it had in the city. A sweet smell of lilac perfumed the air I ran through, but tree limbs had only a green fuzz to them. Assassins are not like workshop participants. They don't just arrive, unpack and kill someone. There's always planning involved. Observing. Waiting. Monitoring. Measuring. Looking for that perfect time to strike a target and then escape.

The Sigma Center was open to the outside by a road. A lake bounded the Center on one side and bare forests surrounded it on the remaining sides. That didn't leave many places to hide, at least during the day. I jogged back to my cabin from the lake, scanning the hillside above Condo Row as I did.

Two thoughts occurred to me. Hire me to stalk Bashir here, and I'd either set up an observation post in those hills, or have someone on the inside of Bashir's organization or in his workshop monitoring the sheikh's movements, then informing me of the best time to move in for a kill. I checked my watch. Hiking up into the hills behind my cabin would have to wait. I needed to get over to the first session of my workshop.

* * *

Phillip Epstein looked every bit the part of a counselor at Camp Granola. Okay, make that a workshop leader at the Sigma Center. A gray-haired man with a bald spot in the middle of his head, and his remaining hair was tied into a ponytail that fell down to his shoulders.

Epstein sat cross-legged on a small riser in front of a large room of nearly one hundred people, mostly women. I sat on the floor in the second of two large semicircular rows in front of him. He started the workshop by closing his eyes and taking long, deep breaths. His glasses, dangling from the end of a silver chain, rose and fell against his chest as he breathed. He invited us to close our eyes. I tried, but found myself peeking.

Finally, Epstein let out a long sigh and said, "Thank you. Please bring your awareness back to the present moment."

A lot of other long sighs echoed around the room and people opened their eyes with smiles on their faces. Then Epstein asked the participants to introduce themselves and in one sentence say why they'd come to his workshop.

"Don't take more than two minutes on your introduction," he said.

I did the math quickly. That meant over three hours of introduction.

A common theme emerged during the introductions: people reported being drawn to the workshop for reasons they couldn't quite explain. One woman said she randomly opened the Sigma Center's catalog to a page with Epstein's picture. Another woman said her karma led her here. One of the few men said his girlfriend suggested he come here to help him "open up" emotionally. From the way he fidgeted, I wondered if she hadn't demanded he come or else. Yet another said she couldn't get enough of Epstein, and wanted to be in his presence whenever she could. From the way she smiled and the way Epstein smiled back, I wondered if being a workshop leader had other perks as well.

When it came my turn to introduce myself, I said, "I came because I've heard the terms 'self-discovery' and 'self-exploration' a lot, and I wanted to learn more about what that really meant."

Epstein seemed to like that answer. He also seemed compelled to say, "Mr. Shannon, it's a welcome change to see a black man in my workshop."

Suddenly, I felt the eyes of the entire workshop on me, and a number of women flashed the same smile at me that I'd seen them flash at Epstein. A handful of people had yet to introduce themselves, when in the distance a gong sounded.

"Dinner," Epstein said. "We'll finish the introductions tomorrow morning, then move into the next phase of the class."

People stood and meandered out of the hall. All in all, so far it seemed like workshop leaders had pretty easy gigs: They closed their eyes and got other people to do the talking. They sat there. Smiled. Listened. Occasionally they nodded their heads. And they never forgot about dinner.

The setting sun turned the tips of the hills surrounding the campus golden. From the direction of the lake a chorus of frogs croaked. When I reached the large eating hall, I found myself at the back of a long line of several hundred people. Far ahead of me, Barbara Cummins stood out in a line. And far ahead of her, I saw another black woman entering the hall—Liz.

It took nearly fifteen minutes before the line reached the dining hall. The drone of hundreds of conversations echoed off the high, peaked ceilings. The rows of tables and chairs, and the steadily moving line of hungry people, reminded me of prison at mealtime. I filed past the salad bar and filled a small plate with lettuce and cucumbers. I bypassed the sprouts. When I got to the section with hot food set under reddish-orange heat lamps, I laughed out loud. How many ways can you fix tofu? One tray had breaded tofu cutlets that reminded me of a square piece of chicken. Another, stir-fried tofu with vegetables. And a third tray had tofu-stuffed egg rolls.

I heaped some steamed vegetables and rice on my plate, then paused at the tray marked, "Tempeh." I turned to the woman behind me and pointed to the diced and cubed pieces of what looked like meat in a red sauce. She stood barely over five feet tall. She'd worn a long, flowing skirt to dinner. Her short-cropped hair faded slowly from black on top to gray around the temples. She had high cheekbones and dark, soft eyes. She was the kind of woman you reserved the term "handsome" for, and meant it as compliment.

"What's tempeh?" I asked.

"Fermented soybeans," she said.

"I thought tofu was made from soybeans."

"It is," she said.

I pointed at the tempeh again. "So that's fermented tofu."

She snapped from her puzzled look with a smile. "Never thought of it that way, but technically, I guess you're right."

"Technically," I said. "I think I'll pass on the tempeh and stick with the breaded tofu instead. It smells good."

"The breading is made without wheat flour," she said. "Spelt, cornmeal—"

I stuck my hand out to stop her.

"I'm a newbie," I said. "I'm just getting past the tofu. Probably better if I didn't know what else I was about to ingest."

She smiled, then drifted off to find a table. I carried my tray around, wondering where to sit. I saw Liz in a far corner of the room, moving her arms, talking intently with a younger man next to her. I headed the other way, toward a table with no one at it. I passed behind Natalie Chen, sitting with other participants in the sheikh's workshop. She kept on eating, and I overheard her tell someone how much she enjoyed the first session of the retreat.

"Mr. Shannon."

I turned to see a woman I recognized from Phil Epstein's class. She patted the bench beside her.

"Come sit by me," the woman said.

En masse, the rest of those sitting on the bench squeezed together to make a place for me.

"Daria," the woman said as I sat down. "Daria Lockhart."

"John Shannon," I said.

"Yes, I know. You're in my workshop. I liked how open and honest you were with your reasons for being at Phil's workshop."

I mumbled, "Thanks," in between bites of tofu.

Daria kept talking. "This is the fourth workshop I've taken with Phil." She held up four fingers. "It only gets better from here," she said.

Daria looked to be in her mid-forties or even older. She had dark-brown hair that fell just below her ears with strands of gray running through it. She wore a deep purple running suit that seemed to bring out the darker tones in her skin.

"What kind of work do you do, Mr. Shannon?" Daria said.

One thing about tofu: it can be very chewy. I pointed to my mouth.

"Sorry," Daria said. "Please finish eating. We'll have plenty of time to talk later."

"I—" I started to answer Daria when a voice blared from behind me.

"John, what the hell are you doing here?"

I whipped around. Everyone at the table looked up. Liz stood over me. I managed a weak smile.

"Why are you here?" Liz asked.

I pointed to by plate. "Let me finish eating, and maybe we can talk about this outside."

Liz huffed. She checked her watch. "Hell, I have an evening session. If you want to talk it'd better be now. I'll meet you outside the hall." She pointed toward the entrance, then stormed away in that direction.

I pushed my tray away and Daria grabbed it.

"I'll bus it," she said. "Former partner?"

"Soon-to-be ex," I said.

Daria rested a hand on my arm. "Don't worry, a lot of that goes on up here. Couples come to a workshop together, leave apart.

Singles come alone, leave coupled. It's a good place to sort your life out. Safe. Secure. Away from the troubles of the ordinary world."

"Thanks," I said. I got up to leave, following the path Liz had woven between tables out of the dining hall.

* * *

I caught a glimpse of Liz marching down the path from the dining hall toward the lake, and I ran to catch up to her. She must have heard me coming, but she didn't turn around. I touched her on her shoulder. She shook me off.

"Wait," I said.

Liz turned around and screamed.

"What the hell are you doing here, John?"

Two women walking across the campus in front of us turned and looked our way. I put my hand out to Liz.

"Can we talk? Quietly?"

"I don't care who hears me," Liz said. "I'm tired of repressing my voice, my needs, for the sake of you or anyone else."

"I'll lower my voice, then," I said. "I'm here working."

"Like hell you are," Liz said. "I'm here for two weeks to get away from the life I had in the city long enough to try to find what I need to be doing for me." She patted her chest. "And here you are . . . in my face. Damn you. Where's JJ?"

"With Nora."

Liz's lips trembled. Tears came to here eyes. "Don't you think about anyone but yourself? You're supposed to be home . . . with

JJ. Or have you forgotten that I left him with you so you two could spend time together? Then, you farm him out to—"

"Nora," I said. "A trusted friend."

"Somehow I don't think you're hearing me. If I wanted to leave my son with a trusted friend I would have done that, and it wouldn't have been with Nora."

"It couldn't be helped," I said. "And maybe you're the one who thinks only of herself. I didn't come up here after you. I came up here because I had to work."

"Bullshit," Liz said. "What work brings you up here?" A sarcastic smile crossed her lips. "You suddenly get the urge to embark on a journey of self-discovery?"

"No," I said. "Though I'm registered in the class."

"What class?" Liz asked.

"Sacred Journeys and the Self."

Liz wrinkled her face. "With Phillip Epstein?"

I closed my eyes, then opened them slowly the way Epstein had done at the beginning of class. "Thank you. Please bring your awareness back to the present moment," I said with a dreamy voice. "So you know the man?"

Liz shook her head. "It's not a joke. Serious people come here. If you're in Epstein's class just to make fun of it—of him—you've wasted your time and your money."

"I'm in Epstein's class as a cover."

Liz squinted. Her voice dropped. "You're serious."

"About what?"

"About being here for work."

"Uh-huh."

"Who? What work? For Nora? Tucker? What could either of them possibly want with the people who come to this place?"

I sighed. "It'd be better if I didn't say."

"Surveillance? Threat assessment?" Liz paused. Her eyes swept the ground before she snapped her head back to look at me. "Sheikh Bashir? That's it, isn't it?"

I put my hand up for her to stop. "I'd rather not say."

"What does Tucker think? That because the sheikh is Islamic he's a terrorist threat?"

I didn't say anything.

"Goddammit. You and the paranoid Homeland Security people you work for. Just because the man's Islamic he's automatically suspect. Don't you know he's a Sufi? That's why he's here. Sufism is the enlightened, spiritual branch of Islam. Not the fundamentalist, suicidal, terrorist branch."

"I've heard something about that," I said.

"Do the people that run this place know why you're here?"

"It's all been arranged," I said.

Liz sucked her teeth. "I bet it has. Yell 'terrorism' and nothing's safe or sacred any longer. Not even a sanctuary like this."

"Isn't that the truth," I said.

Liz checked her watch. "My evening session begins in fifteen minutes," she said. She turned to leave.

I jogged to catch up to her. I touched her shoulder again. This time she didn't shake me off. She did turn around.

"I am here working," I said. "But I'm also glad to be here to understand more about why you're here."

She shook her head. "You don't have a clue." She turned abruptly and walked off.

# TWENTY-TWO

Sometimes I slip into an eerie dream state where part of my mind knows that I'm dreaming yet it's useless to try to wake myself. I felt that way now as agitated waters yanked me under and tumbled me round. I fought desperately for the sunlight-sparkled surface above me, but the swirling waters pinned me down. I held my breath until my chest burst, then I sucked in what I thought would be my death. But instead of water or air, I drew down the glittering particles from above, which, like pixie dust, entered my lungs, transforming them into luminous gold sacs, and from there filling my body with a suffuse golden light as well.

I floated up from beneath the river, which now lolled as a peaceful stream, and when I got to the surface, I drew in a chest full of fresh air, treading water while spinning around to get my bearings. Darkness cloaked the barren shore from which I came. Light bathed the verdant shore ahead of me. I wanted to open my eyes and dispense with this journey, but then I looked deeper into my mind, deeper still toward the opposite shore. Just above the riverbank, a small, dark man hovered over a fire pit, rubbing his hands as if to warm them. He eyed me and waved me toward him. Sheikh Bashir, I first thought.

I swept my hands in wide arcs through the water ahead of me, keeping my head above the water, pulling my feet into my body, then kicking out my legs, whipping them together. I glided toward the man and the shore. The closer I came, the more familiarity washed over me with every stroke. Suddenly, I saw myself swimming not through the water, but through the air, hovering ten feet above the ground and what I swam toward—whom I swam toward. Not the sheikh, but Promise, hunkering down in the cold corner of a winter prison yard.

The scene shifted instantly back to the river, and as I approached the shore, Promise stood up from the fire and walked down to the water to greet me. I rose from the river, but shed no water, and walked toward Promise dry.

"John," Promise said. He smiled.

I couldn't see his lips move, but his voice surrounded me as the water had moments earlier.

"John," Promise said again. "John. I've been waiting for you."

I still couldn't see his lips move, but his words flowed mellifluously toward me as though carried on gently rippling waves.

"Where am I?" I asked.

Promise laughed softly, the way he laughed to let people know that he knew something that they had yet to find out. "At the start of a journey," he said. "A journey you hadn't realized you'd undertaken. A journey—"

"And now, bring your awareness back to your breathing."

At the sound of Epstein's voice, Promise began fading from my mind. I fought hard to bring him back, like trying to retrieve the fragments of a dream slipping away ever more swiftly with each brightening ray of dawn.

"Take a few deep breaths."

"A journey . . . what?" I called out silently to a vanishing Promise. But I was too late.

"And when you're ready," Epstein said, "open your eyes."

A subtle wave of anger flushed through me. Epstein had ripped me from my friend. I blinked, then squinted, as I opened my eyes, a part of me longing now for the adventure I'd tasted within. Epstein stared at me as he spoke.

"From the look in your eyes, it appears that some of you had profound journeys on the way to your mountain." He cleared his throat. "Mr. Shannon, would you like to share yours with the rest of the group?"

I checked my watch, amazed to find that nearly forty-five minutes had passed since I first closed my eyes.

"No," I said. "I'm not ready to share."

Epstein nodded. "Then perhaps after we take a short break."

Epstein called for a fifteen-minute break, but instead of the hum of conversation I'd expected to buzz around the room, a solemn quiet prevailed. People stood up and filed out of the hall. Several women lay down spread-eagle in the grass under a brilliant morning sun with their eyes closed. Perhaps they hoped to travel back to wherever their inward journey had left them. I found a tree and sat with my back against it, still feeling in a daze.

It seemed like no time had passed when Epstein called out, "It's time to resume."

The flock of silent participants headed back toward the hall. I turned in the opposite direction and walked toward my cabin and the hills behind the Sigma Center. My legs wobbled slightly as I made my way across the campus. I shook my head as I walked, trying to loosen the dreamlike hold my mind had on me, trying to regain hold of reality and the real reasons I'd come to the Sigma Center.

Thirty yards to one side of my cabin, a trail led uphill into the woods. Taking the gentle incline, I fought myself from slipping into believing that if I walked long enough beneath these trees I'd come to that magical river where I'd find Promise waiting for me on the other side. The uphill trail ended at a ridge from which another trail took off in two directions. I took the path that wound around the perimeter of the Sigma campus.

Not far along, a small footpath led downhill off the main trail. I took it, ending up at a natural stone slab seat. I sat and gazed at the commanding view through the bare trees of the Sigma Center and the lake. What the hell had happened back there in Epstein's workshop? What did Promise mean about embarking on a journey?

I let my eyes roam the ground at my feet. Suddenly, I started to chuckle, then laugh. A condom lay half buried in the dirt. A hot summer's evening, with the lights of the campus reflecting off the lake . . . I imagined this must be a pretty spot. My head began to clear, and I felt comfort knowing that not all fantastic journeys at this Center took place solely within the mind. I stood up and walked back up to the ridge trail.

I needed to think like a "hit man" after the sheikh. I wouldn't make an attempt in the daylight, and I wouldn't do it from a place as obvious as the lover's slab that I just left. So I took the next footpath down. It came to a seat too. But this one was of hand-made wood, not stone. I stepped around the bench and into the trees on one side. I wandered off-trail in the direction of the large hall where Sheikh Bashir would speak tomorrow night. Buds ready to burst lined the tree limbs that I passed.

Looking down the slope, bare branches framed a view of the hall. I shook my head. I had an almost unobstructed view of the stage and the speaker's podium through a huge window set into one wall of the building. I'm sure the window framed a stunning natural backdrop for a talk, but it also framed a picture-perfect target for a gunman.

Then, something rustled in the brush above me. I sucked in a breath and spun around, crouching low for a better look. A bright sun dazzled in the blue sky above the ridge, partially blinding me. A branch snapped. I flattened my body to the ground. Leaves crackled underfoot. I pressed my face into the damp, cold earth, lifting my head to look up the hill. The sound appeared to come from the other side of the ridge trail. I shimmied forward and to my right, aiming for a large tree stump to hide behind. The sound of the footsteps came closer, and when I pushed my foot off a rock to move forward, the rock gave way, clattering through leaves and fallen branches on its way downhill.

The footsteps stopped. So did my breath.

I lay there looking up, motionless, expecting a hulking form to loom out of sunlight. I scanned the area, searching for a way out. I didn't see one. Suddenly, the footsteps picked up again, and a backlit figure stepped up and over the ridge, lording down on me. I rolled over onto my back and laughed. The large deer pranced away, its white tail switching from side to side. I crawled over to the tree stump, propped my back against it, and laughed some more. So much for a city boy out in the woods. Then I looked down at the ground. On one side of me lay a small pile of cigarette butts. Unlike the condom, the butts looked fresh.

I patted my pockets. I didn't have a bag to place the butts in. Truth is, we didn't have time to run DNA on them now. By the time I got down off the ridge, a long lunch line snaked its way inside from the lawn outside the dining hall. While I waited to get in, I didn't see anyone from Epstein's workshop, and I didn't see Liz. Once inside, I did see familiar sights. Soup. Salad. And more tofu. Natalie Chen looked up from her table as I passed by, but neither she nor I made direct eye contact. I carried my tray of food to a table at a far end of the dining hall.

Over vegetable barley soup and whole grain bread, I pondered the morning, but I hadn't gotten too far into considering who was behind the cigarette butts and where they'd come from, when the journey I took in Epstein's class slammed into my mind. The gears in my mind ground to a halt and a strange sense of sadness and yearning descended on me, as though I ought to be looking for something I hadn't even realized I'd lost.

My body flinched. The hand on my shoulder startled me from my thoughts. When I turned around I saw Phillip Epstein standing over me.

"Can we talk?" Epstein asked.

"Have a seat," I said.

"I thought we might find a more private place," he said.

I waved my hand around the hall. "In here?"

"No." He pointed to a door behind him. "In the faculty dining room in there."

I pushed back from my table and followed Epstein through a door marked "Private." We stepped into a different world, which reminded me of going from a crowded airport gate through the doors of a VIP lounge. Inside the faculty area, soft music played over the speakers, plush carpet covered the floors, and no one lined up for food. A waiter behind a small counter took plates from a few men and women who pointed at entrées that included a lot more than just tofu. Baked fish. Asparagus with hollandaise sauce. Scalloped potatoes au gratin. Beyond the dining area, I spied a room where several men and women sat slumped over massage chairs, while masseuses and masseurs dug their fingers into their necks and backs. I cracked a smile.

"So this is how the other half of self-discovery lives," I said.

"Nice to come back here to relax after hours in a workshop," Epstein said.

"I bet it is."

Epstein took my tray from me and handed it to someone behind the counter. I took a clean plate from a stack at one end of the counter and had the server fill it with the fish, asparagus, and potatoes. Epstein got his meal, and then we both took seats at a small table with a window that looked out to the surrounding hills. I started into my fish. Epstein closed his eyes for a moment before beginning to eat his food. After a few bites he looked up at me.

"What are you doing here?" he asked.

I put my fork down. "You mean why didn't I come back after the break?"

Epstein shook his head. "No. I believe I understand why you didn't come back. What I want to know is why you came to this workshop in the first place?"

"I already said during the introduction that I was curious about self-discovery, self-exploration, self-enlightenment."

Epstein stabbed an asparagus spear with his fork and popped it into his mouth. "And you expect me to believe that?" he said. "Look, I've been teaching these workshops for what, twenty-five, thirty years? You get a good feeling for the type of people who attend."

"So I take it I'm not the type?"

"If by that you mean being a man and being black, then no, you're not the type. But I don't give a damn about gender or skin color. I'm talking about something else. You don't feel engaged with the workshop. Like you're there marking time. Even though this morning you had a profound experience during the guided inner exercise."

I put down my fork. "And what makes you think I had a profound experience?"

"Your breathing slowed. Your facial muscles relaxed. You remained still, calm. Your eyes were glassy when you opened them."

"But I didn't come back."

"That happens to a lot of people. They confront something within they're not ready to deal with yet. Doesn't matter. I'm not here to force people to change or to look at darker parts of themselves they're not ready to look at. That comes when they're ready."

Epstein let his fork bounce gently between his fingers. He eyed me. I stared back.

"You're a secretive man with a great deal to hide," he said. "You project strength, yet I sense underlying vulnerabilities. You have an almost fatherly air about you, yet I also sense great need. Is there something you need to tell me? Something I need to know? About me? The workshop? The Sigma Center? About you, and why you're really here? I thought you might be uncomfortable speaking in front of the entire group. That's why I waited to ask you until we could be alone."

I kept staring at Epstein, even though I had the uncomfortable feeling that, like Promise, he could see more than I wanted him to see. I felt myself starting to say more than I should. About Liz. About Promise. About the inner journey I took. Even about the sheikh.

But I reined myself in. "No," I said. "I'm here because I want to find out about self-discovery."

Epstein's facial muscles twitched. He broke off a piece of fish with his fork and resumed eating. He sighed between bites. "Then I hope you find whatever you came here looking for. Whether it's inside my workshop or not."

# TWENTY-THREE

After lunch, I walked over to Tony Matarazzo's office. I told him what I'd seen in the hills behind the campus. I asked for more security at the Sheikh's talk. His voice leaped an octave higher as he spoke.

"Set up a security checkpoint with metal detectors to screen attendees at Sheikh Bashir's talk?" He pounded his hand on his desk. "And risk word spreading that the Sigma Center's turned into an armed camp? That we've succumbed to the fears of terrorism?" He eyed me with contempt. "Never. We're an institution that preaches openness, tolerance, respect for all people."

"What'll you be preaching if the sheikh's assassinated here?"

"It's your job to see that it doesn't happen," Matarazzo said.

"I could use some help."

"I thought that's why OM . . ." he chuckled as he spoke, then shook his head, "OM. Hell of a name for a place that trades on fear. Around here you only hear OM chanted as a mantra for openness to the divine presence within the universe."

"Fear and fearlessness," I said. "A friend in prison once told me that mystics seek the path beyond both."

Matarazzo cocked his head. "You surprise me," he said. "Now you sound like someone who belongs in one of our workshops instead of snooping around looking for snipers in the woods."

"It's your lack of concern that surprises me," I said. "You have several hundred people here who could get hurt if there is an attack on the sheikh."

"As I started to say before," Matarazzo said, "that's why I agreed to allow you and two other agents to go undercover for the sheikh's protection."

"The three of us may not be enough."

"Then I'll assign some of my staff to help you."

I laughed. "And do what? Sit around and meditate to protect the sheikh?"

"And now you sound like someone who doesn't have a clue to what goes on here." A smirk crossed Matarazzo's face. "Meditation might not be such a bad idea in this case."

"What if I asked the local police force to send in some plainclothes detectives for the sheikh's talk?"

"Like I said when we talked earlier, that'd deplete the entire evening shift."

"But it would sure help us."

"I'll think about it," Matarazzo said, "and get back to you later this afternoon."

\* \* \*

Leaving Matarazzo's office, I thought about heading back to my workshop, but I walked over to the kitchen instead, where I picked up a few small zip-lock bags. Then I hiked back up into the hills behind the campus to gather the butts. The sun had moved south of the ridge and a steady wind blew. Down below me, the surface of the lake looked like a huge rounded swatch of corduroy or herringbone studded with sparkling sequins.

This time, the rustling in the woods on the other side of the trail had me smiling at my skittishness to unaccustomed natural sounds, but when I got to the large tree stump what I saw stopped me in my tracks.

The cigarette butts had disappeared.

I looked around quickly. I ran back up to the ridge trail and scanned the area to make sure I hadn't found my way to the wrong stump, then I hurried over to the opposite side of the trail. From somewhere down below, a car engine started. My hand slammed into my thigh. Damn. I hadn't heard a deer this time, but a person who'd returned to clean up what he or she left.

I started back down the trail toward my cabin when I heard footsteps coming toward me from below. I stopped, stepped off the trail, and hid behind a large boulder. My eyes remained focused on a switchback about fifty yards farther along the trail. A person appeared from around the corner, and it turned out to be Liz. She had a notebook in one hand and water bottle in the other. She wore blue jeans, a khaki shirt, and a short, black jacket. After a quick mental calculation of whether to stay hidden or not, I stepped from behind the boulder. Liz jumped, then let out a yelp.

"Damn you, you scared me," she said.

"Sorry. I didn't realize it was you coming up the trail."

She shook her head. Disgust filled her eyes. "And you're not in your workshop, walking this trail because . . . ?"

"Something I needed to check up on. And you're not in your workshop walking this trail because . . . ?"

"Susan, my workshop leader, gave us an assignment: Find a place you haven't been on campus and travel there." She held up the notebook. "Write down your thoughts, feelings, impressions along the way. What obstacles you encounter. What helps you along the way."

"Sounds like what Epstein had us do," I said.

"Oh? Why didn't you say that's why you were out here? Funny," Liz said. "That we came to the same place."

"No," I said. "He didn't have us take a walk."

Liz wrinkled her face.

"He had us do something similar, but only in our minds."

"At least the obstacle part will be easy," Liz said.

"Me?" I asked.

"Not exactly," Liz said. "More like what you represent for me." She pointed to her chest.

"And what's that?"

"You want to walk?" Liz asked.

"Up the trail?"

"Uh-huh."

I pointed up the hill. "There's a bench along the ridge where we can sit."

"Let's go," Liz said.

We walked in silence back up the trail. Maybe the ease of Liz's footsteps, or the fact that she simply walked without talking, helped. Inside my chest a knot of tension unraveled. I let myself exhale. We made our way to the hand-carved wooden bench that overlooked the campus and the lake. The small seat brought us shoulder to shoulder. I wanted to reach my arm around Liz, but I kept it to myself.

"You remember when we sat in that depression behind a sand dune at your parents' place in Martha's Vineyard?" I asked.

Liz sighed. "And watched the sun rise?"

"Uh-huh. Times were good then."

Liz didn't answer for a moment. "Do you remember what I was doing then?" she asked.

"You'd just finished your residency and we were talking about starting a family."

"Do you remember why I'd chosen gynecology?"

"Because your father had been chairman of the Obstetrics and Gynecology Department at the hospital, and . . . that's the problem isn't it?"

"That's the problem," Liz said. "Daddy wanted me to be a doctor. Daddy wanted me to be an obstetrician and gynecologist like he was. Daddy wanted a son. Daddy wanted to keep his name alive. But he had a girl, and she would have to do."

"Daddy didn't want you to marry me."

"No, he didn't."

"Is that why you married me? 'Cause Daddy didn't want you to?"

"I married you because I loved you," Liz said. A subtle, sly smile then crept onto her lips. "But the fact that Daddy didn't want me to marry you made it all the more sweet."

"So is this separation and divorce about Daddy or about me?"

"Neither," Liz said. "It's about me. Susan, the woman leading my workshop, saw us together after dinner last night. She asked me to do an 'empty chair' session in front of the group."

"'Empty chair?'"

"You face an empty chair and talk to it as though someone you need to speak with is sitting in front of you. At first, I put you in that chair and I had a lot of anger. I felt oppressed by your presence here. Trapped. As though I couldn't escape from you. Angry because you left JJ to be here, when I left him to be with you—"

"But—"

Liz put her hand across my mouth. "Let me finish. Then Susan asked me to close my eyes and recall the first time I'd experienced similar feelings. I'd barely shut them when I felt propelled backward in time to age six. I wanted to have a sleepover at a friend's house. She just lived down the block in Striver's Row, and my parents let me walk there all the time. But at eight o'clock that night, my dad rang the doorbell to check on me. He could have called, but he insisted on making his presence known. 'Don't forget to brush my teeth and wash before going to bed. Don't stay up too late.' Don't do all the things you do when you have a sleepover away from your parents. Same thing throughout high school and even college. You know, the girls in my dorm at Sarah Lawrence set up something we called 'daddy radar' to warn me when he entered the campus, especially if I had a boyfriend in my room. He felt free to drive up to the school whenever he wanted.

"So, Susan asked me to put my daddy in the empty chair and talk to him. I did. I told him I loved him, but I also felt oppressed and controlled by him. I told him he'd never given me the chance to find out who I was as a person because he'd always insisted that he knew what I should do. I told him Mother and I were different. I needed to find out what mattered most to me, what moved me most in my life, even if that meant leaving all the things that he'd helped me accomplish. I needed to accomplish things I could look upon and say, 'I choose to do that because it's meaningful for me.'" A tear rolled down Liz's cheek.

"It sounds like what you've been saying to me for the last several months," I said.

"It is," Liz said, "but even more importantly, the more I spoke to that empty chair, the more I realized it wasn't you or Daddy I was facing there—it was me."

Liz wiped tears from her eyes, and I fought the urge to reach out and comfort her, but after the journey I'd taken in Epstein's class, I knew that Liz needed to do work this out on her own. Liz stared out at the lake, though I had the impression her gaze went far beyond it.

"I sat there," Liz said, "as clearly as you're sitting next to me, and I saw myself as a small child sitting in front of me in that chair. And I spoke to young Elizabeth. I told her that it wasn't her fault, that her daddy did his best, but that now she needed to take control over her life. She needed to discover what she needed to do, not what people around her—even those she loved—wanted her to do."

Liz laughed. "I put you back on the stand next," she said.

"Trouble?"

"No. Susan asked me what I needed to say to you. I needed to apologize."

"For what?"

"You didn't come here to spy on me, to trap me, and as much as I know you love JJ, you wouldn't have left him alone without a good reason."

"Thanks," I said. "That's true."

Liz turned the face me. "You're really here working, aren't you?"

"I am."

"Anything I should know about?"

"Better if you didn't."

"Anything I should worry about?"

"I'll let you know."

"Some of the people in the workshop spoke about Sheikh Bashir being on campus."

"What did they say?"

"Some questioned the wisdom of bringing an Islamic spiritual teacher here given the climate of discrimination against Muslims in this country today. Others said because of that climate, the sheikh needed to deliver his message here at Sigma, that of all the branches of Islam, Sufism was the most enlightened, the most spiritual in a nonreligious sense. Pretty easy to put two and two together. You being here suddenly at the same time as the sheikh."

"Did you tell anyone about me?"

"People know about our separation and pending divorce," Liz said, "but I didn't tell them why I thought you were here."

"Probably good if you didn't."

"I won't," she said. Liz touched my arm, sending a tingle through my body. "I don't know how much time I need," she said. "I don't know how long it will take me to feel comfortable with me." She tapped her chest. "But it wouldn't be right to ask you to 'hang on' while I go about doing now what I should have been doing in my twenties."

A lump welled in my chest. "You know I still love you."

Liz began to cry. "I never doubted that for a minute," she said. She patted herself again. "It's about me, John. It's not about you."

I patted her leg. "I need to get back down the hill." I stood up and started to walk when Liz called out.

"John."

I turned around.

"Whatever's going on up here, I'm glad you're here to help out. It makes me feel safer. But please be careful."

"I will," I said, and turned once more to leave.

# TWENTY-FOUR

SHORTLY BEFORE DINNER, I caught Hamid walking from the sheikh's cottage. He wore a flowing white robe with gold embroidery, a white skullcap, and black sandals with gold socks.

Hamid bristled. "The Sheikh loves to sit in front of the window in the lecture hall," he said. "He likes pictures of him with that backdrop, especially at night when the lights from below illuminate the trees and the plants outside."

"It also illuminates the sheikh for a would-be assassin waiting in the woods outside."

Hamid scowled. "I told you before, the sheikh's protection is our sacred duty."

"How many men do you have for his protection detail?"

Hamid shook his head. "Privileged information."

"Will you post guards in the woods behind the lecture hall?"

"Privileged information."

"Can we at least coordinate our efforts?"

Hamid grinned. "How many undercover agents does OMS have on campus?"

I said nothing.

"You see," Hamid said, "this is what you Americans call working together. We tell you everything and you tell us nothing. Can we work together? No."

Hamid turned, sending his robes fluttering about him, and glided off toward the dining hall.

I called Tucker about sending additional manpower to protect the sheikh. He bristled too.

* * *

Natalie, Barbara, and I had arranged to meet an hour after dinner. I stood at the top of the path leading from the main road down to the lake. I shined my flashlight in the direction of the footsteps coming down the main road. Plumes of smoke rose from Barbara's and Natalie's nostrils as they walked toward me. Barbara slapped her hands together. The muffled sound suggested she had gloves on.

"It's damn cold out here," Barbara said.

"Plenty of stars, but no clouds," I said. "No blanket over the earth."

"Do we have enough people to blanket the sheikh tomorrow night?" Natalie asked.

"No," I said. "We don't."

"Just what I thought," Natalie said.

"Did you try calling Tucker?" asked Barbara.

"Earlier," I said, "and he told me we'd have to make do with what we had, that everyone else was busy protecting the president of Afghanistan, who's in New York for a visit to the United Nations."

"Local law enforcement?" Natalie asked.

"The director of the Center's not sure he wants them on campus. Afraid they'd raise too much negative publicity about the Center."

"And the sheikh's murder would be better?" Barbara said.

"I tried to reason with him. Anyway, up here local law might be like the Dukes of Hazzard."

"Maybe like we'll be better off without them," Natalie said.

"My thoughts exactly," I said. "At least Tucker's intel was on target."

"How's that?" Barbara asked.

I told them about the tree stump above the lecture hall and the cigarette butts there one minute, gone the next.

"The sheikh's people don't seem like they'll be much help either," I said.

"Hell," Natalie said, "the sheikh's people may be the problem."

"How?" I asked.

"This morning, after Hamid led us in a round of dancing, a young man in his late twenties stood up and started railing," Barbara said. "He said that Americans had no business studying the sacred traditions of Islam, the sheikh should be forbidden from teaching anything about Islam or Sufism to Americans, and that the sheikh's form of Sufism came dangerously close to blasphemy."

"What did Hamid do?"

"That's just it. Hamid seemed to know him," Natalie said. "He called him by his first name, Raheem, then he said something in Arabic to him, which seemed to calm him down."

"But it shook up the others in the workshop," Barbara said, "and Hamid spent the remainder of the morning trying to assure us the sheikh had no ill will toward Americans."

"Funny," I said. "It doesn't sound like the Hamid I know."

"Well, the whole thing didn't sit right with me," Natalie said.

"And Hamid's supposed to be protecting the sheikh," I said.

"Like I said, maybe Hamid's the one we need to be protecting the sheikh from," Natalie said.

"Do we have a plan for the sheikh's talk?" Barbara asked.

"Both of you will be inside the hall, wired and armed," I said. "I'll be up in the hills behind the hall, keeping an eye out for whoever left the cigarette butts by the tree trunk."

"Have you seen the lecture hall?" Barbara asked, her voice rising. "There's nothing but an open window behind the lectern."

"And the vegetation on the other side of the window is illuminated at night," I said.

"Maybe we should offer to paint a bull's-eye on the sheikh's back," Natalie said.

"You can't possibly cover all the places a shooter could find with a clear line of sight through that window on your own," Barbara said.

"We'll just have to do our best," I said. "I'll be in radio contact. If I need you, I'll holler."

* * *

I showed up late for Phillip Epstein's workshop the following morning. Everyone sat in a circle, talking. Heads turned toward me as I walked in.

"Come, join us, Mr. Shannon," Epstein said. "We're having a discussion about any challenges we're encountering in the workshop."

I tried to smile, though I cringed inside. I squeezed between two women, who gave me crossed-eyed looks as I sat down.

"Continue," Epstein said, motioning toward one of the few men in the workshop, a tall, thin man who, with his wire-rimmed glasses, reminded me of John Lennon.

"I'm through," the man said.

"Anyone else need to say something before we begin today's session?" Epstein asked.

A woman my age, dressed in a bright floral skirt and dark brown top, raised her hand. She had a dark olive complexion and dark-brown eyes. She wore her jet-black hair down around her shoulders. She also had a pleasant smile. Epstein acknowledged her with a nod. She sat up straight. Her smile vanished and was replaced by a sneer. "I have a problem," she said, "with that man over there." She pointed to me.

All eyes turned my way. A smile rose on Epstein's lips. He motioned the woman on. "Alice," Epstein said, "tell Mr. Shannon the nature of the problem you have with him."

I looked at Alice and she at me. Her face reddened slightly before she spoke. "I . . . I'm . . . well, I guess it's anger," she said. "Yes, I'm angry with you. We've developed something of a community, a family here. And you come and go, flit in and out of this workshop. Yesterday you were gone most of the day."

"And Mr. Shannon's absence, Alice, makes you angry because?"

Alice drew in a deep breath and turned to Epstein. "Well, because I looked forward to him—"

"Speak directly to him," Epstein said. "Directly to Mr. Shannon, not to me."

Alice turned to me. "Because I looked forward to your participation in this workshop."

"Hmmm," Epstein said. He stroked his chin. "Alice, I get this sense that you're not saying all that's there, so perhaps you'd like to close your eyes, take a deep breath, and get in touch with whatever's behind that emotion of anger."

Alice closed her eyes and breathed deeply. I stared at her, still dumbfounded at suddenly being placed on the spot. Maybe this is how that chair felt when Liz spoke to it. When Alice opened her eyes she had tears welling on the inside corner. One tear fell down over her left cheek. Her face had flushed considerably more.

"It's . . . it's . . . I'm having a hard time with it," she said. She huffed. "It's just that it's not often that black men come to workshops like this. I found your opening remarks exciting and intriguing. Most of the men I know haven't the slightest interest in self-discovery. Only now I wonder if you'd simply lied about all that, because you haven't shown up for most of our sessions."

Epstein nodded and smiled. "Good, Alice. Good. You got to tell him how you feel. What's going on now?"

A slight smile returned to Alice's face. "I'm feeling relieved," she said, "as if a burden's been lifted from my chest."

Epstein turned to me with a 'gotcha' grin. "Now, Mr. Shannon, what's that like for you to hear Alice speak about her feelings?"

I contemplated the silver flecks in the otherwise powder-blue carpet, and remained silent at first. Alice may have felt relieved, but the medicine ball had just been tossed at me.

"I didn't lie about my interest in what's going on this workshop," I said.

"Look at Alice when you speak," Epstein said.

A twinge of anger swelled in my chest, but I turned my gaze from the carpet to Alice's face. The eager look in her wide eyes reminded me of a tennis player waiting with tense anticipation for a serve.

"But I have many things on my mind and I needed to be alone to ponder them."

"If you wanted solitude, then why come to a workshop where sharing one's insights and observations is important?" Alice asked.

"I didn't know what to expect," I said. "I take it you've been to workshops like this before?"

Alice nodded her head slowly. "Many."

"It's my first."

"Then you'd better get used to this." She pointed back and forth between us.

"Used to what?"

"Interaction. Engagement. Being held accountable. What'd you think? Self-discovery's just about contemplating your navel?"

"I didn't know what to think," I said, "but I'm glad to know we're not here just to be self-absorbed."

"We're also not here to withdraw from the group," Alice said, "especially on a day like yesterday, when we told each other about the inner journeys we took. That brought all of us closer together."

"I'm glad," I said.

Alice shook her head. "It's more than that. After you share something intimate like that journey with the group, you begin to bond with each other, to feel close. Those who don't share lose out on that bonding. When you left I felt rejected because you didn't want to participate in sharing your journey."

"I had to take care of something important," I said.

"What could be more important than what we were doing in this workshop at the time?" Alice asked.

"I wish I could tell you, but I don't feel comfortable saying anything further."

Alice's voice rose. "And I don't feel comfortable with secrets. It's what's the matter with our society now."

"I want to keep you on track here, Alice," Epstein broke in. "Instead of veering into a discussion about society, stay focused on your feelings about Mr. Shannon's participation in the workshop."

"Well, when he returned to the group this morning—late, I might add—I felt . . . I'm not sure . . . I felt . . . well, I felt intruded upon, watched. Yes, that's it. Like he was a spy simply here to observe us."

My body cringed slightly. I thought about exchanging places with one of the silver specks in the carpet.

"Is there something that Mr. Shannon might do to help you feel more comfortable with his presence here?" Epstein asked.

Alice had curled her bottom lip underneath her top lip. She stared off in space, then returned, nodding. "Yes," she said. "It'd make me a lot more comfortable with Mr. Shannon if he'd share his journey with us."

Epstein turned to me. "Mr. Shannon?"

My leg twitched. "I'm not ready to share that journey," I said.

Epstein's eyes twinkled. "Do I also detect something more there?" he asked.

"More where?"

"Besides not being ready," Epstein said. "Your voice rose. It sounded tight. Your facial muscles tensed. Makes me think that besides not being ready, you might also feel some anger or resentment at even being asked."

This all reminded me of a New Age version of the "Dirty Dozens." That's game we'd play as street kids where everyone would "sound off" on everyone else's mother. "Yo' momma's so ugly, when she tried to work the streets the johns paid her to stay home. Well, yo' momma's so ugly, when she sticks her face out the window, she gets arrested for indecent exposure." And the point wasn't the best "Yo' Momma" joke, but to remain unflapped when someone else came up with a great one about your mother. You lost when you got angry, and usually a fight happened after that.

In prison, the stakes rose even higher. Get angry and someone might lose his or her life. I thought about turning to Epstein and saying, "Yo' momma's so ugly, the doctors put tinted glass on her incubator." But I chuckled to myself instead and said, "I'm sorry, but what happened to me during that inner journey is something I choose to keep to myself for the time being."

"Bravo. Bravo," I heard someone shout, and turned to see Daria—the women who'd warned me away from the tofu—clapping. "I'm perfectly fine with Mr. Shannon sharing what he wants to, when he wants to, and if he needs to be gone from this workshop, I'm fine with that too."

"Well, I'm not," Alice said.

Epstein, sensing the impending conflict, turned away from me and toward Daria.

"And what's that like for you now, Daria, to feel Alice standing up against you?"

Epstein never did get back to asking me what it felt like. In truth, Daria's intervention reminded me of the time Tommy Mervin, the best "dozens" player on my block, came to my rescue when an older kid name Jared began hitting pretty hard on my mother. I remember Jared saying to me, "Yo' momma's so dumb, she thought a quarterback was a refund," to which Tommy stepped in and said, "Jared, yo' momma's so dumb she got hit by a parked car." We all laughed our heads off, and that stopped the show.

I didn't bother getting back into the arena with Daria, Alice, and Epstein. And they apparently didn't miss me. They seemed content playing the "New Age Dozens" by themselves.

# TWENTY-FIVE

The Sheikh's workshop had an evening session, which meant I didn't get to see Natalie and Barbara until well after ten. I sat at a table in the Sigma Cafe nursing a cup of latte—made with real milk and real coffee. Barbara and Natalie came over to me.

"Is anyone sitting here?" Barbara asked, pointing at a chair.

I picked up my coffee cup. "No," I said. "I was actually through."

"Please, you don't have to leave because of us," Natalie said.

"It's a nice night," I said. "I'm going back to my cabin, changing into some warmer clothes, and walking down to the beach by the lake."

I stood up. Natalie and Barbara pulled back chairs.

Twenty minutes later, dressed in a polar fleece jacket with a hooded sweatshirt on underneath, I strolled down toward the lake. Shafts of light from flashlights danced in the darkness. I passed a number of people, mostly couples, as I walked without the benefit of a flashlight. Several shined their lights in my face, and what I heard came as a surprise.

"Good evening."

"It's a crisp but cold night, hope you enjoy it."

"Do you need to borrow my flashlight?"

You see, dressed like this on the streets of the city, I'd probably get stopped by men and women shining flashlights in my face, but they'd be dressed in blue and they wouldn't be wishing me a good evening.

In the dim starlight, I saw a hammock slung between two trees and headed in that direction. I swung up and into the knotted mesh, folded my hands behind my head, and peered at the stars shimmering above me. Living in the city you sometimes forget that there is anything but the tops of skyscrapers and smog overhead. In the background, I heard soft whispering, then a female voice say, "Bill, not here. It's too cold. Let's go back to my room." Now that brought a smile to my face, knowing that people who came to places like this were as motivated by the discovery of others as they were by the discovery of self.

The next female voice seemed to come from the walkway I'd taken to get down to the lake. It was louder than the voices around me. "It's my first time in a class like this."

Unmistakably, that voice belonged to Natalie Chen.

I tipped the hammock to one side and spilled out. I slowly moved in the direction of Natalie's voice, and when I heard her say, "Like, there are so many stars in the sky up here."

I replied by saying, "There are the same number of stars in the sky everywhere, only we can't see them."

Barbara whispered, "John, is that you?"

"Yes," I said.

"Should we talk here?" Natalie asked.

"No," I said. "Let's walk along the road that cuts through the campus. It leads to a state road away from here."

Flashlights, like fireflies, twinkled as we walked along the campus road. Then, one quarter of a mile away from the center of the campus, the flashlights stopped.

"Like, people pay for stuff like this?" Natalie asked.

"Frankly, I kind of enjoyed what Hamid had to say," Barbara said.

"Look within. Find yourself within. Find God within. Oh, pl . . . leez," Natalie said.

"Your assessment of the workshop participants?" I asked.

Natalie laughed. "Like, we saw you with a participant from another workshop after dinner yesterday. You two didn't seem to be having such a friendly conversation, or did your workshop leader have you practicing expressing your anger to strangers?"

"She wasn't a stranger," I said.

Barbara sucked in a breath. "Oh. Then who was she?"

"My soon-to-be ex-wife."

"Ex-wife?" Both women chimed together.

"Personal involvement in a case?" Barbara said. "Why'd Tucker assign you to this one?"

"I was already working it," I said. "I had no clue it would lead here and that Liz would be here at the same time."

"And you're okay with it?" Barbara asked.

"I am," I said. "Let's get back to your assessments."

"If were talking stereotypes," Natalie said, "then none of the participants looks the role of a hired gun. Certainly not one from the Middle East."

"There's 150 people in the workshop," Barbara said. "Mostly white. Mostly women. Lawyers. Doctors. Stockbrokers. At least that's what they said in the introductions. The few men that are in the workshop look like they'd be more comfortable squeezing teddy bears than triggers."

"Maybe we're dealing with an informant inside the sheikh's workshop, or entourage, planted to provide information on when he'd be most vulnerable," I said.

"Or someone within his organization," Natalie said.

"Hamid?" I asked.

"Or that fellow named Ali," Barbara added.

"Or the half dozen women I've seen go into and come out of the sheikh's cabin at various times," I said.

"Must be his bodyguards," Barbara said, her sarcasm cutting through the crisp night air.

"Must be," I said.

"Thought these guys were supposed to be celibate," Natalie said.

"Sufis aren't like fundamentalist sects of Islam," I said. "Apparently there's a lot of room for interpretation of religious doctrine."

Barbara started to laugh, then stifled it. "Oh, that explains it. He needed a lot of interpreters," she said.

"His bodyguards needed to understand what they had to do." I added.

We all subdued our laughs.

"Day after tomorrow is Sunday," Natalie said. "The sheikh addresses everyone here at the Sigma Center in an evening lecture."

"Good time for a hit," I said.

"That's when I'd move," Natalie said.

"And we've heard that people travel from as far as New York City and Boston just to hear the sheikh's lecture," Barbara said. "Apparently, it's a treat for him to give an open lecture like this."

"How many people do you guess are on campus?" I asked.

"Three to four hundred," Barbara said.

"That'd be my guess too," I said.

"The hall we're in could easily hold five hundred seated," Natalie said, "and that's where the sheikh's lecture will be held."

"The hall backs up against the hills that surround the campus," I said.

"Have you swept the hills for signs of an observation post?" Barbara asked.

"It's on my list for tomorrow," I said.

"But you'll be in your workshop all day," Natalie said.

"On a sacred journey to find my self," I said.

"You haven't told us what your workshop's like," Barbara said.

"Nothing to tell. All we did was spend three hours introducing ourselves."

"Must be a fun place to be a guy," Barbara said.

"How's that?" I asked.

"I figure the ratio of women to men is about four to one. From the talk I've overheard, most women consider this a pretty good place to find men. You know, any man that'd come here on his own is the kind of man a lot of these women would like to find, and they're not just looking in their workshops. You're already on the radar screens of the women here." She chuckled softly.

"I am?"

"After dinner, a couple of women asked me if you and I were a couple. You know, right now you're the only African American man on campus, and outside of your ex, I'm one of the few black women."

"Guess diversity hasn't struck the self-discovery movement," I said.

"From the way the women talk, more than a few would be up for affirmative action," Barbara said.

We exchanged a round of soft laughter.

"We'll meet here on the road tomorrow night after your workshop is over," I said.

"Tomorrow the sheikh is supposed to address our workshop for about thirty minutes," Natalie said. "We'll keep monitoring the workshop participants and the people close to the sheikh."

\* \* \*

The next morning Phillip Epstein started his workshop with another round of eyes-closed deep breathing. Sitting cross-legged on the floor, I gave in this time, and kept my eyes closed. Then, when I'd expected him to tell us to open our eyes, he invited us to keep them closed.

"Imagine yourself at one end of a very long plain," he said. "At the other end is a tall mountain. Take a moment to be aware of some issue in your life that needs your attention. When you discover that issue, take the time to also discover how you would like that issue to be resolved. Now symbolize the resolution in some way. It doesn't have to be fancy—a circle, a shining star, a flower—whatever symbol stands for resolution to you. Then place that symbol on top of the mountain."

I'm glad Epstein paused. It gave me time to catch up to him. Funny, the first thing that came to mind was Promise. I smiled to myself. I bet this is something that he'd love to do. Then I brought myself back to Epstein's task. The issue popped immediately into my head: preventing an attack on Sheikh Bashir. The symbol came quickly as well, and I placed a shield—like the ones knights carried into battle—on top of the mythical mountain.

Epstein picked up where he left off.

"Now, remaining with your eyes closed, imagine a path that leads from where you are to that distant mountain where your symbol lies. Take that path. Be aware of what or whom you meet along the way—obstacles that suddenly appear; people that emerge to help or hinder you on your way. Take however long you need to reach the base of that mountain."

As I began the journey in my mind, the first thing I noticed was that the plain had turned into a forest, and like the shooting galleries I practiced in to hone my reflexes and skills, it seemed as though figures appeared then disappeared randomly from behind the trees. My body tensed, and the thought that crossed my mind was to check the hills surrounding the Sigma campus. But suddenly a large boulder cropped up in the middle of the path, and as I walked toward it, trying to figure out how I'd get around it, Liz popped from behind the boulder, screaming at me, "What are you doing here? What are you doing here?" I reared back.

I started to mouth a response when Liz just as suddenly disappeared and JJ appeared from the other side of the boulder. "You don't have to find out who killed al-Salaam," he said. "I don't want you to get hurt."

I reached out toward JJ, but he disappeared as well.

The only way to get around the boulder was stepping off of the path and making my way through the forest. I didn't see any paths there, just dark patches between the boughs of green trees. I headed into the forest, thinking I'd simply scamper around the boulder, then resume walking on the path. But when I walked back to where the path should have resumed on the other side of the boulder, neither the boulder nor the path was there. A strange smell permeated the air around me. It took me a moment to place, but when I did, the smell grew stronger and unmistakable: the pungent chlorine-filled odor of the chemicals used to wash down the floors of the prison cellblock I was on for two years.

I stumbled amidst the trees now, unsure of which direction to take. I just kept walking. Suddenly, the image of a hard-assed prison guard named McNamara popped up from behind a tree. He was wielding a baton, and swung at me. I ducked. He twirled handcuffs above his head like a cowboy spinning a lasso. I dove at his legs, which turned into a shimmering vapor, and I sprawled headlong onto the ground. I looked around, but couldn't see my tormentor.

And then I heard something moving through the brush behind me. It sounded like an animal. The rustling stopped. I scanned, but I couldn't see anything. I heard a few twigs break and turned in that direction. Nothing. Then the movement started again, circling around me now. I felt like prey. I took off in a direction opposite of where I thought the sound came from, still not knowing where I was going. The sound of running footsteps grew louder behind me. The mountain with the shield seemed a distant memory. Survival. Escape. Those seemed real inside this world I'd descended into. And even though I knew I could open my eyes if wanted to, or at least I believed I could, a powerful force kept my eyes closed, wedded me to this adventure playing out in my mind. I kept running, high-stepping over fallen tree limbs, while behind me a still invisible presence kept coming toward me.

I couldn't stop running—didn't dare to stop running. Afraid that if I did, I would be consumed by the monstrous presence behind me. Then, to my surprise, fifty yards ahead of me a mighty river roared, its current like the sound of a freight train, sunlight glinting off the bubbling waters. Behind me, the sound of my pursuer grew ever louder. I pulled up at the side of the river and looked behind me. Still, I couldn't see anything, but I heard the brush breaking, felt the pursuit like a wave of humid air growing hotter, heavier.

I ran along the river's edge and my pursuer seemed to follow me from the brush along the bank above, always just out of sight, yet always present in the sound of breaking branches and plodding, unrelenting footsteps. Up ahead came a bend in the river, which I approached only to find a large rock outcrop projecting from my side of the shore into the water. I couldn't pass it, and it seemed I had only two choices: take my chances with whatever force or freak of nature followed me, or plunge into the turbulent water. I didn't have time to think. I ran up to the rock wall, looked behind me again, then pushed off the rocks into the raging river.

# TWENTY-SIX

It must have been three-thirty that afternoon when I first noticed the cloud of blue exhaust fumes hovering over the line of cars clogging the main thoroughfare. From the buzz of the conversation swirling around, it didn't take being enlightened to figure out that most people had driven here for Sheikh Tariq Bashir's talk at seven thirty tonight. It also didn't take enlightenment or Epstein's prodding to realize we were undermanned and undergunned—well, considering the surroundings, make that underpersoned and undergunned.

Women made up most of the newcomers, and most looked harmless. Lots of flowing white cotton skirts. Matted dreadlocks here and there. I have nothing against dreadlocks, mind you, but on white folks with fair skin and straight hair they just don't work for me. I spotted a guy in a business suit stepping out from a brand new BMW, looking around as though he wanted to find the valet. I tracked him as he walked toward the Sigma Cafe, and made sure our paths intersected. I held the door open for him as he stepped through. We stood at the end of a long line.

"No flowing white cotton," I said.

The man turned around and laughed. He ran his hand from a bald spot on the back of his head down an invisible line along his back. "I cut off my ponytail and traded in my white cotton clothes for a suit, tie, and a briefcase long ago. Arthur Williamson," he said. He stuck out his hand. Arthur had smooth skin and a baby-faced look that lied about his age.

"John Shannon," I said, shaking his hand.

"You up here for the sheikh's talk?" Arthur asked.

"Actually, I'm here taking a workshop."

"Really?"

"Really."

Arthur checked his watch. "Workshop's over?"

"No," I said. "I'm taking a self-discovery break."

He swayed his head back and forth. "This workshop, that workshop, different name, same material . . . after a while they all seem to blend together." He laughed to himself. "I've thought about writing *The Dummy's Guide to Leading a Workshop*. You know? Have people close their eyes, discover what's inside, then talk about it among themselves. Not much for the workshop leader to do other than throw in a few, 'How do you feel about this? What's that like for you? What do you need most right now?'"

I started laughing too. "Have you been spying on my workshop?" I asked.

"No," Arthur said. "Been to so many myself I could lead one blindfolded."

"So whaddya do?" I asked.

"Lead workshops," Arthur said, deadpan.

"But I—"

He pushed up his wire-frame glasses, then elbowed me. "Just kiddin'. I'm an investment banker."

"Up here?"

"Hey, one of my largest clients invited me."

"The Sigma Center?"

He shook his head. "No. Although I've tried for years to get their business. I've been investing the sheikh's money since he arrived in this country back in the early '70s." Arthur looked at me. "Care to eat with me, Mr. Shannon?"

I checked my watch. I wanted to talk to Barbara and Natalie before the sheikh's program. "Maybe some herb tea," I said. I winced when I heard the words come out of my mouth. They sounded so. . . well . . . so appropriate for the Sigma Cafe.

Arthur got a tofu plate with vegetables and rice. I thought about warning him off the stuff, but he seemed like a man who knew his way around the New Age. I changed my mind and went with a cup of coffee.

The cafe hummed with conversation. With no seats open at any of the tables, we stepped outside to a patio with hand-carved wooden tables and chairs. The late afternoon air danced crisply around us, laced with a piquant, sweet smell from the wood. Arthur began carving up the rectangular, spongy cake of tofu in strips the way some people carve up a steak. He must have caught me staring. He stabbed a piece, plunged it into his mouth, and smiled.

"Take it you don't care for tofu?" he said.

"Not much."

"It's an acquired taste," he said.

"Didn't taste like much of anything when I tried it," I said. "Sheikh's investment banker. Well-heeled place like the Sigma Center. This New Age, spiritual, self-exploration stuff's big money, huh?"

Arthur held up his hand, finished chewing another bite of tofu, then dabbed his lips with a napkin. "Depends," he said. "Sigma got into the game early. In fact, the sheikh got them into it."

"How's that?"

"The sheikh came to this country right at the tail end of the Peace and Love generation. Here was a man educated at Eaton and Cambridge. His father was not only a revered Sufi leader in the Middle East, he was also the head of a major Middle Eastern equipment firm. He—"

"So money and spirituality ran together in the family's blood?"

Arthur chuckled. "I guess you could say that. Anyway, his father wanted the sheikh to come to the West to spread Sufism to a new generation of young people."

"He figured hippies would have an easier time of digesting Sufism than anyone else."

"Yes. You'll remember in those days, there was a sense of openness and welcoming for Eastern spiritual ideas."

"Just a little before my time," I said. "I was playing the 'Dozens' with kids on my block in the Bronx."

Arthur scrunched his face. "The Dozens?"

"You know, 'Yo' momma's so stupid she called a store and asked when Mr. Clean was available to clean her house.'"

Arthur had a blank stare. "Oh," he said.

He took a few more bites of tofu, and I sipped my coffee.

"So the sheikh met up with the folks that ran the Sigma Center?" I asked.

Arthur laughed. "No. The sheikh was dropped into New York City and immediately a group of kids who smoked dope and dropped acid gathered around him. They nodded to the 'groovy' things the small, brown man from the Middle East had to say." Arthur shook his head. "He could speak better English than most of us. Had better manners than all of us. And, still, he tolerated us blowing smoke in his face while he spoke at length about spirituality."

"So I take it you were among them?"

"I was," Arthur said.

"Eventually, the sheikh moved out of New York City to a place upstate not far from here."

I raised my coffee cup to my lips. "I thought he lived in Brooklyn?"

"Oh, he still has that place, but he also has an estate about thirty miles from here. It was supposed to become a retreat center. And it did for several years. We called it the Habitat. But then the '80s happened and hippies became yuppies."

"Let me guess. You saw the growing appetite for spirituality as a way to make big bucks."

Arthur scowled. "Some of us did. Personally, I would have rather continued with the Habitat and had my job on Wall Street, but a group of people broke off from the Habitat and founded the Sigma Center. And, well, look around you. They've been successful."

"And the Habitat?"

"Still the sheikh's estate, but that's all. He uses it to get away from the city. For special events. To entertain occasionally. He's a jazz aficionado. He's got an extensive collection of vinyl there, along with a sophisticated sound and recording studio. He mixed his own CDs from vinyl. Sometimes he'd seclude himself in his music library for hours with earphones on, looking out the window over the lake."

"Did you know Yousef al-Salaam?" I asked.

Arthur's head bobbed. "Funny you should ask that. The sheikh hosted Yousef at the Habitat for almost two weeks shortly before he was murdered. Yousef fell in love with the sound system and the recording studio. He made a few demo recordings with the Sheikh playing the oud in the background."

"And an educated man like the sheikh didn't look down his nose at Yousef's rapping?"

"Some around the sheikh did, but what would you rather have, young people blowing grass in your face, or young people rapping?"

"Got a point there."

"The sheikh wanted to influence Yousef so that he'd include a more uplifting, spiritual message in his music."

"Based on his last album, apparently he did."

Arthur lowered his head. "It's sad what happened to Yousef. When I ask myself what would I rather have, kids blowing grass in my face or kids blowing a semiautomatic; the answer's easy."

"You got a point there too," I said. I patted the table. "Nice talking with you."

"I'll see you at the sheikh's talk tonight," Arthur said.

I smiled. "That's one of the main reasons I'm here."

* * *

An early dinner line had already formed by the time I got to the dining hall. I looked for Barbara and Natalie, but I didn't see them. I'd just stepped across the threshold of the dining hall, when two short gongs went off. The large clock high up on a wall said five thirty, and when I turned back to look across campus, a mass a people swarmed out of buildings, heading toward the dining hall.

I sighed. A steaming tray of tofu sat under the first set of heat lamps I came to. Then I smiled. Under the second set, I spied a tray of baked turkey. I also noticed how readily people ahead of me went for the turkey, which made me laugh. I put an extra helping of turkey on my plate, then dropped a mound of mashed potatoes and a pile of green beans beside it. I retired to a seat with a good view of the door and a dinner that at least looked familiar.

I first recognized Daria and Alice walking through the dining hall door, arm-in-arm, laughing, talking. I guess Epstein's New Age 'Dozens' therapy group could boast a success. Then I saw Liz come into the hall and I swallowed hard, forcing a piece of turkey down that I hadn't chewed well. She walked in with a young, hippie-looking guy. Both were talking and laughing. Before they picked up their trays and empty plates, they stopped and gave each other a big hug. She kissed him on the cheek.

Damn. Epstein's voice crept into my head. "What's that like to see Liz and that guy hugging?"

Forget about playing the New Age "Dirty Dozens" with Hippie Guy. I stabbed a few green beans, shoved them into my mouth, and chewed hard. Promise's voice, soft and steady, also drifted through my thoughts.

"John, good or bad, it's hard to let go. It's easier to hold on to hurt and suffering than to cast them off, just as it's easier to hold on to happiness and joy than to give them up. Easier to wrap yourself in anger and pain than to step away from them. Joy and sorrow. Pleasure and pain. They're prison bars. Even if some are made of gold and the others of cruder metal, both still bind. The only truly free man is the one who walks a middle path between pleasure and pain, between joy and suffering. He who experiences both but is unaffected by either. You carry your prison with you, and only you can set yourself free."

I shook my head and laughed to myself. A seventy-year old inmate who'd not seen the outside of prison since he was a teenager made more sense than a lot of the counselors and campers I'd encountered here at Camp Granola.

"Something funny?"

The voice startled me, and I looked up. Barbara stood above me holding a tray. Natalie wasn't with her.

"Is this seat taken?" Barbara asked.

"No, please be my guest," I said.

I scooted over and Barbara sat down. She looked right at home in blue jeans and a sweatshirt, though I noticed she wore earrings, and I detected the subtle fruity scent of her perfume. She'd gone for the tofu instead of the turkey.

"First time here?" Barbara asked.

"It is, and you?"

"Mine too," she said. "Hi, my name is Barbara. Barbara Cummins."

"John Shannon," I said.

Barbara carved up the tofu into small squares and popped a few in her mouth.

I pointed to the plate. "They say that stuff's an acquired taste."

Barbara laid her fork down, then made a brief sweeping gesture around the room with her hand. "I'd say all of this is an acquired taste." She turned to me and winked. "But I could get used to having someone cook for me while I spend most of the day dancing and talking, and meditating on the meaning of life."

"I'd miss reality," I said.

"Funny," Barbara said. "Today, our workshop was all about how reality is part perception and part projection. Either way," she tapped the side of her head, "it's all up here."

"Tell that to some guy ready to use a gun."

"Excuse me," a woman across the table spoke up, "but I couldn't help overhearing your conversation. Even with the man and his gun, it'd all still be in his mind—I mean the reasons for using it in the first place. And even if you wanted to get to him and prevent him from using that gun, that's your reality, and it'd be in your mind."

Barbara and I exchanged quick bemused glances. "Thanks," I said to the woman across from us. "Guess I never thought of it that way."

"Are you going to hear the sheikh's lecture tonight?" Barbara asked me.

"I am," I said.

"Would you like to walk after dinner, and then wander over to the talk together?"

"I would."

# TWENTY-SEVEN

Natalie didn't join us for our after-dinner walk. Out the corner of my eye I noticed Liz watching Barbara and me as we walked across the dining room floor and out the door. With all the people now on campus for the sheikh's talk, the main road looked more like Times Square at lunch hour. Barbara and I didn't have much to say to each other. We checked in briefly once more. I'd patrol the woods behind the lecture hall while she and Natalie took up opposite stations inside.

At the edge of the Sigma campus, we turned back. Barbara went off toward her dorm and I toward my cabin to pick up some gear. I pulled on a warm jacket, slipped my Browning 9 mm into one pocket, and my radio into the other. When I stepped back outside, dusk had descended, washing out the view and turning blossoming spring colors into bland shades of brown and gray. I started up the trail behind the hall, smacking my hands together to get some blood flowing against the chill. I winced. I couldn't have better announced my presence than that.

I had no night-vision binoculars, but with no clouds over-head, when darkness finally came it meant that at least the stars and the moon, if it came out, would provide a little light. I moved slowly in the dim light along the trail. When I reached the path along the ridge, light from the large lecture hall window helped to guide me to the tree stump where I'd seen the mound of cigarette butts. I propped my back against the stump. I had a good view of the stage where the sheikh would be speaking—and so would anyone else up here. I stuck an earbud in and bent the stem with the microphone so it barely touched the side of my face. I switched on my radio and listened. Silence. From the view into the hall, people had just begun to file in.

A high-pitched crinkling noise came over the earphone. It sounded like hair brushing against a microphone. Suddenly, a blast of Middle Eastern music twanged. I ripped out the earbud.

"John."

I could hear Natalie with the earbud several inches away. I placed my thumb over the earbud and pulled the microphone close.

"Turn the damn thing down," I whispered.

Then I slipped the earbud back into my ear.

"Sorry," Natalie said. "Like, I guess you can hear me?"

"I can."

"I'm online too," Barbara's voice said.

"I've got a clear view of the podium," I said.

"Both of us are close to the door," Barbara said, "watching hands, pockets, and faces as people come into the hall."

"Okay," I said.

The cold, damp earth pressed against me through my pants. My earbud distorted the music. Still, the tinny, wavering harmonies of the strings and the reverberated pops of the drumbeat had me half-expecting to see a line of belly dancers undulating across the stage. Ten minutes passed before the music faded and the lights dimmed with the exception of a spotlight on the stage. Hamid stepped into that cylinder of light. Natalie and Barbara must have still been at the rear of the hall. I could barely make out what Hamid said, though it sounded like an introduction.

Then, suddenly, a drumbeat cracked in my ear. The music grew louder and a line of men in flowing white robes and white fezzes whirled onto the stage. They twirled around the stage like human spinning tops unwound and let go. Sometimes each dervish moved in place, and sometimes they moved into and out of each other like a set of human gears. These dervishes reminded me of Yousef al-Salaam on his last music video. They danced for a half hour.

When Hamid came back on the stage, Barbara or Natalie must have moved closer to the front of the hall. I clearly heard Hamid say, "The dervishes are not even warmed-up yet. They can perform like this for hours at a time, but now it is time for us to welcome Sheikh Tariq Bashir."

I yanked the earbud off. The applause seemed to shake the walls of the lecture hall, and the hills as well. Hamid disappeared from view. Then, like stagehands between acts, four men pulled a raised dais with a large seat onto center stage. The seat had been draped with white, and around it several bouquets of flowers rested.

The applause dimmed. Sheikh Bashir, dressed also in white, appeared, walking slowly and regally across the stage. With studied movements, he lowered himself to the seat and folded his legs under him. His white hair and beard struck a sharp contrast with his bronze skin. I swore I could smell the fragrant plumes of smoke curling upward from small pots of incense on either side of the him.

Sheikh Bashir reached for one of the long-stemmed roses, bent it toward him, and took a long sniff. He raised his head and spoke, looking around the assembled crowd as he did, "It is such a joy to be among all you beautiful flowers, scented with the sweet perfume of your desire for the divine."

The hall erupted in applause again.

From there, the sheikh launched into words that appeared to flow from a stream of consciousness, the general subject being the soul's quest for the sacred and how he likened that quest to a moth's flight toward a lamp's flame. How so many of us had glass enclosures around our lamps, up against which our souls beat themselves again and again, desperate for the light but not realizing the impediment in between. At times the sheikh's voice reminded me of a bird in flight, swooping down toward the earth, then rising higher into the sky. I found it hard to follow his logic, especially given the poor quality of the transmission over my headset.

"Are you taking notes on this?" I asked Natalie.

"Hell," she whispered, "following this guy's logic is like trying to nail Jell-O to a wall."

"Good. At least I'm not—"

The sudden rustle above me had me pushing my back into the stump, whipping my Browning from my pocket.

"John," Natalie said.

I waited. I'd already been fooled twice up here.

"John," Barbara said. "What's happening?"

A twig broke. A man sighed.

"I've got company," I whispered. "Talk to you after I find out who it is."

I pulled the earbud out and groped along the cold ground beneath me until my fingers found their way over a small branch. I tossed it in the direction of the manmade bench. The footsteps responded, moving in that direction. I rolled to the other side of the stump, bounced up, and scurried to the ridge. I couldn't see anything before me, but I could sense the presence of a person near me. I found a rock this time and chucked it in the same direction I'd thrown the branch, hoping for more footsteps or even a flash of gunfire—something I could use to locate whoever was up here with me. Nothing moved.

I angled my head from side to side, trying to pickup an outline of a human form in the starlight, or the rays of light heading uphill from the lecture hall. I didn't see anything.

Best, I thought, to lead this person away from the sheikh, or at least force him to contend with my presence. So I stooped low to the ground and headed into the brush on the other side of the ridge trail. If I looked toward the sky at the right angle, I could at least make out the shapes of several large boulders. I stopped behind one and waited to see if footsteps would head my way, but I still heard nothing. I grasped the crosshatched metal handle of my Browning tighter. Even in this cold, sweat pushed from my pores.

I decided to make a long, deep arc down the hill and up around the area where I thought this other person now stood. I made a noise as I traveled, hoping that would draw his gunfire. In the dark, I picked my way downhill, crawling over fallen tree limbs, stumbling through the brush, slowly. With my shoulder turned in front of me, I slid through a stand of trees, caroming off trunks like a blind man walking through a field of tall manikins with limbs rooted deep into the earth.

Looking uphill now, light from the lecture hall painted a thin corona where the ridge met the dark, starry sky. I headed toward the edge of that light. "A moth crawling toward the flame," I thought as I moved slowly.

The incline steepened. Then, about fifty yards below the ridge trail, I came to an outcrop of rocks. I tried to find a way around them, but it occurred to me that climbing the rocks might make the least noise as I worked my way back up to the ridge.

I stuffed my gun back into my pocket and stretched my arms and fingers out, searching for handholds to pull myself up. When I found one, I dug in my fingers, propped myself on one leg, and searched for a toehold with the other, partially suspending myself off the ground. I'm not a rock-climber, and this may have been a foolish thing to attempt alone in the dark, but I'd barely had time to contemplate my poor judgment, when I heard the loud crack of a branch directly behind me. I dropped down, but too late.

A hand buried the cold, hard muzzle of a pistol into the base of my skull. A gruff voice whispered in the darkness. "You so much as twitch, and you're a dead man."

He pulled the pistol away from my skull, though the impression still remained. I heard the man take a few steps back, then suddenly, light burst from the darkness. The flame had found the moth. My eyes squinted under the powerful flashlight beam and I tried to raise my arms over my face.

"Keep your eyes open and do not move," the voice said.

I tried to see behind the light, but the man kept the flashlight in front of his face.

"Look my way," the voice said.

The man had a deep, slightly raspy voice. I had the impression that he was tall, perhaps heavy. I squinted again as I looked toward into the beam.

"Now turn around and place your hands over your head, high up on the rocks."

The moment I did, the man jumped behind me, patting down the side of my jacket, pulling my Browning out.

"Put your hands behind your back, slowly, one at a time."

I knew the pattern well.

"My name's John Shannon," I said. "I work for the Office of Municipal Security in New York City."

I heard the cuffs come out of the man's pocket. In an instant, he'd snapped them around my wrists.

"Turn around," the man ordered.

He stepped back as I turned around, then he trained the flashlight on my face once again. I rolled my right hip toward him.

"Hip pocket," I said. "Wallet has my ID."

He didn't say anything.

"Look," I said, "you seem like law enforcement. You're not a gunman or you probably wouldn't have bothered with the handcuffs. You'd have just shot me."

The man in the shadows remained silent.

"My hip pocket," I said again.

He huffed. "Turn around. Put your hands on the rocks."

I did, and he slipped his fingers into my back pocket, fighting with my wallet until it shook free. The flashlight beam jiggled, then it grew dim. I twisted my head around slightly. The man stared at my wallet, his face illuminated in a ghastly glow of light. He shined the light back in my face.

"Office of Municipal Security?"

"Uh-huh."

"Never heard of it."

"Only been around since 9/11."

He huffed. "Why the fuck didn't they call us and tell us what's going on up here?"

"Seems you found out anyway."

"Hell, Tony's a friend. Known him since he started this place. He called and said some undercover guys from New York came up here protecting the life of a sheikh. Must be you, but what the hell are you doing out in the woods?"

"Take the cuffs off and I'll tell you."

"Sorry," he said. "Name's Evan. Evan Briggs. Local Chief of Detectives."

Briggs's keys clanged as he fumbled with them. He pulled my wrists to him, jabbed a key into the lock, and the cuffs sprung back. My wrists stung. I rubbed them.

"How the hell you going to protect the sheikh from out here?"

"Got some people on the inside."

"Hmmm. Big operation? Control center? Infrared? All that high-tech shit?"

I laughed. "Right. The other day I found a fresh mound of cigarette butts near a stump on the other side of the ridge," I said. "I thought it might make a good nest for a sniper."

"Hell, it's a straight shot from the ridge into the back of that lecture hall. Glass window. Plenty of light inside. Make a perfect nest. That's why I came up here the back way. Old deer trail. Been using it ever since we were kids. So why'd you come down this far? Looked like you were trying to climb that rock wall."

"I heard you up on the ridge," I said. "Didn't know what to make of it, so I thought I'd circle around and come up on you from behind."

"Hell," Briggs said. "One big problem with that plan."

"What's that?"

"You mighta heard someone up there, but it wasn't me. I just came up here behind you. Heard you making all this noise and thought I should have a look."

"Wasn't you up there?" I asked.

"Nope," Briggs said. "Wasn't me."

"So we do have company," I said.

"Here, you might need this."

Briggs switched on his flashlight, then handed me my Browning. I reached for it when suddenly a small explosion sounded, followed by a ping off the rocks. Dust and a few rock chips flew into my face. Briggs killed his light.

# TWENTY-EIGHT

"This way," Briggs said. He grabbed my arm and yanked me along the rock wall. "Shot came from above and to one side. There's an alcove at the other end of this wall. Shooter won't have us in his sights there. Sonofabitch probably has a night vision scope."

Briggs slid his back along the rock wall. I followed him. Suddenly, the rock wall opened up and swallowed him.

He reached for my arm. "Duck down," he said.

I did, and he pulled me in.

"Where are we?"

"Place we used to play in as kids. Used it to get out of the rain, or later as a blind when we'd hunt deer. Sucker tries coming after us now, we got him. Be quiet. Let's see what he does."

I rested on my haunches with my back against the wall of the small cave. A damp, dank smell hovered in the air. I strained to see. I closed my eyes, then opened them. I could barely discern a difference, but I did notice that the cave seemed to amplify the sounds of wind rustling through the tree limbs and the chirping of small critters in the night. A branch broke, and my body stiffened against the rock.

Briggs laughed. "Don't do much huntin,' do ya?"

"No."

"It's only a deer."

Then a faint sound of crunched leaves filtered in from above.

"Let's go," Briggs said. "That's our man, and he's on the move."

I rose to my feet when we stepped outside the cave.

"You think you can find your way back the way you came?" Briggs asked.

"Sounds like you got a plan," I said.

"When you get up to the ridge trail, head back my way. If this guy wants a clear shot into that hall he'll be somewhere between us. Maybe we can get to him before he sets up."

"Just don't shoot me on the trail," I said.

"You don't do much huntin'," Briggs said. "Already got the sound of your tracks in my head. Doubt both of you sound the same. But I'll holler before I fire if that makes you feel any better."

"It does," I said.

Briggs laughed before disappearing into the brush.

I worked my way back along the rock wall and back into the brush. I high-stepped over tree limbs again, pulling my earbud from my pocket and stuffing it into place. I switched on my radio.

"Natalie," I said. "We've got a shooter up here and also a local cop. We're trying to reach the gunman before he has time to set up."

"You want us to pull the sheikh off the stage now?"

"Not yet," I said. "These folks might have a plan B as well. Let's see if we can scratch plan A first, to eliminate at least one shooter. I'm going silent again. I'll be in touch."

"John," Barbara broke in, but I lost her words amidst a round of applause that erupted in the hall. I switched off my radio.

A crescent of light from the lecture hall guided me up through the trees to the ridge trail. Overhead, a layer of clouds moved in, covering the stars, plunging the night further into darkness. I stopped and listened. I heard nothing, not even Briggs. In his own way, Briggs reminded me of Promise—A man who knew his environment so well he could navigate through it with ease on a starless night; only where Briggs walked a path through the darkest parts of the woods, Promise often tread through the darkest parts of the soul.

"After fifty years in prison," Promise loved to say, "you learn that the places inside of yourself that you fear most are the very places you must travel to if you're ever to become free."

The lecture hall finally came into view. Its light blinded me. I walked quickly toward Briggs along the ridge trail. Looking down, the sheikh raised one hand, then the other, in animated gesticulation as he talked.

"Shannon, that you?"

"I didn't even hear you."

Our arms touched. We both whispered.

"Like I said, you don't do much huntin'."

"He's not between us," I said.

"Means he's down there below us on the other side of the ridge," Briggs said.

"Gimme your flashlight," I said.

"Sounds like you gotta plan now," Briggs said.

"Uh-huh. Gimme the light."

Briggs handed it to me.

"Go back down the trail a little ways," I said. "When the light comes on, be ready."

I waited for Briggs to move away, then I lay down on my stomach and perched the flashlight between two rocks. I pointed it in the general direction of the handmade bench. I took a deep breath. The moment I switched it on I rolled away down the trail, gun in hand, and a moment after that, a gunshot rang out, plowing into the earth near the flashlight, raising a tiny cloud of dust. Briggs fired back first, then the gunman fired at Briggs. I watched the muzzle flash and fired at it. But the gunman spun and fired not at the flashlight, but at me. I heard him moving. It sounded like a man crawling on all fours coming my way. Briggs remained still. I waited. I thought about firing at the sound, but that would only alert the gunman to my position.

The gunman's movement stopped, but I couldn't locate him. Then what Briggs said about a nightvision scope flashed into my mind. I saw my face in the middle of crosshairs bathed in an eerie greenish-yellow light. My instincts told me to roll down the other side of the ridge trail. But just as I started to move, a loud wail arose from the lecture hall.

I looked downhill. The lecture hall lights had dimmed, and the raucous buzz of the fire alarm reverberated through the night.

Briggs bellowed. "Get down there. I'll take care of this one."

Briggs must have been following the sound of the gunman's movements as well because he fired repeatedly in that direction. I jumped up into a low crouch and hurried back along the trail.

Behind me, several different weapons reported to each other. I pulled out my flashlight and switched it on. I didn't want to miss the trail down to the campus.

I fumbled for my earbud and jammed it in, then groped for the radio's "On" switch. Natalie and Barbara spoke excitedly with each other.

"What's taking place?" I said.

Barbara sounded out of breath. "Fire alarm went off. The hall's clearing. There's chaos down here. Sheikh's being hustled out a side entrance by Hamid and some others."

"Stay with the sheikh," I said. "Both of you stay with him."

"We're on him. Where are you?" Natalie said.

"Coming down."

"And the shooter?" she asked.

"Local guy's after him," I said.

"You can't go any farther." I heard the male voice through my headset.

"Like hell I can't," Natalie said. "We're here to protect the sheikh."

"A woman?" The male voice sounded incredulous.

"Two women," Barbara said.

"Now get out of our way," Barbara said. "The sheikh could be in danger out there."

The man laughed. I walked hurriedly down the trail. A few grunts and groans came over the headset. It sounded like a struggle.

"Barbara? Natalie?"

No answer, but a wave of voices now swept over the campus: more groans, and then a deep sigh over the headset.

"Barbara? Natalie? Where are you?"

Still no answer.

Then, finally, "John, we're outside looking for the sheikh and his entourage."

"What happened?" I asked.

Barbara huffed. It sounded like she was running. "A couple of guys are going to have difficulty pleasing their girlfriends for the next several weeks."

"Sheikh's headed toward his car," Natalie said.

"Where is it parked?" I asked.

"Looks like a parking lot behind the administration building."

"I know where it is," I said. "I'm headed that way . . . Hamid with him?"

"I think so," Natalie said.

The fire alarm still rang as I raced past the long path leading up to the dining hall. I pushed my way through people wandering around in the dim glow of the lamps lining the pathways that crisscrossed the campus. They stumbled, dazed and unsure. Off to one side, I saw two figures running along a path that angled to meet mine. Ahead of me, a huddle of bodies moved toward the administration building's parking lot, now blazing under the blue-green glare of a tight cluster of tall overhead streetlights with long, curved necks.

Natalie and Barbara both had their pistols out when our paths met. The sheikh moved in the middle of the circle, a bright white flame surrounded by a wall of eight men. The drone of conversation, mostly in Arabic, arose from the circle.

A man yelled at the three of us as we ran up to the sheikh's human shield. "Stay away. Go back to the Center." He flicked us away with the back of his hand.

I turned to Barbara and Natalie. "Stay here."

Hamid walked out in front of the group, looking furtively one way, then the other. I ran around the circle to get to him, but a man stepped out with his gun in his hand to block my way. I didn't have time to explain. I also didn't have time for amateurs. With a quick sideways sweep of my arm, I knocked his gun from him, then I grabbed his arm, bent slightly, and tossed him over my hip.

Suddenly, the group stopped close by the sheikh's idling car. Guns came out, leveled at me. Hamid turned around. Ali, the receptionist from the Brooklyn Sufi Center, shook his head.

"Hamid, don't let the sheikh get into the car."

The sheikh turned to face me. A puzzled, stunned look on his face.

"Don't let him get into that car," I said.

"Are you crazy?" Hamid said. He pointed back toward the lecture hall. "Someone set off an alarm. If we'd have stayed there, someone could have tried to shoot the sheikh."

"And out here at night he's even more vulnerable."

"That's why we're leaving with him," Hamid said.

"What? To drive out the main road into the Center?"

Hamid said nothing.

"A long, dark road on which you must drive slowly," I said. "You haven't cleared the woods on either side of the road. It'd be an easy place for an ambush."

Hamid remained silent, but a murmur of Arabic moved through the other men.

"Brother Hamid," a man called out. "You would let this one tell you what to do?"

"It's not safe, Hamid," I said. "We'd be better off putting the sheikh in his cabin and protecting him there."

"No," another man shouted. "We should follow the plan we laid out with the sheikh."

Ali stepped out of line, walked over to the car, and opened the back door. The group of men broke their circle and gently shoved the sheikh toward the car from behind.

"Wait," Hamid said. "We will—"

Suddenly, Natalie cried out, "Gun. Gun."

I turned to see Ali pointing a pistol at the sheikh, a grim smile on his face. His lips moved in a silence utterance. I bowled over two men aside and raced toward car. Before I could reach the sheikh, Natalie flew through the air in a blur, arms outstretched, gun in hand, her face torqued and distorted with strain.

An explosion followed. The sheikh's eyes popped wide open, his white garment spattered with red. Ali stood by dazed, his trigger arm limp by his side. The other men seemed unable to move as well. I grabbed the gun from Ali's hand and threw a hard punch into his stomach and he crumpled.

When I looked back, I saw Natalie lying in a pool of blood on the ground.

Barbara grabbed the sheikh and tossed him to me like a basketball player making a forward pass. I yanked the car door open, pushed the sheikh inside, then lay over the top of him.

I yelled at the driver, "Go. Go."

He didn't move. I raised up and pointed my gun at his head. "Go," I said again.

Outside, Barbara kneeled over Natalie, her gun pointed at the other men. Hamid stood beside her, his gun drawn at the men as well. Hamid looked over his shoulder at us and angrily waved the driver away. Finally, the driver pressed the gas pedal and we moved along the road from the parking lot. The sheikh's body trembled under me. Whatever we'd face making our way out of here seemed better than facing the certain danger we'd just left.

When the car came to the main campus thoroughfare, the driver turned right. A sea of red taillights pulsated brighter, then dimmer, as a line of drivers waiting along the road tapped their brakes. Something went off inside me.

"No. No." I tapped his shoulder with my pistol and pointed in the other direction.

"This the way out," he said.

I tapped him harder. "But that's the way we're taking."

"That way don't know."

"Doesn't matter," I said. "Back up and take that road." I motioned behind us, then pointed.

"That way don't know," the man said again.

I slammed the butt of my pistol down on the top of his shoulder. "You'll follow my instructions. Now take that road."

The man huffed, then looked up into the rearview mirror with a deadly grimace. The tires screeched as he backed up, then screeched again as he lurched forward. A woman crossing the main road jumped out of the way. She pounded on the hood as we made our way slowly past her. We drove through people still walking the campus.

"It'll be okay," I said to the sheikh.

"May I sit up?" he asked.

"I'd prefer it if you remained down," I said, "so you'll make less of a target."

"Was she killed?" he asked.

"I don't know."

"Who is she?"

"Natalie. Natalie Chen."

"And she risked her life to protect me?"

"Yes, she did," I said. "It's her job."

"And you people work with the Office of Municipal Security?"

"Yes, we do."

"I owe you a debt of gratitude."

I looked behind us. Against the backdrop of red taillights, two blinding white headlights moved our way, like the glowing eyes of a nocturnal beast on the hunt. "Hold on to your gratitude," I said. "We haven't gotten out of here yet."

People thinned out as the road neared the edge of the campus. The driver sped up, but so did the car behind us. The driver hit his high beams once the road plunged into the darkness beyond the campus. I sat up and the sheikh moved to sit up too, but I held him down. I scanned the road and the woods we drove through, looking for anything that seemed out of the ordinary. Our headlights illuminated two red marblelike eyes ahead. The driver slammed on the brakes while the deer in our headlights stared at us impassively before scampering into the night.

The headlights behind us grew brighter.

"Go," I said. "Go."

We started again but the driver didn't seem in a hurry.

"What is happening, Sir?" The sheikh asked.

I glanced out the window. The other car came on fast.

I rapped the driver's shoulder with my pistol barrel. "Faster."

Then, in the rearview mirror, I caught his grimace dissolving into an eerily serene state while his lips moved as though praying. I smashed my gun with all my force into the side of his head. He slumped over onto his window, and the car careened wildly to one side of the road. I tried to steer over his shoulder, but the man's foot lay heavy on the gas pedal, his limp arm preventing me from fully turning the wheel.

With one hand on the wheel, I slithered into the front seat. With the other hand, I groped for the driver's side door handle. I pushed the door open, but it flopped back. Still trying to steer the out of control car, I raised a leg to the driver's body and kicked him from the moving vehicle. His body hit the gravel and rolled to the side of the road. I slid behind the wheel and gunned the accelerator.

I yelled toward the sheikh. "Stay down."

And a moment later, out of the side-view mirror, I saw the driver's body erupted in a huge explosion.

# TWENTY-NINE

THE PRESSURE WAVE FROM the blast slammed painfully into my eardrums. I stomped on the brakes and squeezed my eyes closed. The car's windows shattered. Glass showered over me. I had the sensation of a huge invisible force moving up from behind the car, pushing us forward, even with my foot on the brakes. The car came to a head-snapping halt. Cold air barreled in. When I opened my eyes I realized we'd been thrown into the ditch. I looked over at the sheikh, lying still on the rear seat.

"Are you all right, Sir?"

He lifted his head, and though I couldn't see the expression on his face, his voice shook slightly. He mumbled, "Yes. I think so."

I'd hoped the blast caught the car behind us. It shattered our rear-view mirror. I looked back. Headlights slowly emerged from a dense plume of smoke, like a phoenix rising from the ashes. I turned the ignition key, but our car had stalled.

I twisted the key in the ignition. The engine whined, but it wouldn't turn over. Our headlights illuminated the road. My fingers fumbled around, looking for the light switch to shut them off. I twisted the end of one arm coming from the steering column and the wipers went on, beating out a surreal rhythm. Behind us the headlights drew closer. I twisted another lever arm and our headlights clicked off. I cranked the key so hard this time I feared that I might break it. Still, the engine wouldn't engage. I looked behind us again. The car had nearly reached us. Then another set of lights came at us through what remained of the windshield. Much further down the road, a car sped our way.

I yelled to the sheikh, "Get out!"

"What?" he said. "Here?"

"Get out or get killed."

I scooped my gun from the floor and shouldered the door open. I raced around to the opposite side of the car, nearly ripping the handle from the passenger door as I yanked it open and pulled the sheikh out. I pushed him farther down into the ditch, then up the side of a small incline into the woods. The car behind us came to a screeching halt with its headlights pointed toward the woods, trapping us in their beams. I fell to the ground and brought the sheikh down with me. Then, grabbing my pistol with two hands and propping my arms along the ground, I fired twice at the headlights and restored the darkness of the night.

I pulled the sheikh to his feet. "Come quickly," I said.

He stood, but when he tried to move, his robe snagged on a downed tree limb. I sighed and shook my head.

"Sorry, Sir," I said.

I reached down and with one jerk, tore off the bottom of his robe. He touched my hand and said softly, "Thank you."

I grabbed the sheikh's hand and moved as quickly as I could in the darkness, heading us deeper into the woods, but also back toward the Sigma Center, away from the men who'd just stopped and the other car barreling down the road toward us. Suddenly, flashlight beams swept through the darkness, searching for us. The sheikh's robe would glow like a torch once the beams found us, drawing these gnats to the flame.

I counted five flashlight beams and heard multiple voices speaking Arabic. The sheikh heard them too. He squeezed my hand.

"Wait," he said. "The leader's name is Ibrahim. He's telling the others to spread out to shine their lights through the trees and look for my white robe."

"We've got to keep moving," I said. "Let's try to find a rock on a large tree stump. We can hide behind it and use it as a defense."

"But should we move? I'm an easy target," the sheikh said.

Fabric ripped. Then the Sheikh leaned an arm on my shoulder.

"I have street clothes on underneath the robes," he said.

I shimmied out of my jacket. "It's cold out here," I said. "Take this. And give me your robe."

I bundled the fabric under one arm and we made our way slowly, clumsily, through the woods, feeling for trees with our arms out, picking our way through the shadows created by the car's headlights. A man's voice called out in Arabic and lights fanned out through the trees.

"This Ibrahim's telling them to spread out and try to encircle us," the sheikh said.

I stopped and hung the sheikh's robe on a low-lying tree limb. I thought about waiting until the flashlights came closer, then picking off the men one at a time. But in the darkness of the woods, shooting at a beam with so many trees in the way didn't make sense.

Tires screeched, and through the trees I saw a car come to a stop along the road. The voice in Arabic called out gleefully.

"He says that others have come to join the hunt for the Infidels," the sheikh said.

I curled my bottom lip into my mouth and rested my teeth on it. I had to decide where to take a stand, and I had to decide soon. I had nine rounds left in my Browning, and who knew how many men now on the hunt. I didn't like the odds of heading deeper into the woods, so I pulled the sheikh straight down toward the road. His body stiffened.

"Where are we going?" he asked.

"We can't see in these trees, and I don't have a clear shot at any of these men. Our best bet is to head back to the road and maybe use one of the cars as cover."

"We are in Allah's hands now," the sheikh said. "May he be merciful with us."

"Amen to that, brother," I said in my mind.

We'd moved about fifty yards through the woods toward the road when two flashlight beams lit up the trees behind us. A volley of shots rang out and I pushed the sheikh to the ground. Some men called out in Arabic. The sheikh laughed, then whispered to me, "The man said, 'You idiots. You've just killed the sheikh's robe. Now find the sheikh and kill him instead.'"

We continued making our way toward the road, voices scattered in the woods around us. Suddenly, the sheikh grabbed my arm and stopped me.

"Wait," he said. "This Ibrahim's onto us. He's just sent three men back to the car on the road in case we try to head that way."

Flashlights and footsteps crashed through the woods. We couldn't turn back now, and I think the sheikh knew that. I heard him uttering softly in Arabic as we stepped over twigs and branches, and I prayed that someone else listened to his prayers. I watched flashlights bouncing through the trees back toward the road. Behind us and on both sides, flashlights drew closer as we neared the road and Ibrahim herded us toward our fate. When we reached the ditch beside the road, I turned to the sheikh and whispered. "If you keep low you can stay in this ditch and head back to the campus. By now, law enforcement and emergency vehicles will have arrived and someone will help you there."

"And what will you do?" the sheikh asked.

"Hold these guys at bay as long as I can."

"I don't even know your name, Sir," the sheikh said.

"Shannon," I said. "John Shannon."

I thought about running with the sheikh for the cover of one of the cars parked in the road, but that meant a hundred yards with little protection. Right now, staying in this ditch seemed like the best choice. I looked both ways, tracking flashlights as they bounced through the trees. Three beams shone farther back in the trees, two closer to us. One beam reached the ditch about fifty yards away. I grabbed my pistol with both hands and aimed at the light, but when I glanced over my shoulder, another beam had reached the ditch near the cars on the other side of us. I switched my aim back and forth, waiting for whichever man got closer.

I faced the cars when suddenly, behind me, someone called out in Arabic. I turned and fired once at the light. I never saw the man, but his beam faltered, shining haphazardly up at the sky, then into the woods, until it fell to the ground and became a small glow. I whipped back around to the other beam, but before I could take aim a shot cracked the night from that direction. A split second of eternity followed as I braced for the impact of a bullet nearby. I heard none. Felt none. The light died.

Footsteps rushed toward us. I aimed, ready to pull the trigger, when a voice whispered, "Shannon? That you?"

The voice belonged to Evan Briggs.

"You got the sheikh with you?" Briggs asked.

"Here," I said.

"Hell, can't see a thing."

"Keep walking in the ditch. You'll find us," I said.

"That's what I figured."

When Briggs got up to us, I reached out and grabbed his leg. He kneeled down.

"How'd you get here?" I asked.

"You're not a hunter," Briggs said. "I am."

"That was you driving by in the car?"

"Yep. Hell, son, you got yourself in one helluva mess."

"Who is this?" the sheikh asked.

"Name's Evan Briggs."

"Local law enforcement," I said.

"How'd you want to handle this?" Briggs asked.

"Got a flashlight?" I asked.

"Right here," Briggs said. "Didn't want to turn it on."

"When I tell you, turn it on."

I leaned back to the sheikh.

"Can you yell out in Arabic that he shot one man and he's taken the sheikh back into the woods?"

"Tell me when."

"After you do, I want you to stay here," I said. I turned to Briggs.

"When the sheikh calls out, you switch on your flashlight and head up into the woods."

"You'll follow the lights headed my way?" Briggs asked.

"Uh-huh."

"Sounds like a plan," Briggs said.

"Get ready with the flashlight."

I tapped the sheikh on the shoulder and said, "Now."

He screamed at the top of his lungs, sounding not at all like the mild-mannered man I heard talk to hundreds. Briggs clicked on his flashlight and raced into the woods. I watched as the three beams turned in his direction and Ibrahim called out in Arabic.

"What'd he say?"

"They're following the other man's flashlight."

"Good. Whatever happens, stay here until one of us comes back for you."

I raised up and headed into the woods, following the flashlights, angling to place myself behind them. Ibrahim bellowed toward Briggs, whose flashlight beam kept moving ahead, luring the men deeper into the woods.

Suddenly, Briggs's beam died. Ibrahim's voice sounded strained and high-pitched. The other flashlights never even turned in my direction. They didn't know I was there. Thirty yards away, I called out, "Drop your weapons on the ground and raise your hands above your heads."

All three beams turned toward me now.

Then Briggs shouted, "I'd do as the man asked."

The beams turned the other way. A shot rang out toward Briggs. He fired back, and a man sighed low before a flashlight beam jerked over the woods. One man turned toward me and fired. He missed by a mile. I shot back, but heard nothing. Briggs fired as well. Then, suddenly, both beams went out. But I didn't think Briggs or I had hit either of the two men still standing. Footsteps crashed through the brush, running away from the road, deeper into the woods.

Briggs's flashlight popped on. I walked toward it.

"They're on the run," Briggs called out. "Assholes. They're running deeper into the woods. There's a rise about a quarter of a mile from here, then a steep drop from a cliff about an eighth of a mile beyond that."

By the time I reached him, Briggs was on his knees over a man lying on the ground.

"He's still breathing," Briggs said. He pulled the man's flashlight from his hand and offered it to me. "Take it. Go back and help the sheikh. Get him out of here. Take their car." He laughed. "Road leads to State Route 19 about five miles ahead. Make a left on 19, and follow it till you get to the freeway. I'll stay here and call for backup. I'll be okay. I'm a hunter. These are my woods. Those fools don't have a clue what they're doing out here."

I grasped Briggs's shoulder as he rose. "Thanks," I said.

I turned and started walking away when Briggs called out, "Hey, Shannon . . ."

I stopped and turned around. Briggs shined his light toward me.

"Good plan. You're not such a bad hunter after all."

I tipped my head to one side and gave Briggs a two-fingered salute, then turned again and headed back to the sheikh. When I got to the ditch, I shined my flashlight on the sheikh, lying face down. My heart clenched.

Suddenly, the sheikh raised his head and turned toward me with a big grin. "One's prayers are sometimes answered."

# THIRTY

Apparently, the sheikh wasn't taking chances. He sat up front as we drove the dark back road, and every time I looked over at him, he appeared to be praying.

Once we turned onto Route 19, I pulled out my cell phone and called Tucker.

"Where the hell've you been?"

"Hunting," I said.

"Sheikh with you?"

"He is. How's Natalie?"

"Shot in the shoulder. High. She's in a hospital up there. She's a tough kid. She'll make it. And the sheikh?"

I turned to my right. The sheikh flashed me a thumbs-up.

"Fine," I said. "I'm thinking we should take him to his country estate up here. It's about thirty miles away."

"I'll have a welcoming party there for you," Tucker said.

And he did.

We drove up a dark, winding road to the sheikh's estate, but when we reached the stone wall that surrounded the property, it looked like a laser light show inside the gates. State Patrol cruisers, with red and blue lights pulsing, sat just outside the gate and in a ring around the house. Overhead, a helicopter made circles with its spotlight pointed down at the sheikh's stone mansion, which reminded me of a castle. And the sheikh could have easily passed for a kid at the circus, whipping his head one way, then the other, taking in the sights.

He chuckled, "You Americans do things with such pomp and circumstance . . . especially after the fact."

A uniformed officer holding a leash with a large German shepherd at the other end met us at the door. After the sheikh opened the door, the officer barked, "Sweep Brutus," and the dog scurried inside the house. I turned to the officer.

"Brutus?"

The man grinned. "It'll only take him a minute or two to make sure there are no perps or pops inside."

The sheikh turned to me, his face wrinkled.

"Bad guys or explosives," I said.

We waited, and a several minutes later Brutus loped downstairs, sitting at his handler's feet, a self-satisfied look in Brutus's eyes. The officer pulled a biscuit from his pocket. Brutus wolfed it down.

"House's clear," the officer said.

The sheikh's country home had slate floors downstairs and a wide staircase that spiraled up to the second floor. A crystal chandelier hung from a long chain in the middle of the downstairs hall.

"Mr. Shannon," the sheikh said, "I don't know about you, but after tonight, I need a shower. There's a guest room straight back that way." He pointed down the hall. "I'll meet you in the library after we've both cleaned up."

The sheikh left for the steps and I walked down the hallway, past doublewide, floor-to-ceiling sliding wood doors, partially cracked, revealing wall-to-wall cases of books.

I leaned back into the overstuffed tan leather sofa, scanning titles along the shelves. Past the leather-bound editions of Shakespeare, Dickens, and Melville, I spied a large-format picture book on the history of jazz. I pulled it out and thumbed through grainy black and white prints of Kid Oliver, Jelly Roll Morton, and Fats Waller. I flipped to the back. I smiled. John Coltrane, on one page, faced Miles Davis on the other, sweat rolling off their brows, talking to each other through their horns.

"Do you like jazz, Mr. Shannon?"

The sheikh surprised me. He'd entered through another door with a tray of fruit and cheese and two glasses of wine. He wore a red silk sitting robe with black lapels embroidered in gold. Give him a pipe or a cigar and we could have been somewhere in the English countryside ready to chat over a "spot of tea."

"I do like jazz."

The sheikh's face lit up. He set the tray down on an end table and picked up a remote control. He punched a few buttons, and a plaintive sax blew through the speakers, like a wailing wind off the ocean. The sheikh took a seat and closed his eyes, his head bobbing slightly to Dolphy's beat. I stared at the sheikh and shook my head. Somehow, the entire scene seemed so unlikely.

"I recognize Dolphy's sound, but not the piece," I said.

The sheikh opened his eyes slowly and smiled. He pushed another button on the remote and the volume lowered. He grinned like a kid holding a rare baseball card.

"It's a live recording I made on an old tape recorder when I heard Dolphy play once in Stockholm—an original composition that never made it onto any of his albums. I love jazz." He paused with the thought. "It's music that speaks to me as a Sufi. Dancing with one's spirit through unbridled creative expression. Finding God by searching deep inside, then expressing the joy of that discovery through improvisation. It's why I believe dervishes twirl and Dolphy blows the way he does. Jazz is also the perfect music for two men who have just escaped with their lives thanks to the grace of God. Don't you think?"

The sheikh handed the tray to me. I took a slice of apple and a wedge of cheese. After a sip of red wine, I said, "Is that also why you liked Yousef al-Salaam and his rap music?"

The sheikh sighed. "Poor boy. Caught between two worlds. His soul reaching beyond the circumstances of his life." He smiled. "Do you know that Yousef came here to record? Downstairs I have a complete studio and excellent recording equipment. I've spent the last few years converting my collection of 2500 LPs to CD. Yousef liked recording up here."

"Do you have a master of the last session that Yousef recorded?"

He shook his head. "Probably. I haven't been up here since Yousef's last session several weeks before his death. Would you be interested in hearing it?"

"I would."

"Would you also like to see the studio?"

"I would."

The sheikh's eyes sparkled like a young boy with baseball cards now about to get into mischief. He waved me toward him with his finger. "Follow me."

We walked through a door at the back of the library, and from there into the hallway, through another door, and down a set of stairs. At the bottom of the stairs, the sheikh stopped and swept his hand around the large space.

"When I acquired this place it was a game room, filled with a billiard table, ping-pong table, and card table."

It now looked like a modern-day recording studio. We stood in an open space lined with acoustic tiles and a microphone that dropped down from the ceiling. I followed the Sheikh across the room to a door into the control room. I reared back as he opened the door. The control room measured half the size of the room outside, and two walls of the control room had old vinyl LPs lined from floor to ceiling. Alphabetized lettered tags stuck out from the sheikh's cache of records.

The sheikh took a seat behind the control board as though slipping into the pilot's seat of a plane. He sighed. "I'd always envisioned that someday I'd bring famous jazz musicians here to record, but I'm not sure that will ever happen now. A few groups recorded up here many years ago. I like to keep up with technology. Yousef helped me bring the equipment up to the latest digital standards."

The sheikh pulled open a metal drawer with several cases of CDs in it. He fumbled through the collection, then finally emerged holding a CD labeled: "Y.A.S. Recording Session 1. First Take. Gotta Tell the Truth."

"Gotta Tell the Truth," I said.

The sheikh shook his head. "I haven't heard it."

He slipped it into a CD player and hit some switches. He reached for two sets of headsets and handed me one. The CD began with al-Salaam talking to someone, but no one replied, and I wondered if he spoke to himself. But an acoustic guitar began playing with a funky rhythm and lively chords. Al-Salaam began to sing. The sheikh and I both sat there, tapping our feet to his rhythm.

Suddenly, I heard al-Salaam's words beyond the music. The sheikh must have heard them as well. We both turned to each other, wide-eyed, listening in rapt attention. After the song ended, the sheikh pulled off his headset. I took of mine as well.

"I'll play it again with the voice highlighted and the music further in the background," the sheikh said.

He moved a few dials on the player and I listened to al-Salaam as though he were standing in front of me reciting poetry. When the piece ended, we laid our headsets down.

I pointed to the CD. "Is it true?" I asked.

The sheikh nodded. "I wouldn't be surprised."

"Then I know who killed Yousef. Can you make copies of this CD?"

"For you?"

"No. I mean can you make lots of copies?"

"How many?"

"A hundred, maybe two."

The sheikh smiled, then patted a machine to his side. "It's the latest CD burner," he said. "Two hundred will not take long at all. I could re-master it, add a bass and drum track . . . even one of those scratchy record tracks. I could sample it from Yousef's other CDs."

"That'd be even better," I said.

The sheikh worked through the night on the project.

* * *

Driving back to New York City the following morning with two hundred remastered CDs of Yousef al-Salaam's last recording session, I stopped first at Ken Tucker's office. Charlene waved me in. Tucker stared at his keyboard when I entered. He looked surprised.

"Put this in a CD player," I said.

He rolled his chair over to the edge of his desk, pushed a button and the drawer of his CD player opened. He looked at al-Salaam's CD before he slipped it in.

"I don't like rap," he said.

"Listen to it," I said.

He leaned back in his chair, and folded his arms behind his head. When Yousef finished, Tucker sprung back to an upright, seated position. He picked up his telephone and made a call. Tucker wasn't shy with words. He let the person on the other end of the line know of his extreme displeasure. When he finished, he jabbed the button on the CD player, pulled the disk out, and waved it at me.

"You got more of these?"

"Plenty," I said.

"Good. They'll be on the air by tonight. You want me to send someone to pick up Harmon?"

"I'll do it," I said.

# THIRTY-ONE

I SWERVED TO THE curb outside Harmon's office building at 54th Street and Third. I stuck an Office of Municipal Security tag on top of the dashboard and raced into the building, flashing a badge and walked through the security checkpoint without stopping. I stopped at the security desk in the lobby. A man in a blue uniform with three yellow stripes stepped forward. I flashed my badge again.

"John Shannon, Office of Municipal Security. I need a private car up to the twentieth floor, and when I get off I want the floor closed to elevator traffic until I call down."

The officer nodded. "Yes, Sir. Here's the number."

The officer walked with me toward the elevator bank. A dozen people crowded into a car with open doors. The officer stepped inside and cleared the passengers from it, then he stuck a key into a lock on the elevator's control panel, hit the button marked "twenty" and stepped aside.

"Private car to the twentieth floor," he said.

I walked into the car. The doors closed and in no time they opened again. I turned right and pushed opened the doors to H&M Records. A rap artist played on the office speakers. I made out "'ho" from the torrent of his words, but didn't bother listening to the rest. I didn't recognize the receptionist at the front desk, and I didn't stop to ask for Harmon, either.

"Yo, mister," the receptionist said. "Where do you think you're going?"

I didn't answer. I walked fast down the hallway and pushed open Harmon's office door. He sat behind his desk, chewing on the end of an unlit cigar. He pulled the cigar from his mouth.

"What the fuck're you doing here again?"

The door burst open behind me. "Mr. Harmon, this man just ran past me. Do you want me to call security?"

"Goddamn, Lucinda. I want you to get back to the front desk, where you belong."

The door closed softly behind me.

"New help," Harmon chuckled. "Just breaking her in. You seem like a man on a mission. What're you so goddamned hot to trot about?"

"Arresting you for conspiracy in the murder of Yousef al-Salaam."

Harmon threw his cigar at me. "You fucking lost your mind? Besides, I told you I don't know no one named al-Salaam."

I waved a CD at him. "Well, this says otherwise."

"What, some goddamned rap song? Hell, they write any damn thing they want."

"But Yousef didn't write this," I said. "It's your voice on the recording. He wove a telephone call from you into his recording."

300

I saw Harmon's hand moving toward a desk drawer. I whipped out my gun and pointed it at him.

"What are you, some gangster?" Harmon said.

"No. I want you step out from behind your desk."

Harmon reached for his phone. "The hell with you, pal. I'm calling building security."

"I already notified them. Now step from behind your desk with both hands out."

Harmon didn't move.

"Now." I barked.

Harmon flinched. "Okay. Okay."

He held his hands out. I grabbed an arm, spun him around and snapped cuffs on his hands behind his back. I pushed him down onto his couch, walked over to his desk, and opened the top drawer. I pulled out a Smith and Wesson .38, which I dangled between two fingers.

"I suppose you use this as a letter opener."

"Look, the kind of business I'm in, you can't take chances. Some two-bit hoodlum might come in here and try to rob the place."

A CD player sat to one side of Harmon's desk. I hit "Stop." The rapper on the overhead speakers went silent. I slipped al-Salaam's disk in and hit "Play."

The sheikh had recorded a driving bass beat leading up to al-Salaam's entry. "*Salaam Alaikum . . . Salaam Alaikum . . . Salaam Alaikum . . . ,*" he began. Then, in a quiet voice that grew ever more powerful, al-Salaam sang, "*Got to tell the truth. Even if it gets me killed. Got to tell the truth . . .*"

On the recording, a telephone rang. "Is this the Deuce?" the male caller said.

I looked over to Harmon. His eyes grew wide at the sound of his voice.

*"Got to tell the truth"* al-Salaam sang. *"Even if it gets me killed. Got to tell the truth . . ."*

"Deuce, look this is how it goes down. There's two million in it for you. Two million in it for T-Mo."

"Stop it. Stop it," Harmon said.

*"Got to tell the truth . . ."* al-Salaam sang.

"All they want us to do is cut a CD where T-Mo plays the 'bad boy' and you play the 'good boy.'" Harmon's recorded voice continued.

*"Got to tell the truth . . ."*

"T-Mo takes the side of a suicide bomber. You take the side of a Muslim who says the United States is in Iraq to help Arabs, not to hurt them."

*"Got to tell the truth. Even if it gets me killed . . ."*

"Dammit, Deuce. We're talking a lot of fucking money the government's willing to throw at us. We make the recording. They flood the Middle East with it. That's it. We go to the bank. Everyone's happy."

*"Got to tell the truth. No peace until the troops leave the Middle East. Got to tell the truth . . ."*

"My dear brother, al-Salaam," another recorded voice said. "This is Imam Sayd Aziz of the Brooklyn Mosque."

*"Got to tell the truth . . ."*

"I understand that you have been given a wonderful opportunity to spread a message of peace. I am fully behind this recording and will help to ensure that young people in the Middle East get to hear your words. I hope you won't let us down."

*"Got to tell the truth. Will not sell my soul. Got to tell the truth . . ."*

"Look you little bastard. I made you what you are. Without me there'd be no Deuce F. No Grammies. No houses in New York and L.A. No trips to the Middle East. No name change to Yousef. You'd still be fucking Edgar Koontz. Contract says that either you do the recording with T-Mo or the government goes somewhere else."

*"Got to tell the truth . . ."*

"Hey, homey. Heard you messin' wit my money. So here's how it goes. You play or you pay. You dig? This is T-Mo!" The phone clicked. Al-Salaam came on again.

*"Got to tell the truth. No peace until the troops leave the Middle East. Got to tell the truth . . ."*

"I asked T-Mo to give you a call, to see if he could talk some sense into your damn head." Harmon said. "My advice. You'd better listen to him before you get hurt."

Harmon slumped into the couch.

*"Got to tell the truth. Even if it gets me killed . . ."*

"Home boy. You a dead man," T-Mo cackled.

*"Got to tell the truth."*

\* \* \*

303

I dropped Phil Harmon off at the 17th Precinct, where they arraigned him on conspiracy to murder. Walking from the station house, my cell phone rang.

"I'm at NYU Medical Center with Natalie," Ken Tucker said. "Thought maybe you'd come over."

First I stopped to get a bouquet of flowers, then I drove over to the medical center. Tucker stood outside of Natalie's room.

"She's doing well," he said. "Sure she'd be glad to see you."

Barbara stood at Natalie's side, holding her hand. Natalie cracked a weak smile when she saw me.

"Sheikh doing okay?" she asked.

"He is," I said. "Thanks for what you did."

"I only did my job," she said.

"Thanks just the same." I set the flowers in an empty vase. "What's the damage?"

"They pulled a slug from my shoulder. It fractured my clavicle, shattered a portion of my humerus. I'll be out of here in a few days. Then several months of rehab. She helped me, you know."

"Who?"

Natalie grimaced. "It's still painful."

"Elizabeth," Barbara said. "She pulled out a medical bag and stabilized Natalie until the EMS unit arrived."

"I'm glad she was there."

I stayed and talked with Natalie and Barbara. I told them what happened at the sheikh's house and about finding al-Salaam's last recording. When I left the room, Tucker still stood outside.

"Al-Salaam's last recording will be played starting tonight on MTV," Tucker said.

"Why?"

"Why, what?"

"Why'd you step in like that? I thought he was nothing more than another terrorist in your books."

"You were convinced he wasn't. Figured I'd better play the devil's advocate."

"You play that pretty well."

Tucker chuckled. "I don't like it when I'm lied to. I asked about al-Salaam but Washington didn't tell me they had a 'hearts and minds' campaign designed around his rap music. Al-Salaam wouldn't go along with the program. It cost him his life. I figure he oughta get the last word. Lies. That's what got us into this whole mess to begin with."

"Someone pick up T-Mo?" I asked.

"NYPD," Tucker said.

"Harmon will get charged with murder?"

"Or a smart ADA will cut him a deal to testify against the rappers that actually pulled the trigger." Tucker tapped me on the shoulder with the back of his hand. "There's someone else in here you may want to visit."

"Who?"

"Next floor down. Room 513."

Tucker turned and walked back into Natalie's room. I took the stairs down two at a time. Faint strains of a saxophone seeped from under the door of room 513. A uniformed officer guarded the door. I showed him my shield. He stepped aside. I knocked.

"Come in," a woman answered.

When I opened the door, Sam Adams sat up in bed. My legs trembled. Her eyes had dark circles around them. I tried to find words. Sam found them before me.

"When I went jogging the morning that you left, a man attacked me and threw me to the ground. I hit my head. Another man came running up and apprehended my attacker. Someone named Tucker visited me in the hospital. He said he wanted me to stay here under guard. He also said he wanted to spread the word that I was killed during the attack as a way of keeping me safe."

I reached into my pocket and pulled out a copy of al-Salaam's final recording. I slipped it into the CD player next to Sam's bed. I sat beside her and reached for her hand. She grasped mine and we held hands in silence. Sam smiled. So did I. And al-Salaam sang, "Got to tell the truth . . . *Salaam Alaikum . . . Salaam Alaikum . . . Salaam Alaikum.*"